Thom Jones is the author of *Cold Snap* and *Sonny Liston was a Friend of Mine*. He lives with his family in Olympia, Washington. He is currently at work on his first novel.

Further acclaim for Thom Jones:

'A writer as brave as he is gifted.' Michael Herr

'Thom Jones has stormed the scene like an angry doberman at a garden party. He is shocking, he is gorgeous . . . A voice so relentless and felonious at once – that you ought to need a permit to carry it.' *Boston Globe*

'Thom Jones' stories are propelled by an amazing blend of knowledge and skill, terror and release.' Robert Stone

'Writers as good as Thom Jones appear but rarely. The original poetry of his fictional world is irresistible, and the sense that he knows this world absolutely has cleansed his prose and produced an affectless sheen . . . Thom Jones is a wonderful writer.' *New York Times*

'He is not only a quirkily gifted, exceptionally powerful writer but – and this is much rarer at a time when originality often has a derivative quality about it – a vital one too.' *Guardian*

by the same author

COLD SNAP
SONNY LISTON WAS A FRIEND OF MINE

THE PUGILIST AT REST

Stories

THOM JONES

faber and faber

First published in the UK in 1994
by Faber and Faber Limited
3 Queen Square London WC1N 3AU
This paperback edition first published in 1995

Printed and bound by Mackays of Chatham PLC,
Chatham, Kent

© Thom Jones, 1993

The characters and events in this book are fictitious.
Any similarity to real persons, living or dead, is
coincidential and not intended by the author.

Grateful acknowledgement is made to the following
publications in which some of these stories were first
published: *The New Yorker*: 'The Pugilist at Rest',
'A White Horse', 'The Black Lights'; *Esquire*: 'Wipeout'; *Harper's*: 'I want to
live!'; *Buzz*: 'As of July 6, I am Responsible for No Debts Other than My
Own'; *Story*: 'Mosquitoes'; *Mississippi Review*: 'Rocket Man'.

'Purple Haze' by Jimi Hendrix. Copyright 1967 Bella
Godiva Music. All rights reserved. Used by permission.

Thom Jones is hereby identified as author of this work
in accordance with Section 77 of the Copyright,
Designs and Patents Act 1988.

A CIP record for this book is
available from the British Library

ISBN 0-571-17135-4

6 8 10 9 7 5

For Sally

The author wishes to acknowledge the assistance and inspiration of Roger Donald, Jordan Pavlin, Geoffrey Kloske, Mike Mattil, Beth Davey, Mih-Ho Cha, and the rest of the people at Little, Brown and Company who made this collection possible. In addition I would like to express my heartfelt gratitude to the best friend and literary agent any writer could hope for — Candida Donadio, and the wonderful staff at Donadio & Ashworth.

Contents

Part

I

The Pugilist
at Rest

HEY BABY got caught writing a letter to his girl when he was supposed to be taking notes on the specs of the M-14 rifle. We were sitting in a stifling hot Quonset hut during the first weeks of boot camp, August 1966, at the Marine Corps Recruit Depot in San Diego. Sergeant Wright snatched the letter out of Hey Baby's hand, and later that night in the squad bay he read the letter to the Marine recruits of Platoon 263, his voice laden with sarcasm. *"Hey, Baby!"* he began, and then as he went into the body of the letter he worked himself into a state of outrage and disgust. It was a letter to *Rosie Rottencrotch*, he said at the end, and what really mattered, what was really at issue and what was of utter importance was not *Rosie Rottencrotch* and her steaming-hot panties but rather the muzzle velocity of the M-14 rifle.

Hey Baby paid for the letter by doing a hundred squat thrusts on the concrete floor of the squad bay, but the main prize he won that night was that he became forever known as Hey Baby to the recruits of Platoon 263 — in addition to being a shitbird, a faggot, a turd, a maggot, and other such standard

appellations. To top it all off, shortly after the incident, Hey
Baby got a Dear John from his girl back in Chicago, of whom
Sergeant Wright, myself, and seventy-eight other Marine
recruits had come to know just a little.

Hey Baby was not in the Marine Corps for very long. The
reason for this was that he started in on my buddy, Jorgeson.
Jorgeson was my main man, and Hey Baby started calling him
Jorgepussy and began harassing him and pushing him around.
He was down on Jorgeson because whenever we were taught
some sort of combat maneuver or tactic, Jorgeson would say,
under his breath, "You could get *killed* if you try that." Or,
"Your ass is *had*, if you do that." You got the feeling that
Jorgeson didn't think loving the American flag and defending
democratic ideals in Southeast Asia were all that important.
He told me that what he really wanted to do was have an artist's loft in the SoHo district of New York City, wear a beret,
eat liver-sausage sandwiches made with stale baguettes, drink
Tokay wine, smoke dope, paint pictures, and listen to the wail-
ing, sorrowful songs of that French singer Edith Piaf, otherwise known as "The Little Sparrow."

After the first half hour of boot camp most of the other
recruits wanted to get out, too, but they nourished dreams of
surfboards, Corvettes, and blond babes. Jorgeson wanted to be
a beatnik and hang out with Jack Kerouac and Neal Cassady,
slam down burning shots of amber whiskey, and hear Charles
Mingus play real cool jazz on the bass fiddle. He wanted to
practice Zen Buddhism, throw the I Ching, eat couscous, and
study astrology charts. All of this was foreign territory to me.
I had grown up in Aurora, Illinois, and had never heard of
such things. Jorgeson had a sharp tongue and was so supercil-
ious in his remarks that I didn't know quite how seriously I

should take this talk, but I enjoyed his humor and I did believe he had the sensibilities of an artist. It was not some vague yearning. I believed very much that he could become a painter of pictures. At that point he wasn't putting his heart and soul into becoming a Marine. He wasn't a true believer like me.

Some weeks after Hey Baby began hassling Jorgeson, Sergeant Wright gave us his best speech: "You men are going off to war, and it's not a pretty thing," etc. & etc., "and if Luke the Gook knocks down one of your buddies, a fellow-Marine, you are going to risk your life and go in and get that Marine and you are going to bring him out. Not because I said so. No! You are going after that Marine because *you* are a Marine, a member of the most elite fighting force in the world, and that man out there who's gone down is a Marine, and he's your *buddy*. He is your brother! Once you are a Marine, you are *always* a Marine and you will never let another Marine down." Etc. & etc. "You can take a Marine out of the Corps but you can't take the Corps out of a Marine." Etc. & etc. At the time it seemed to me a very good speech, and it stirred me deeply. Sergeant Wright was no candy ass. He was one squared-away dude, and he could call cadence. Man, it puts a lump in my throat when I remember how that man could sing cadence. Apart from Jorgeson, I think all of the recruits in Platoon 263 were proud of Sergeant Wright. He was the real thing, the genuine article. He was a crackerjack Marine.

In the course of training, lots of the recruits dropped out of the original platoon. Some couldn't pass the physical-fitness tests and had to go to a special camp for pussies. This was a particularly shameful shortcoming, the most humiliating apart from bed-wetting. Other recruits would get pneumonia, strep throat, infected foot blisters, or whatever, and lose time that way. Some didn't qualify at the rifle range. One would break a leg. Another would have a nervous breakdown (and this was also deplorable). People dropped out right and left. When the recruit corrected whatever deficiency he had, or when he got better, he would be picked up by another platoon that was in the stage of basic training that he had been in when his training was interrupted. Platoon 263 picked up dozens of recruits in this fashion. If everything went well, however, you got through with the whole business in twelve weeks. That's not a long time, but it seemed like a long time. You did not see a female in all that time. You did not see a newspaper or a television set. You did not eat a candy bar. Another thing was the fact that you had someone on top of you, watching every move you made. When it was time to "shit, shower, and shave," you were given just ten minutes, and had to confront lines and so on to complete the entire affair. Head calls were so infrequent that I spent a lot of time that might otherwise have been neutral or painless in the eye-watering anxiety that I was going to piss my pants. We *ran* to chow, where we were faced with enormous steam vents that spewed out a sickening smell of rancid, super-heated grease. Still, we entered the mess hall with ravenous appetites, ate a huge tray of food in just a few minutes, and then *ran* back to our company area in formation, choking back the burning bile of a meal too big to be eaten so fast. God forbid that you would lose control and vomit.

If all had gone well in the preceding hours, Sergeant Wright would permit us to smoke one cigarette after each meal. Jorgeson had shown me the wisdom of switching from Camels to Pall Malls — they were much longer, packed a pretty good jolt, and when we snapped open our brushed-chrome Zippos, torched up, and inhaled the first few drags, we shared the overmastering pleasure that tobacco can bring if you use it seldom and judiciously. These were always the best moments of the day — brief respites from the tyrannical repression of recruit training. As we got close to the end of it all Jorgeson liked to play a little game. He used to say to me (with fragrant blue smoke curling out of his nostrils), "If someone said, 'I'll give you ten thousand dollars to do all of this again,' what would you say?" "No way, Jack!" He would keep on upping it until he had John Beresford Tipton, the guy from "The Millionaire," offering me a check for a million bucks. "Not for any money," I'd say.

While they were all smoldering under various pressures, the recruits were also getting pretty "salty" — they were beginning to believe. They were beginning to think of themselves as Marines. If you could make it through this, the reasoning went, you wouldn't crack in combat. So I remember that I had tears in my eyes when Sergeant Wright gave us the spiel about how a Marine would charge a machine-gun nest to save his buddies, dive on a hand grenade, do whatever it takes — and yet I was ashamed when Jorgeson caught me wiping them away. All of the recruits were teary except Jorgeson. He had these very clear cobalt-blue eyes. They were so remarkable that they caused you to notice Jorgeson in a crowd. There was unusual beauty in these eyes, and there was an extraordinary power in them. Apart from having a pleasant enough face, Jorgeson was small and unassuming except for these eyes. Anyhow, when he caught me getting sentimental he gave me this look that penetrated to the core of my being. It was the icy look of absolute contempt, and it caused me to doubt myself. I said, "Man! Can't you get into it? For Christ's sake!"

"I'm not like you," he said. "But I am into it, more than you could ever know. I never told you this before, but I am

Kal-El, born on the planet Krypton and rocketed to Earth as an infant, moments before my world exploded. Disguised as a mild-mannered Marine, I have resolved to use my powers for the good of mankind. Whenever danger appears on the scene, truth and justice will be served as I slip into the green U.S.M.C. utility uniform and become Earth's greatest hero."

I got highly pissed and didn't talk to him for a couple of days after this. Then, about two weeks before boot camp was over, when we were running out to the parade field for drill with our rifles at port arms, all assholes and elbows, I saw Hey Baby give Jorgeson a nasty shove with his M-14. Hey Baby was a large and fairly tough young man who liked to displace his aggressive impulses on Jorgeson, but he wasn't as big or as tough as I.

Jorgeson nearly fell down as the other recruits scrambled out to the parade field, and Hey Baby gave a short, malicious laugh. I ran past Jorgeson and caught up to Hey Baby; he picked me up in his peripheral vision, but by then it was too late. I set my body so that I could put everything into it, and with one deft stroke I hammered him in the temple with the sharp edge of the steel butt plate of my M-14. It was not exactly a premeditated crime, although I had been laying to get him. My idea before this had simply been to lay my hands on him, but now I had blood in my eye. I was a skilled boxer, and I knew the temple was a vulnerable spot; the human skull is otherwise hard and durable, except at its base. There was a sickening crunch, and Hey Baby dropped into the ice plants along the side of the company street.

The entire platoon was out on the parade field when the house mouse screamed at the assistant D.I., who rushed back to the scene of the crime to find Hey Baby crumpled in a fetal position in the ice plants with blood all over the place. There was blood from the scalp wound as well as a froth of blood emitting from his nostrils and his mouth. Blood was leaking from his right ear. Did I see skull fragments and brain tissue? It seemed that I did. To tell you the truth, I wouldn't have cared in the least if I had killed him, but like most criminals I was very much afraid of getting caught. It suddenly occurred to me that I could be headed for the brig for a long time. My heart was pounding out of my chest. Yet the larger part of me didn't care. Jorgeson was my buddy, and I wasn't going to stand still and let someone fuck him over.

The platoon waited at parade rest while Sergeant Wright came out of the duty hut and took command of the situation. An ambulance was called, and it came almost immediately. A number of corpsmen squatted down alongside the fallen man for what seemed an eternity. Eventually they took Hey Baby off with a fractured skull. It would be the last we ever saw of him. Three evenings later, in the squad bay, the assistant D.I. told us rather ominously that Hey Baby had recovered consciousness. That's all he said. What did *that* mean? I was worried, because Hey Baby had seen me make my move, but, as it turned out, when he came to he had forgotten the incident and all events of the preceding two weeks. Retrograde amnesia. Lucky for me. I also knew that at least three other recruits had seen what I did, but none of them reported me. Every member of the platoon was called in and grilled by a team of hard-ass captains and a light colonel from the Criminal Investigation Detachment. It took a certain amount of balls to lie to them, yet none of my fellow-jarheads reported me. I was well liked and Hey Baby was not. Indeed, many felt that he got exactly what was coming to him.

*   *   *

The other day — Memorial Day, as it happened — I was cleaning some stuff out of the attic when I came upon my old dress-blue uniform. It's a beautiful uniform, easily the most handsome worn by any of the U.S. armed forces. The rich color recalled Jorgeson's eyes for me — not that the color matched, but in the sense that the color of each was so startling. The tunic does not have lapels, of course, but a high collar with red piping and the traditional golden eagle, globe, and anchor insignia on either side of the neck clasp. The tunic buttons are not brassy — although they are in fact made of brass — but are a delicate gold in color, like Florentine gold. On the sleeves of the tunic my staff sergeant's chevrons are gold on red. High on the left breast is a rainbow display of fruit salad representing my various combat citations. Just below these are my marksmanship badges; I shot Expert in rifle as well as pistol.

I opened a sandalwood box and took my various medals out of the large plastic bag I had packed them in to prevent them from tarnishing. The Navy Cross and the two Silver Stars are the best; they are such pretty things they dazzle you. I found a couple of Thai sticks in the sandalwood box as well. I took a whiff of the box and smelled the smells of Saigon — the whores, the dope, the saffron, cloves, jasmine, and patchouli oil. I put the Thai sticks back, recalling the three-day hangover that particular batch of dope had given me more than twenty-three years before. Again I looked at my dress-blue tunic. My most distinctive badge, the crowning glory, and the one of which I am most proud, is the set of Airborne wings. I remember how it was, walking around Oceanside, California — the Airborne wings and the high-and-tight haircut were recognized by all the Marines; they meant you were the crème de la crème, you were a recon Marine.

Recon was all Jorgeson's idea. We had lost touch with each other after boot camp. I was sent to com school in San Diego, where I had to sit in a hot Class A wool uniform all day and learn the Morse code. I deliberately flunked out, and when I was given the perfunctory option for a second shot, I told the colonel, "Hell no, sir. I want to go 003 — infantry. I want to be a ground-pounder. I didn't join the service to sit at a desk all day."

I was on a bus to Camp Pendleton three days later, and when I got there I ran into Jorgeson. I had been thinking of him a lot. He was a clerk in headquarters company. Much to my astonishment, he was fifteen pounds heavier, and had grown two inches, and he told me he was hitting the weight pile every night after running seven miles up and down the foothills of Pendleton in combat boots, carrying a rifle and a full field pack. After the usual what's-been-happening? b.s., he got down to business and said, "They need people in Force Recon, what do you think? Headquarters is one boring moth-erfucker."

I said, "Recon? Paratrooper? You got to be shittin' me! When did you get so gung-ho, man?"

He said, "Hey, you were the one who *bought* the pro-gram. Don't fade on me now, goddamm it! Look, we pass the physical fitness test and then they send us to jump school at Benning. If we pass that, we're in. And we'll pass. Those dog-gies ain't got jack. Semper fi, motherfucker! Let's do it."

There was no more talk of Neal Cassady, Edith Piaf, or the artist's loft in SoHo. I said, "If Sergeant Wright could only see you now!"

We were just three days in country when we got dropped in somewhere up north near the DMZ. It was a routine reconnaissance patrol. It was not supposed to be any kind of big deal at all — just acclimation. The morning after our drop we approached a clear field. I recall that it gave me a funny feeling, but I was too new to fully trust my instincts. *Everything* was spooky; I was fresh meat, F.N.G. — a Fucking New Guy.

Before moving into the field, our team leader sent Hanes — a lance corporal, a short-timer, with only twelve days left before his rotation was over — across the field as a point man. This was a bad omen and everyone knew it. Hanes had two Purple Hearts. He followed the order with no hesitation and crossed the field without drawing fire. The team leader signaled for us to fan out and told me to circumvent the field and hump through the jungle to investigate a small mound of loose red dirt that I had missed completely but that he had picked up with his trained eye. I remember I kept saying, "Where?" He pointed to a heap of earth about thirty yards along the tree line and about ten feet back in the bushes. Most likely it was an anthill, but you never knew — it could have been an NVA tunnel. "Over there," he hissed. "Goddamn it, do I have to draw pictures for you?"

I moved smartly in the direction of the mound while the rest of the team reconverged to discuss something. As I approached the mound I saw that it was in fact an anthill, and I looked back at the team and saw they were already halfway across the field, moving very fast.

Suddenly there were several loud hollow pops and the cry "Incoming!" Seconds later the first of a half-dozen mortar rounds landed in the loose earth surrounding the anthill. For a millisecond, everything went black. I was blown back and lifted up on a cushion of warm air. At first it was like the thrill of a carnival ride, but it was quickly followed by that stunned, jangly, electric feeling you get when you hit your crazy bone. Like that, but not confined to a small area like the elbow. I felt it shoot through my spine and into all four limbs. A thick plaster of sand and red clay plugged up my nostrils and ears. Grit was blown in between my teeth. If I hadn't been wearing a pair of Ray-Ban aviator shades, I would certainly have been blinded permanently — as it was, my eyes were loaded with grit. (I later discovered that fine red earth was somehow blown in behind the crystal of my pressure-tested Rolex Submariner, underneath my fingernails and toenails, and deep into the pores of my skin.) When I was able to, I pulled out a canteen filled with lemon-lime Kool-Aid and tried to flood my eyes clean. This helped a little, but my eyes still felt like they were on fire. I rinsed them again and blinked furiously.

I rolled over on my stomach in the prone position and leveled my field-issue M-16. A company of screaming NVA soldiers ran into the field, firing as they came — I saw their green tracer rounds blanket the position where the team had quickly congregated to lay out a perimeter, but none of our own red tracers were going out. Several of the Marines had been killed outright by the mortar rounds. Jorgeson was all right, and I saw him cast a nervous glance in my direction. Then he turned to the enemy and began to fire his M-16. I clicked my rifle on to automatic and pulled the trigger, but the gun was loaded with dirt and it wouldn't fire.

Apart from Jorgeson, the only other American putting out any fire was Second Lieutenant Milton, also a fairly new guy, a "cherry," who was down on one knee firing his .45, an exercise in almost complete futility. I assumed that Milton's 16 had jammed, like mine, and watched as AK-47 rounds, having penetrated his flak jacket and then his chest, ripped through the back of his field pack and buzzed into the jungle beyond

like a deadly swarm of bees. A few seconds later, I heard the
swoosh of an RPG rocket, a dud round that dinged the lieutenant's left shoulder before it flew off in the bush behind him.
It took off his whole arm, and for an instant I could see the
white bone and ligaments of his shoulder, and then red flesh of
muscle tissue, looking very much like fresh prime beef, well
marbled and encased in a thin layer of yellowish-white adipose
tissue that quickly became saturated with dark-red blood.
What a lot of blood there was. Still, Milton continued to fire
his .45. When he emptied his clip, I watched him remove a
fresh one from his web gear and attempt to load the pistol with
one hand. He seemed to fumble with the fresh clip for a long
time, until at last he dropped it, along with his .45. The lieutenant's head slowly sagged forward, but he stayed up on one
knee with his remaining arm extended out to the enemy, palm
upward in the soulful, heartrending gesture of Al Jolson doing
a rendition of "Mammy."

A hail of green tracer rounds buzzed past Jorgeson, but
he coolly returned fire in short, controlled bursts. The light,
tinny pops from his M-16 did not sound very reassuring, but I
saw several NVA go down. AK-47 fire kicked up red dust all
around Jorgeson's feet. He was basically out in the open, and
if ever a man was totally alone it was Jorgeson. He was dead
meat and he had to know it. It was very strange that he wasn't
hit immediately.

Jorgeson zigged his way over to the body of a large black
Marine who carried an M-60 machine gun. Most of the recon
Marines carried grease guns or Swedish Ks; an M-60 was too
heavy for traveling light and fast, but this Marine had been big
and he had been paranoid. I had known him least of anyone in
the squad. In three days he had said nothing to me, I suppose

because I was F.N.G., and had spooked him. Indeed, now he was dead. That august seeker of truth, Schopenhauer, was correct: *We are like lambs in a field, disporting themselves under the eye of the butcher, who chooses out first one and then another for his prey. So it is that in our good days we are all unconscious of the evil Fate may have presently in store for us — sickness, poverty, mutilation, loss of sight or reason.*

It was difficult to judge how quickly time was moving. Although my senses had been stunned by the concussion of the mortar rounds, they were, however paradoxical this may seem, more acute than ever before. I watched Jorgeson pick up the machine gun and begin to spread an impressive field of fire back at the enemy. *Thuk thuk thuk, thuk thuk thuk, thuk thuk thuk!* I saw several more bodies fall, and began to think that things might turn out all right after all. The NVA dropped for cover, and many of them turned back and headed for the tree line. Jorgeson fired off a couple of bandoliers, and after he stopped to load another, he turned back and looked at me with those blue eyes and a smile like "How am I doing?" Then I heard the steel-cork pop of an M-79 launcher and saw a rocket grenade explode through Jorgeson's upper abdomen, causing him to do something like a back flip. His M-60 machine gun flew straight up into the air. The barrel was glowing red like a hot poker, and continued to fire in a "cook off" until the entire bandolier had run through.

In the meantime I had pulled a cleaning rod out of my pack and worked it through the barrel of my M-16. When I next tried to shoot, the Tonka-toy son of a bitch remained jammed, and at last I frantically broke it down to find the source of the problem. I had a dirty bolt. Fucking dirt everywhere. With numbed fingers I removed the firing pin and worked it over with a toothbrush, dropping it in the red dirt, picking it up, cleaning it, and dropping it again. My fingers felt like Novocain, and while I could see far away, I was unable to see up close. I poured some more Kool-Aid over my eyes. It was impossible for me to get my weapon clean. Lucky for me, ultimately.

Suddenly NVA soldiers were running through the field shoving bayonets into the bodies of the downed Marines. It was not until an NVA trooper kicked Lieutenant Milton out of his tripod position that he finally fell to the ground. Then the soldiers started going through the dead Marines' gear. I was still frantically struggling with my weapon when it began to dawn on me that the enemy had forgotten me in the excitement of the firefight. I wondered what had happened to Hanes and if he had gotten clear. I doubted it, and hopped on my survival radio to call in an air strike when finally a canny NVA trooper did remember me and headed in my direction most ricky-tick.

With a tight grip on the spoon, I pulled the pin on a fragmentation grenade and then unsheathed my K-bar. About this time Jorgeson let off a horrendous shriek — a gut shot is worse than anything. Or did Jorgeson scream to save my life? The NVA moving in my direction turned back to him, studied him for a moment, and then thrust a bayonet into his heart. As badly as my own eyes hurt, I was able to see Jorgeson's eyes — a final flash of glorious azure before they faded into the unfocused and glazed gray of death. I repinned the grenade, got up on my knees, and scrambled away until finally I was on my feet with a useless and incomplete handful of M-16 parts, and I was running as fast and as hard as I have ever run in my life. A pair of Phantom F-4s came in very low with delayed-action high-explosive rounds and napalm. I could feel the almost unbearable heat waves of the latter, volley after volley. I can still feel it and smell it to this day.

Concerning Lance Corporal Hanes: they found him later, fried to a crisp by the napalm, but it was nonetheless ascertained that he had been mutilated while alive. He was like the rest of us — eighteen, nineteen, twenty years old. What did we know of life? Before Vietnam, Hanes didn't think he would ever die. I mean, yes, he knew that in theory he would die, but he *felt* like he was going to live forever. I know that I felt that way. Hanes was down to twelve days and a wake-up. When other Marines saw a short-timer get greased, it devastated their morale. However, when I saw them zip up the body bag on Hanes I became incensed. Why hadn't Milton sent him back to the rear to burn shit or something when he got so short? Twelve days to go and then mutilated. Fucking Milton! Fucking second lieutenant!

Theogenes was the greatest of gladiators. He was a boxer who served under the patronage of a cruel nobleman, a prince who took great delight in bloody spectacles. Although this was several hundred years before the times of those most enlightened of men Socrates, Plato, and Aristotle, and well after the Minoans of Crete, it still remains a high point in the history of Western civilization and culture. It was the approximate time of Homer, the greatest poet who ever lived. Then, as now, violence, suffering, and the cheapness of life were the rule.

The sort of boxing Theogenes practiced was not like modern-day boxing with those kindergarten Queensberry Rules. The two contestants were not permitted the freedom of a ring. Instead, they were strapped to flat stones, facing each other nose-to-nose. When the signal was given, they would begin hammering each other with fists encased in heavy leather thongs. It was a fight to the death. Fourteen hundred and twenty-five times Theogenes was strapped to the stone and fourteen hundred and twenty-five times he emerged a victor.

Perhaps it is Theogenes who is depicted in the famous Roman statue (based on the earlier Greek original) of "The Pugilist at Rest." I keep a grainy black-and-white photograph of it in my room. The statue depicts a muscular athlete approaching his middle age. He has a thick beard and a full head of curly hair. In addition to the telltale broken nose and cauliflower ears of a boxer, the pugilist has the slanted, drooping brows that bespeak torn nerves. Also, the forehead is piled with scar tissue. As may be expected, the pugilist has the musculature of a fighter. His neck and trapezius muscles are well developed. His shoulders are enormous; his chest is thick and flat, without the bulging pectorals of the bodybuilder. His back, oblique, and abdominal muscles are highly pronounced, and he has that greatest asset of the modern boxer — sturdy legs. The arms are large, particularly the forearms, which are reinforced with the leather wrappings of the cestus. It is the body of a small heavyweight — lithe rather than bulky, but by no means lacking in power: a Jack Johnson or a Dempsey, say. If you see the authentic statue at the Terme Museum, in Rome, you will see that the seated boxer is really not much more than a light-heavyweight. People were small in those days. The important thing was that he was perfectly proportioned.

The pugilist is sitting on a rock with his forearms balanced on his thighs. That he is seated and not pacing implies that he has been through all this many times before. It appears that he is conserving his strength. His head is turned as if he were looking over his shoulder — as if someone had just whispered something to him. It is in this that the "art" of the sculpture is conveyed to the viewer. Could it be that someone has just summoned him to the arena? There is a slight look of befuddlement on his face, but there is no trace of fear. There is an air about him that suggests that he is eager to proceed and does not wish to cause anyone any trouble or to create a delay, even though his life will soon be on the line. Besides the deformities on his noble face, there is also the suggestion of weariness and philosophical resignation. *All the world's a stage, and all the men and women merely players.* Exactly! He knew this more than two thousand years before Shakespeare penned the line. How did he come to be at this place in space and time? Would he rather be safely removed to the countryside — an obscure, stinking peasant shoving a plow behind a mule? Would that be better? Or does he revel in his role? Perhaps he once did, but surely not now. Is this the great Theogenes or merely a journeyman fighter, a former slave or criminal bought by one of the many contractors who for months trained the condemned for their brief moment in the arena? I wonder if Marcus Aurelius loved the "Pugilist" as I do, and came to study it and to meditate before it.

I cut and ran from that field in Southeast Asia. I've read that Davy Crockett, hero of the American frontier, was cowering under a bed when Santa Anna and his soldiers stormed into the Alamo. What is the truth? Jack Dempsey used to get so scared before his fights that he sometimes wet his pants. But look what he did to Willard and to Luis Firpo, the Wild Bull of the Pampas! It was something close to homicide. What is courage? What is cowardice? The magnificent Roberto Duran gave us *"No más,"* but who had a greater fighting heart than Duran?

I got over that first scare and saw that I was something quite other than that which I had known myself to be. Hey

Baby proved only my warm-up act. There was a reservoir of malice, poison, and vicious sadism in my soul, and it poured forth freely in the jungles and rice paddies of Vietnam. I pulled three tours. I wanted some payback for Jorgeson. I grieved for Lance Corporal Hanes. I grieved for myself and what I had lost. I committed unspeakable crimes and got medals for it.

It was only fair that I got a head injury myself. I never got a scratch in Vietnam, but I got tagged in a boxing smoker at Pendleton. Fought a bad-ass light-heavyweight from artillery. Nobody would fight this guy. He could box. He had all the moves. But mainly he was a puncher — it was said that he could punch with either hand. It was said that his hand speed was superb. I had finished off at least a half rack of Hamm's before I went in with him and started getting hit with head shots I didn't even see coming. They were right. His hand speed *was* superb.

I was twenty-seven years old, smoked two packs a day, was a borderline alcoholic. I shouldn't have fought him — I knew that — but he had been making noise. A very long time before, I had been the middleweight champion of the 1st Marine Division. I had been a so-called war hero. I had been a recon Marine. But now I was a garrison Marine and in no kind of shape.

He put me down almost immediately, and when I got up I was terribly afraid. I was tight and I could not breathe. It felt like he was hitting me in the face with a ball-peen hammer. It felt like he was busting light bulbs in my face. Rather than one opponent, I saw three. I was convinced his gloves were loaded, and a wave of self-pity ran through me.

I began to move. He made a mistake by expending a lot of energy trying to put me away quickly. I had no intention of going down again, and I knew I wouldn't. My buddies were watching, and I had to give them a good show. While I was afraid, I was also exhilarated; I had not felt this alive since Vietnam. I began to score with my left jab, and because of this I was able to withstand his bull charges and divert them. I thought he would throw his bolt, but in the beginning he was tireless. I must have hit him with four hundred left jabs. It got so that I could score at will, with either hand, but he would counter, trap me on the ropes, and pound. He was the better puncher and was truly hurting me, but I was scoring, and as the fight went on the momentum shifted and I took over. I staggered him again and again. The Marines at ringside were screaming for me to put him away, but however much I tried, I could not. Although I could barely stand by the end, I was sorry that the fight was over. Who had won? The referee raised my arm in victory, but I think it was pretty much a draw. Judging a prizefight is a very subjective thing.

About an hour after the bout, when the adrenaline had subsided, I realized I had a terrible headache. It kept getting worse, and I rushed out of the NCO Club, where I had gone with my buddies to get loaded.

I stumbled outside, struggling to breathe, and I headed away from the company area toward Sheepshit Hill, one of the many low brown foothills in the vicinity. Like a dog who wants to die alone, so it was with me. Everything got swirly, and I dropped in the bushes.

I was unconscious for nearly an hour, and for the next two weeks I walked around like I was drunk, with double vision. I had constant headaches and seemed to have grown old overnight. My health was gone.

I became a very timid individual. I became introspective. I wondered what had made me act the way I had acted. Why had I killed my fellowmen in war, without any feeling, remorse, or regret? And when the war was over, why did I continue to drink and swagger around and get into fistfights? Why did I like to dish out pain, and why did I take positive delight in the suffering of others? Was I insane? Was it too much testosterone? Women don't do things like that. The rapacious Will to Power lost its hold on me. Suddenly I began to feel sympathetic to the cares and sufferings of all living creatures. You lose your health and you start thinking this way.

Has man become any better since the times of Theogenes? The world is replete with badness. I'm not talking about that old routine where you drag out the Spanish Inquisition, the Holocaust, Joseph Stalin, the Khmer Rouge, etc. It happens in our own backyard. Twentieth-century America is one of the most materially prosperous nations in history. But take a walk through an American prison, a nursing home, the slums where the homeless live in cardboard boxes, a cancer ward. Go to a Vietnam vets' meeting, or an A.A. meeting, or an Overeaters Anonymous meeting. *How hollow and unreal a thing is life, how deceitful are its pleasures, what horrible aspects it possesses.* Is the world not rather like a hell, as Schopenhauer, that clearheaded seer — who has helped me transform my suffering into an object of understanding — was so quick to point out? They called him a pessimist and dismissed him with a word, but it is peace and self-renewal that I have found in his pages.

About a year after my fight with the guy from artillery I started having seizures. I suffered from a form of left-temporal-lobe seizure which is sometimes called Dostoyevski's epilepsy. It's so rare as to be almost unknown. Freud, himself a neurologist, speculated that Dostoyevski was a hysterical epileptic, and that his fits were unrelated to brain damage — psychogenic in origin. Dostoyevski did not have his first attack until the age of twenty-five, when he was imprisoned in Siberia and received fifty lashes after complaining about the food. Freud figured that after Dostoyevski's mock execution, the four years' imprisonment in Siberia, the tormented childhood, the murder of his tyrannical father, etc. & etc. — he had all the earmarks of hysteria, of grave psychological trauma. And Dostoyevski had displayed the trademark features of the psychomotor epileptic long before his first attack. These days physicians insist there is no such thing as the "epileptic personality." I think they say this because they do not want to add to the burden of the epileptic's suffering with an extra stigma. Privately they do believe in these traits. Dostoyevski was nervous and depressed, a tormented hypochondriac, a compulsive writer obsessed with religious and philosophic themes. He was hyperloquacious, raving, etc. & etc. His gambling addiction is well known. By most accounts he was a sick soul.

The peculiar and most distinctive thing about his epilepsy was that in the split second before his fit — in the aura, which is in fact officially a part of the attack — Dostoyevski experienced a sense of felicity, of ecstatic well-being unlike anything an ordinary mortal could hope to imagine. It was the experience of satori. Not the nickel-and-dime satori of Abraham Maslow, but the Supreme. He said that he wouldn't trade ten years of life for this feeling, and I, who have had it, too, would have to agree. I can't explain it, I don't understand it — it becomes slippery and elusive when it gets any distance on you — but I have felt this down to the core of my being. Yes, God exists! But then it slides away and I lose it. I become a doubter. Even Dostoyevski, the fervent Christian, makes an almost airtight case against the possibility of the existence of God in the Grand Inquisitor digression in *The Brothers Karamazov*. It is probably the greatest passage in all of world literature, and it tilts you to the court of the atheist. This is what happens when you approach Him with the intellect.

It is thought that St. Paul had a temporal-lobe fit on the road to Damascus. Paul warns us in First Corinthians that God will confound the intellectuals. It is known that Muhammad composed the Koran after attacks of epilepsy. Black Elk experienced fits before his grand "buffalo" vision. Joan of Arc is thought to have been a left-temporal-lobe epileptic. Each of these in a terrible flash of brain lightning was able to pierce the murky veil of illusion which is spread over all things. Just so did the scales fall from my eyes. It is called the "sacred disease."

But what a price. I rarely leave the house anymore. To avoid falling injuries, I always wear my old boxer's headgear, and I always carry my mouthpiece. Rather more often than the aura where "every common bush is afire with God," I have the typical epileptic aura, which is that of terror and impending doom. If I can keep my head and think of it, and if there is time, I slip the mouthpiece in and thus avoid biting my tongue. I bit it in half once, and when they sewed it back together it swelled enormously, like a huge red-and-black sausage. I was unable to close my mouth for more than two weeks.

The fits are coming more and more. I'm loaded on Depakene, phenobarbital, Tegretol, Dilantin — the whole shit load. A nurse from the V.A. bought a pair of Staffordshire terriers for me and trained them to watch me as I sleep, in case I have a fit and smother facedown in my bedding. What delightful companions these dogs are! One of them, Gloria, is especially intrepid and clever. Inevitably, when I come to I find that the dogs have dragged me into the kitchen, away from blankets and pillows, rugs, and objects that might suffocate me; and that they have turned me on my back. There's Gloria, barking in my face. Isn't this incredible?

My sister brought a neurosurgeon over to my place around Christmas — not some V.A. butcher but a guy from the university hospital. He was a slick dude in a nine-hundred-dollar suit. He came down on me hard, like a used-car salesman. He wants to cauterize a small spot in a nerve bundle in my brain. "It's not a lobotomy, it's a *cingulotomy*," he said.

Reckless, desperate, last-ditch psychosurgery is still pretty much unthinkable in the conservative medical establishment. That's why he made a personal visit to my place. A house call. Drumming up some action to make himself a name. "See that bottle of Thorazine?" he said. "You can throw that poison away," he said. "All that amitriptyline. That's garbage, you can toss that, too." He said, "Tell me something. How can you take all of that shit and still walk?" He said, "You take enough drugs to drop an elephant."

He wants to cut me. He said that the feelings of guilt and worthlessness, and the heaviness of a heart blackened by sin, will go away. "It is *not* a lobotomy," he said.

I don't like the guy. I don't trust him. I'm not convinced, but I can't go on like this. If I am not having a panic attack I am engulfed in tedious, unrelenting depression. I am overcome with a deadening sense of languor; I can't *do* anything. I wanted to give my buddies a good show! What a goddamn fool. I am a goddamn fool!

*   *   *

It has taken me six months to put my thoughts in order, but I wanted to do it in case I am a vegetable after the operation. I know that my buddy Jorgeson was a real American hero. I wish that he had lived to be something else, if not a painter of pictures then even some kind of fuckup with a factory job and four divorces, bankruptcy petitions, in and out of jail. I wish he had been that. I wish he had been *anything* rather than a real American hero. So, then, if I am to feel somewhat *indifferent* to life after the operation, all the better. If not, not.

If I had a more conventional sense of morality I would shitcan those dress blues, and I'd send that Navy Cross to Jorgeson's brother. Jorgeson was the one who won it, who pulled the John Wayne number up there near Khe Sanh and saved my life, although I lied and took the credit for all of those dead NVA. He had created a stunning body count — nothing like Theogenes, but Jorgeson only had something like twelve minutes total in the theater of war.

The high command almost awarded me the Medal of Honor, but of course there were no witnesses to what I claimed I had done, and I had saved no one's life. When I think back on it, my tale probably did not sound as credible as I thought it had at the time. I was only nineteen years old and not all that practiced a liar. I figure if they *had* given me the Medal of Honor, I would have stood in the ring up at Camp Las Pulgas in Pendleton and let that light-heavyweight from artillery fucking kill me.

Now I'm thinking I might call Hey Baby and ask how he's doing. No shit, a couple of neuropsychs — we probably have a lot in common. I could apologize to him. But I learned from my fits that you don't have to do that. Good and evil are only illusions. Still, I cannot help but wonder sometimes if my vision of the Supreme Reality was any more real than the demons visited upon schizophrenics and madmen. Has it all been just a stupid neurochemical event? Is there no God at all? The human heart rebels against this.

If they fuck up the operation, I hope I get to keep my dogs somehow — maybe stay at my sister's place. If they send me to the nuthouse I lose the dogs for sure.

Break on
Through

APART from Sergeant Ondine, all the members of Force
Recon Team *Break on Through* were sitting in the interrogation hootch at Camp Clarke waiting for our team leader to
come out of the op shack. The word was out that we were
going up-country for a quickie, a little "sneak and peek."
Except for Mason, our corpsman, we were, to the man, hungdown, drug-down and crashing hard after five days of in-country R&R.

China Beach, with its free-flowing booze, air conditioning and in-house latrines was Captain Barnes's special present
to us after eight weeks in the field — way out there up north
in no-man's-land, at the ass-end of the monsoon season, where
the nights had been so cold and my fingers had been so numb,
I had to keep my safety in the "off" position as I lay in the
night, watching my fire lanes through spooky surreal drifting
mists.

As I sat on the floor of the interrogation shack, with my
CAR-15 cradled on my lap, I wondered if it had been an alcoholic nightmare at China Beach, or if in fact on one of those

last nights in the jungle that I *had seen* the apparition of a man, cloaked in a trench coat, emerge from the fog, like Humphrey Bogart in a felt hat, tan Burberry, pipe-in-mouth until he lifted his head and showed the face of Lucifer. I remember watching dumbstruck as he removed a doeskin glove to reveal an eagle's talon rather than a hand, and then make an effeminate model's swivel to lift the back of his coat, like someone flashing me the moon with a silly grin while he showed me his tail to prove that it was indeed he. The head swiveled a full 180° and I looked at the tail — muscular, purple, and thick with spines — before he walked off into the fog on cloven feet.

Just after the vision I remember a python shoot through the brush in front of me, sliding past my face. I could feel the weight of it through the earth and remember thinking, "This shouldn't be happening." It was too fucking cold for snakes.

It was a number ten pucker factor, but I had not spooked. I had a pair of claymores in that fire lane and nobody but a ghost could tread lightly enough to get past them, so I had held my fire on the vision and I held my fire on the snake even though I was convinced that something very bad was in the air and that something *bad* was going to happen on that patrol. I was oddly frightened and unconnected, but then as the snake passed, the black night turned purple and I felt such an infusion of power that I wanted to put down my rifle and dance a shaman's dance. I knew nothing was going to kill me on this mission.

If you tap into the purple field you get a sixth sense, heightened hearing, a field of vision that picks up anything that shouldn't be there, the smell of Charles, and even on some of the blackest nights on earth, I had the ability to *see* Charles in fields of purple — literally sense his location, *see* his energy and assume control of it and be the first to kill. I didn't need a

Starlight Scope. The purple force was no boonie voodoo, it was something real, and if you didn't pick up on it and use it there was only one thing that could happen to you — you ended up dead. I often wondered if it was the gift of Satan. Had we done some sort of deal? If so, what would be the price? I never did get any MasterCard bill. Had he come and left it for me personally that night in the jungle, had I somehow sold him my soul?

I checked out my CAR-15 and found it spotless. I must have cleaned it immediately after the last patrol, instinctively. I couldn't remember. I was drawing blanks. The thing about recon was that you got drunk or high whenever possible; it was mandatory unless you were a zero, like Mason. It was part of the package, and as I sat in the hootch waiting for Ondine I almost began to hate Captain Barnes for giving us a party.

Gerber, our machine gunner, was squinting hard at a little wax-paper "Archie and Veronica" comic jacket, from a bubblegum wrapper. He was shucking the jackets off the bubblegum and stuffing the gum in his face, reading the cartoons, passing out gum and chewing the shit out of his own, five pieces at least. Nerves, butterflies. He started to show me the cartoon but saw that I was lost in dark thoughts and instead turned his head away from me, laughing cynically as he passed a little comic strip to Baggit, who studied it a moment and laughed, "Yaawwh!"

Baggit was a Navy SEAL who came to *Break on Through* via the Phoenix Program. Baggit showed up a few days prior to our last operation in a Class A sailor's uniform, slick-sleeved, frightened, like a new guy, and when we stood inspection a few days later, the major walked past him, noticed the small blue insignia with five white stars above Baggit's breast pocket, popped Baggit a salute, and asked him how and where he had

won the Medal of Honor. *The Medal of Honor!* Baggit returned
the salute and said, "Vietnam — somewhere in III Corps . . .
I think."

I saw a look on Ondine's face, like, "Oh, shit! Here's a
motherfucker with three days in-country wearing a Medal of
Honor insignia that he had picked up in a pawnshop or something." While all of us might have *seen* it, should have seen it
since it was there for all to see, no one could really believe it.
Your eye saw it but your brain didn't really take it in. And now
Ondine was going to catch hell because it was his job to see
things like that. After the inspection he hustled Baggit off to
the op shack, but it turned out that the story was true.

Baggit had gone into some deep shit with a Ranger
Company down in III Corps, his platoon catching most of the
trouble while Baggit, himself badly wounded, was calling in
medevacs, directing artillery fire, charging bunkers, killing
two men bare-handed when his rifle jammed, picking up an
enemy's rifle, using that, clearing a jam in the machine gunner's 60 and using *that,* and when a relief company finally did
arrive, they found that it's not a platoon holding off a company
of VC, but one guy, and a week later Baggit personally gets a
Medal of Honor from the commander of MACV while he is in
the hospital recovering from wounds.

Ondine said he knew the story was true once they got
back and started talking to the guy. And then when Baggit's
201 jacket came in a couple of days later, it turned out that not
only did he hold the Medal of Honor but he also had won two
Silvers and three Bronze Stars all with valor — all within
something like four months in-country.

But wait! Baggit is an E-6 who killed a Navy officer, was
convicted of murder, stripped of his rank and medals and sent
to the Long Binh Jail in Saigon where he was waiting process-

ing back to Fort Leavenworth, Kansas . . . where he was to be scheduled for hanging.

Phoenix had sent us jailbirds before, but never a guy who had just been popped from death row, which is why Baggit was so shy at that inspection; why he was pale, timid, and all the rest of it. He told Ondine that he didn't think it was fair having to surrender America's highest commendation since he had won it at great risk and he told Ondine that he told the spooks in the Phoenix Program they could take his stripes but he would rather go to Leavenworth, Kansas, and take death than give up his medals.

It was hard to believe but those crazy Phoenix bastards promised Baggit leniency if he could hold it together, but as soon as he came to the team and this Medal of Honor thing was straightened out and he knew he wasn't going back to jail, the scare wore off. Pretty soon Baggit was walking around in a pair of tiger-striped fatigues with his SEAL badge and jump wings, cocky-like, and he started in on everybody with his shit, including Ondine, and I remember thinking, *That's just fine*. Let him go one-on-one with Ondine. I knew that Ondine would fuck him faster than a mouth full of razor blades. Baggit was just plain crazy but Ondine was smart crazy. Ondine was dangerous, capital "D."

We sat in the interrogation shack, Baggit looked at Gerber's comic a moment more and said, "I wouldn't kick her out of my bed. How 'bout you, *Ahab?*"

He passed the comic strip to Dang Singh, who studied it carefully. Baggit knew the word *Ahab* would raise a red flag and he was testing Singh to see what would happen. Singh chose to ignore the remark. Singh was easy until you crossed the line with him. When that happened he was lethal; the scariest man on the team.

"I am liking the blond one, Betty; she is the sweet one, but Veronica does have the money," Singh said, pausing to deliberate, as if it were a real dilemma. "Archie liking Veronica, wanting to be rich, social climbing."

"No way," Gerber says. "If Archie is some kind of snob, why would he hang out with a dude like Jughead?"

"True," Singh says, "Jughead a social liability."

Baggit threw his head back and roared. "Yaawww!"

In the middle of the interrogation shack there was a large mahogany Morris chair complete with armrests. It was a very large chair, the kind you could imagine an Orson Welles or latter-day Brando going for, substantial, with plenty of hip and thigh room. The kind of chair that not even the fattest of men could collapse. How it ever got to Vietnam, I can't say, but sitting in the room alone, bolted to a heavy pallet, the only piece of furniture, it looked very much like an American electric chair. I thought it would make Baggit nervous. For a guy that was a hairbreadth away from death row, I thought that Baggit either had a high tolerance for difficult situations or that he was too stupid or too fucking crazy to be scared, and that scared me more than anything. Scared me more than the wild stunts he had pulled at China Beach, flashing knives and shit, performing karate exercises in the streets, punching holes in hotel room walls, beating the crap out of prostitutes and so on. Normal enough in recon. Standard, really. But I didn't want to go out into the field with some motherfucker who thought he was invulnerable or who would be just as happy to kill me as Charles.

Baggit had quickly made it known that he thought the Marine Corps was a piss-poor green motherfucker and that the SEALS had it all over Force Recon, but he got no argument on this. *Break on Through* was a varied bunch. Our machine gunner, Gerber, and myself were the only ones who had been through stateside recon training — just a lot of Mickey Mouse jive — push-ups and forced marches.

One of our best people, Jack Jensen, for instance, had been a rear echelon Marine cook, a heavyweight boxer that I had known at Pendleton and had sparred with. Jensen had no combat training beyond the standard four weeks of ITR, but he was very good in the field — a natural — so when Baggit came along with his SEAL bullshit, no one said too much. This kind of thing was permitted to a degree, although Baggit went too far with it; he and Jensen almost got into it on the first day. It was never entirely clear why headquarters assigned him to a Marine Corps recon team and not back to the SEALS. I guess the murdered officer had a lot of good buddies in the Navy.

A few days after receiving his assignment, Baggit hung a pair of wet socks on the frame of Jensen's bunk, and the next thing you knew there was a shoving match and a few punches thrown but Captain Barnes came into the hootch before there was a real fight and read both men off, especially Baggit. He threatened to send Baggit back to jail. That cooled him down for a while, but I could see that Baggit was going to rag Jensen and vice versa until one or the other established himself as top dog. I knew that if Baggit persisted with this attitude any one of us would have straightened him out, each in our own way. When I think back on it, I'm thinking we were some of the most dangerous people going in Vietnam.

Dang Singh came to the Marine Corps via Bombay–London–Canada–Los Angeles. He was becoming a naturalized U.S. citizen thanks to the Marine Corps and hoped one day to buy a convenience store in Los Angeles, the city he called his home although he had spent less than two months there altogether. Singh was about twenty-seven years old, about Ondine's age, and like Ondine, he was cool under fire, courageous without being reckless. Singh had saved my ass twice. He liked to play the fool but he was a good Marine. Humor was his way of dealing with Vietnam.

Singh was tall for an Indian, about five-eleven, slender, with a light complexion. He had a handsome face and was quite distinguished looking in his tailored tiger-striped fatigues and red beret, a uniform that he had compiled all on his own. You could do that in Force Recon, wear a uniform of choice and more than anywhere in Vietnam, ignore Mickey Mouse regulations.

In the hootch Singh removed his beret and smeared his long thick blue-black hair with a sweet-smelling hair dressing he bought in Saigon called Christopher J's Tiger Rose Pomade. "Keep away mosquito bug, try sometime and you be hook, that for sure."

Gerber, his mouth jammed with bubblegum, said, "Singh, got him a *head full of hair!*"

"Is an otter pelt, I'm telling you; hotter than hell in this place. Is a damn nuisance keeping beautiful all day long," Singh said. "But when I cut it short, ducktail style, everybody always mistaking me for Elvis. 'Oh, Elvis, nice tan you got. Oh, Elvis, what you doing in Vietnam? Oh, Elvis, please be singing 'Heartbreak Hotel.' Elvis, when you be giving me one free Cadillac El Dorado? Elvis, how the Colonel doing these days?' An' I never liking Elvis no how. Is a curse, I'm telling you. Ask Hollywood." ("Hollywood" was my nickname because I went through boot camp in San Diego. It was a little dig. There was an impression that you weren't a *real*

Marine unless you had been through recruit training at Parris Island.)

"Elvis, shit," Baggit said. "You look like fucking Ahab the Arab."

"I'm thinking you one Jerry *Lee* Lewis look-alike," Singh said, finally offended by the nickname *Ahab*. "And how come you all-the-time saying 'yawww'? Get on a man's nerves real quick."

"Well, if you think that's something," Baggit said. "I've just about had it with "ah-roo-ga!' What kind of shit is that?"

"That's fucking recon," Gerber said. "Don't *ever* fuck around with that."

"That's right. That's our fucking battle cry. That's like fucking *Geronimo!*" Jensen said with real heat.

"Well, fine," Baggit said. "In the SEALS we had a thing called 'Hell Week.' I hear they sent you to cook school, Mr. Hotshot PFC. Yawww!"

"Don't laugh." Singh said. "Jensen one esteemed graduate. Certificate in foot locker. Jensen knows *how* to break eggs. Doesn't you, Jensen?"

"And my *salami* is really worth a try —" Jensen said.

"Knock it off. That is some of the most immature shit I have ever heard," Ondine said, standing at the entrance of the hootch with his ruck on and a Remington pump-action twelve-gauge in his hands. "We've got five minutes. Let's motate."

Jensen shook a couple of "greenies," powerful amphetamines, from a small vial and handed them to Ondine. "This will cure what ails. You're such a meany bear when you're hung over."

"Jensen is right, Ondine. You Mr. Grouchy Bear," Singh said.

Ondine gave a little smirk. Jensen offered me the vial and I popped two of the capsules. I hadn't thought of "greenies" but I knew from experience they were the only hangover cure that was certain, and I was so grateful I passed Jensen a spare bottle of insect repellent. He offered me two more of the pills and then let the whole vial go around. That was the rule — everything was shared freely, everyone was trusted completely. You could leave five hundred dollars on the top of your rack, go out into the field, come back six weeks later, and that money would still be there covered with layers of fine red dust, untouched, unmoved.

At last the vial came to Baggit and we saw him pop six capsules at once. This was unheard of, and Singh laughed and said, "Baggit don't be needing helicopter, him can fly by his own self."

Baggit laughed, too. "Yawwh!"

Pretty soon we were all laughing, even Ondine. Six greenies was a very serious matter. So serious, it was funny.

Our corpsman, Mason, shook his head in disbelief. Mason was a "born-again" Christian and, almost worse, he liked the Beach Boys. The main reason he was avoided was because he would dog it under fire and when someone cried, "Corpsman up!" Mason was slow on the draw. Mason didn't seem to know it, but he had more to fear from team *Break on Through* than he did from Charley. He had the life expectancy of a mosquito.

"You are going to have heart rhythm trouble behind all of that speed," Mason said. Everyone laughed and Mason shrugged his shoulders. "What can I say?" He began handing out the large orange "weekly" malaria pills and the little white "daily" ones. Then he started passing out salt tablets. I

stepped outside and swallowed mine with a half can of flat
Budweiser and then the birds came in. I clamped my hand on
top of my bush hat and ran for the chopper, hopped inside last,
and sat back hoping the speed would kick in faster than the
fear. The slick lifted off, dipped away from the base, and
started picking up the lush green vegetation of the countryside — royal palms, banana stalks, and much else botanical.
In the cool of the chopper, looking down, if you didn't know
better, you would have thought you were in paradise, not hell.

Baggit sat next to me and joked with the chopper pilots.
Singh and Gerber, across from me, were grim. It was they who
took the prisoner on our last mission and I remembered that
man and the way they threw him out of the bird when we came
in and how they hustled him into the interrogation shack, and
how they strapped him to the large mahogany chair. The way
they were giving it to him, I knew he had either insulted them
or he had something good, was an officer or something. It was
one of the rare times I had seen Dang Singh out of control and
it wasn't pretty.

In the chopper I watched Singh continue to fuss with his
hair, combing it forward until he tied it together in a topknot
fixed with a rubber band. He set his beret down firmly and
held it in place with a long hat pin as he blew little pink bubblegum bubbles and then sucked them back in his mouth and
popped them. Nerves. The scent of Christopher J's Tiger Rose
Pomade was so strong it flavored the taste of my bubblegum
and I chunked it out the door and watched it float down into a
jade-green sea of jungle.

Whenever we were out in the field and took a prisoner,
Singh would immediately get close with the man and talk to
him in genial, soothing tones on the way in, promising to make
the prisoner a Kit Carson scout if the man defected and went

Chieu Hoi. By acting friendly, Singh was getting a fix on whether or not the prisoner would cooperate or whether he would lie; whether he was a true believer, or just some innocent caught up in a war that meant nothing to him.

The nice-guy routine changed when the prisoner was taken into the interrogation shack. None of the Marines on the team wanted anything to do with it, not even Ondine. Usually our Vietnamese people did all the dirty work — kicking the shit out of the prisoners, taking the fight out of them before Dang Singh even began.

A prisoner would be tightly bound in the Morris chair so that movement was impossible. Securing them took some doing since most of them were relatively tiny in the first place and the chair was really massive, but this ultimately was a good thing, since it must have made them feel smaller and more inconsequential than ever before. What worked best was rope around their chest, neck, forehead, legs, elbows, and on the wrists, duct tape.

Dang Singh liked to question a prisoner and extract "hot" information before Intelligence had their run at him. What Singh would do is remove the hat pin from his beret and run it under the man's thumbnail all the way down to the base. He would do it slowly, taking several minutes — sometimes, I heard, he would take a solid hour. He didn't even bother asking questions as he did this although I saw them volunteer information after the pin was run in just a few milimeters. If the screaming got too bad, one of the ARVN Rangers would duct-tape the man's mouth shut and sometimes lay a handkerchief over the prisoner's face, splashing water on it from a canteen. This was said to replicate the sensation of drowning.

Only when Singh got down to the base of the nail did the questions start, and if the answers weren't forthcoming he would take a bayonet and tap on the pin. He was cool, methodical, almost friendly as he did the job, but whatever the man had been — a Communist ideologue, patriot, soldier, husband, father, son — whatever — all of it went out the door until he had become little more than a vessel of pain and the only thing in the world that mattered to him was to make the pain go away. Singh could get the "hot" stuff quicker and in a less dirty way than anyone. If the prisoner did well, gave us something good, Singh would give him a Marlboro cigarette to smoke before he turned him over to the spooks in Da Nang with their Sodium Penthothal, tape recorders, and polygraph machines. Our last prisoner had given good but not until Singh hauled out a rat-tail file and ground the prisoner's lower front teeth down to the gum line. After a three-hour session they dragged him out of the shack with shit in his pants and let him sit in the dirt and smoke a half pack of Marlboros before a truck came along to take him off to Da Nang. He was a tough little fucker and had earned Singh's grudging admiration.

As our choppers moved inland, we began picking up steep mountains with rainbowed crystal waterfalls and triple-canopy jungle in seven shades of green. I was grooving on the ride, hoping it would never end, when I heard the pilot point out the valley that was our destination and watched the first bird circle the valley before it dipped down low and finally set down.

Our Kit Carson scout, Ondine, Jensen, and two Vietnamese Rangers jumped out of the slick and moved quickly through the elephant grass. Then it was our turn. I'm not sure if my brain was being hammered by all the amphetamine or if it was just adrenaline, but I was glad to get off the bird and glad for the heft and feel of my rifle. The choppers swung up and out of the valley, their blades beating sharp and heavy at the same time — *whop, whop, whop, thup, thup thup* — *Here we go*, I thought. *One, two, three, ca pup, ch, ch . . . come on, baby!*

The enemy was waiting for us, and in seconds we were getting chewed up by .31-caliber machine-gun fire. Charles began firing rockets at the choppers, and I knew that if they had rockets they had to be there in numbers. I had seen hot LZs before, but never anything like this.

Mason got hit just as we cleared the whorls of elephant grass laid flat by the chopper blades. I was running just behind him and got a faceful of hot sticky blood. I grabbed his wrist and rather than feeling the dead weight of a corpse, Mason felt like a feather. I ran full bore dragging Mason into the cover of the tall grass.

The NVA had set up an L-shaped ambush but the team immediately went away from it toward our secondary LZ in the hopes that the birds could come around and extract us. Blood was pulsing out of a wound from Mason's chest — sucking chest wound. I slapped the cellophane wrapper from a pack of Camels over the exit wound and put field dressing on it.

One night while we were setting up in the field, I remember Mason telling me that his head didn't believe in God. "My head doesn't get it," Mason said, "but my heart bleeds for Jesus." While the rest of us were getting drunk and rowdy at China Beach, Mason had stayed in the air-conditioned base recreation center eating hamburgers and french fries as he studied *Science and Health: A Key to the Scriptures*. Now he was seized by the grip of death. Choking in his own blood he cried my name, "Hollywood!" and died. I remembered my purple force, felt its surge, and remembered thinking that it was a funny universe where God couldn't keep the faithful alive but the Devil could.

The .31-caliber fire was flying all around me. Not in bursts but continuously. This must have gone on for several minutes. I was afraid to move. I remember having glanced at my Rolex as we set down, and now, as I lay in the tall elephant grass, I could feel the sting of the little cuts the razor-sharp leaves had made on my face and hands, like paper cuts.

Time was doing strange things to me. It seemed like the sun had sunk behind a mountain, that I had experienced a night, that the sun had risen and set, that there was another night and that this happened again and again and again, but suddenly the machine gun stopped and I realized that the gunner, in his excitement to nail us, had burned out the barrel. When I looked at my watch I saw that only seven minutes had passed. Looking up, I could see a column of NVA spreading out to encircle the team; I got up and began to sprint. I knew that Mason was dead and I didn't even care. I just wanted to haul ass. There was triple-canopy jungle about two hundred meters ahead of me but the NVA was moving that way, too. I was going to have to get there first. Behind me I could hear the dull *bap, bap, bap* of AK-47 fire, and as I ran, I hoped that if I had to take a round, that it wouldn't be a sucking chest wound like Mason's, that it would be in the back of my head and that I wouldn't hear it or feel it.

As I ran it seemed that time had played its other trick — slow motion. On full automatic, an AK-47 puts out 600 rounds per minute but I was able to count each of those rounds. *Purple haze all in my eyes, don't know if it's day or night — tomorrow or the end of time?* The purple field. Safety in purple field. I finally made the tree line near the floor of the valley and had to start moving up the mountain. In spite of the density of the jungle, Charley was everywhere. I saw five troopers hustle past me on a narrow speed trail. I was lying on a little hill with my ass up in the air and couldn't believe in my luck — they hadn't seen me. That was the beauty of the tiger-striped fatigues; if you had your face painted, all you had to do was step three yards in the jungle and freeze and nobody saw you. I turned around as quietly as possible and began to crawl away from the trail and looked up to see three soldiers hacking their way through the brush with machetes — they were coming at me dead ahead and I was trapped between them and the speed trail.

I couldn't really get a shot at them because of the heavy brush, but a sunbeam angled down on me illuminating a kind of hole between the second and first layer of jungle canopy. I reached for a frag and a smoke grenade and at the same moment read the time on my watch — two hours ago we were discussing the possibilities of screwing comic-book Veronica and now I was caught alone in the jungle a million miles from anywhere I wanted to be.

I flung the frag up into the sunlight and when it blew, I popped my smoke and darted out to the high speed trail. I ran to the left in the opposite direction I had seen the first bunch of soldiers moving and after a few long strides I dropped to the ground, rolled over to the side of the trail, and leveled my weapon. The three soldiers, unhurt by the grenade, jumped out on the trail almost simultaneously. I placed a single round into each of their chests with my CAR-15, then jumped up and ran back exactly to the place where I had come from. The next thing I knew I was laying down a claymore mine with infinite care, patience, and skill, and then greasing the detonation cable with a tube of camouflage paint, leaves, and twigs — it was invisible.

A strange kind of calm had descended over me, and as I looked at my sunbeam I could see the sun flare like an orange ball on the horizon. It was like in my high school Golden Gloves fights. The first punches had been thrown, the butter-flies had vanished, and I was in control of my fear, riding atop it, using it to my own advantage. It was like a movie. Unreal.

I was glad to get the mine down, it was one less thing to carry, and I was amazed to hear my smoke grenade continue to hiss. I was very much in the here-and-now yet at the same time I was sitting on my grandmother's lap in her grocery store down on the south end of Aurora, Illinois. We were sitting up near the front of the store, ten o'clock at night, and every time a car passed my grandmother would twist around arthritically and look down Lake Street to Lombardo's Store on the adjacent corner to see how much business Anthony Lombardo was getting.

My grandmother. She was scarcely five feet tall. Her hands and elbows were rough with calluses. Her hair was thin and gray and she always smelled vaguely of Ben-Gay. They called her "Mag" and said that in her day she was a "looker" and that she loved to dance. She didn't seem the dancing type to me. To me she was "Gram." Every day for forty-five years she dragged herself from bed at 5 A.M. and set her aching body to work. The store opened at 6 A.M.

The Rainbow breadman came early with fragrant still warm bread wrapped in gaily colored plastic bags. The Oatman's milkman came in his short refrigerated truck with chinking clear glass bottles of milk; the meatman, a Groucho Marx look-alike in a knee-length, bloody white lab coat and with a strong cigar; and then customers began filing in, in a steady procession — I could see them all before me. See, hear, taste, smell.

It was there for me. Like Proust with his tea biscuit. Here and now — real. I could see the cheerful, boozy Francesco Sacco coming in the back door on his way to a ten-hour shift at the Durabuilt. He left his bulldog, Pete, waiting on the back porch, while he departed through the front door, strolling up Jericho Road, lunch pail in hand, in love with life and the whole world. The dog guarded Mag's back porch for years.

The people came to buy and they came to visit. There was no television in those days. There was no hurry. Mag was a skillful conversationalist as well as a hardworking storekeeper. The work got done: shelves were stocked, the coal stove was stoked, laundry was washed and hung to dry on lines out in the back parking lot, meals were made, four daughters were raised, so were innumerable grandchildren and even an orphan who walked in off the street with tears in his eyes and instantly became a part of the family. Mag could not stand the sight of hunger or suffering. She saw the Great Depression come and go and she also saw that her neighbors were fed. Food was sold "on time" and it was freely given away. The filthiest hoboes were privileged to hot meals in her kitchen. Located as it was near the railroad yard, the store was known to hoboes all across the country — and the hours were convenient. Mag didn't close the store until eleven in the evening, when she ritualistically ate a dish of crackers and milk in the dark of the kitchen. A burning light invited customers to bang on the door. I can remember selling pork chops to an uncompromising drunk on a hot, steamy midnight in July. After the long day was done, Mag hobbled up the stairs to bed, where she rubbed her legs with Ben-Gay and read her prayer book until she fell asleep.

Mag had started the store with an eighth-grade German-language education and fifty dollars to her name. She loved the work and she loved her customers. In my turn I helped with the store. I sacked red and white potatoes in ten-pound bags. I colored tubs of margarine and spooned out peanut butter by the pound. I helped Mag butcher chickens in the basement. I swatted the huge jumping spiders that came in banana crates from Central America. I swept the floor and lugged pop bottles up and down the basement stairs on dark nights, fearful of the bogeyman. One day I longed to run the store myself. I thought it was my destiny.

The best part, after the crackers and milk in the kitchen, was when we'd go upstairs together and I'd turn on the night light while Mag slowly hobbled up the steps, and I'd have the sheets down and my face in a comic book, a "Little Lulu" or an "Uncle Scrooge," while she rubbed herself down with Ben-Gay and then log-rolled into bed and opened her prayer book.

"Gram, when we die do we really go up to heaven?"

"No. When we die, we just die."

"Then how come you read prayers every night."

"Because I believe in God."

"I love you, Gramma. I hope you never die."

"You'll show them, Tommy. Someday you'll grow up and you'll show them all."

I glanced at my Rolex, which read 20:46. Six minutes. It was fast growing dark. I inched over to a red mound where I was able to lay off the weight of my ruck. I got some bug juice from my breast pocket and started dousing the leeches on my hands, face, and neck. As soon as the insect repellent hit them, they recoiled, pulled their heads out of my skin, shrunk, and dropped off.

I heard a soft rustling and grabbed my rifle only to see another enormous python race across my path. It seemed like he was doing fifteen miles an hour. Not again. I did not want to see Satan again, but I needed the field of purple.

The night was black as ink and the sounds of the jungle took over, punctuated sporadically by the distant sound of mortar fire. Occasionally there were multiple bursts of AK-47 fire followed by the heavy thunking of Gerber's 60. It sounded very far away. I heard a couple of small explosions and more 60 fire and then silence. *That's good*, I thought. *Git some, Gerber, git some, man; you're one hard-core motherfucker.*

Willard G. Kegly aka Gerber. We called him "Gerber" because he looked like the kid on the baby food jars. Back at China Beach after I told Gerber about my vision of Satan, he told me he also had a dream or a vision where he saw his ticket getting punched on this next mission. For a moment I thought he was about to cry, but then he took on a reckless air. "I don't give a ratfuck," he said. That was how you did it. You did not cry or whine. That was not permissible. You just had to take it, like in the cowboy movies.

Mason, who often said he was covered in the blood of Jesus and cloaked in the armor of God, and who jeopardized the team with his self-concern, was dead. Gerber, who conceded his life and didn't give a ratfuck, had uncanny luck. It was the field of purple. He had found it. He didn't say so, but I knew that he had it and I hoped he would hold on to it and I hoped that I would hold on to it and that *Break on Through* would manifest it then and forever. Over and over again when the shit got heavy, what the guys would say would be, *"Not this time, oh dear God. Don't let it be this time!*" No one said, don't let it be "this tour," or "this month," or "this week"; they said, don't let it be "this time."

The 60 continued to rattle far, far away. I knew everything there was to know about Gerber. The first girl he kissed. The first time he made love. I knew of his best friends, his parents and family, that the GTO he claimed to own was actually his brother's and that Gerber drove a Morris Minor that his father had handed down to him. I knew the one meal he would eat if he had to eat the same meal for the rest of his life — cheeseburger and fries, chocolate shake. I knew the way he wore his hair in civilian life, the type of clothes he wore — Dobie Gillis; the grades he got in high school, what made him laugh, what made him crazy, what his dreams were. I knew all these things about Gerber and I loved Gerber, would have laid my life down for Gerber, done anything for Gerber, and yet I somehow didn't really *like* him. Back in the world I might have even hated him. But on that night, on that mission, the sound of Gerber's machine gun was the nicest lullaby I have ever heard. "Go on, Gerber, git some!"

Suddenly my claymore blew and I heard a muffled cry. I spun around and fired the two magazines I had taped together on full automatic. I flipped a frag into the direction of the explosion, locked in another magazine, and ran out to the high speed trail toward the sound of Gerber's machine gun.

Everything seemed detached and far away. I flashed back to Copley Playground. I remembered Carlo Cesare, my first friend, and the sweetness of his friendship. "God bless you, Carlo, wherever you are; I hope you aren't here in the fucking Nam."

On summer mornings I would leave the store with my baseball mitt and walk up the block to his window and tap on the screen. He would come around and let me in and I would wait for him to eat his cereal and then we would go off to the ballpark. Mario Vittorio was at the playground, Peter Perillo, all of the ballplayers. One time Vittorio asked me if he could see my tonsils, like he was doing a medical survey, and when I opened my mouth, he spat a hocker into the back of my throat and then ran away, laughing. I caught up to him, dragged him down in a chicken wing until he started crying and then his brother, Paulo, younger but fat and tough, shoved me off. "Leave my brother alone." So I gave Paulo a few but he was crazed and immune from pain. I boxed him easily but he put his head down and ran in through my punches, grabbing me. I pulled away and punched. He grabbed at me and clawed at me and pretty soon had me scared badly.

I was the better runner. I made it to the store, but Vittorio had the audacity to run in after me and kick the shit out of me. Mag had to run him off. The old man heard about it and came by with his old heavybag, liquor on his breath.

"Boxing is the science of controlling fear; it's not a perfect science, alas, but I'm going to show you how to control fear. Let's go. Put your hands up. Set yourself up. Your feet are too close together. Okay, that's better. Now pop a jab. Stick and move, baby. Get your elbows in. Jab. Everything works off of your jab, remember that. C'mon, jab — snap it. Keep your chin down, you're holding your head too high. That's better. Jab. C'mon, jab. There's nothing to be afraid of. It's only a fight. It's only a fight."

"Uncle John. How good of a fighter was my dad?"

"Your dad? Well, he was very good. A boxer, very slick and he had guts. Number five in the world. That's not too bad, is it, considering he wasn't really much more than a blown-up light-

heavy? He used to fight drunk. Pretty good, too, in a way, but horseshit, really."

"He told me that Joe Louis promised him a shot."

"That's how he got to be number five. They rated him so the fight would seem legitimate. I mean Louis was his friend and wanted to give him a payday, that's all."

"So he wouldn't have had a chance?"

"Tom, he wouldn't have had a chance if they put handcuffs on Louis. On the worst night of his life, Joe Louis would have beat him, but that isn't taking anything away from your father. On his best day he didn't have the speed or the firepower to cope with Joe Louis, but I don't think he was afraid. I don't think the son of a bitch was afraid of anyone."

Voices coming up the trail. Quick, jump in the bushes. Shut the fuck up, Tommy; your heart is pounding, Tommy, every fucking gook in the jungle can hear it, Tommy; and if Charles doesn't hear you, Tommy; he's going to smell your rotten-meat, dead-flesh Caucasian smell.

Oh, fuck, here they come. How many of them are there? Five? I think I saw five.

I pull the pin on my last frag. *One, two, three, ca pup, daca, ch ch, come on, baby.* Throw it, now! Boom! Okay, step into your fire lane and waste those motherfuckers!

Pop pop pop pop pop pop . . .

Okay, good, slap in a fresh magazine, good, now run. Come on, motherfucker, pick them up, pick 'em up, pick 'em up, lay 'em down, lay 'em down, lay 'em down. Move.

Run.

Boom boom boom boom boom! Ondine's shotgun. Good to hear it. Git some, Ondine, you motherfucker!

Ondine, in a voice ranging from baritone to falsetto. "Fuck-ing, Hollywood, man, you cain't say the word right, don't fucking

*say it at all. Three years in the fucking Crotch and you cain't even
say motherfucker! Jive time, watch this, hey! Check it out."*

*Ondine cups his right hand almost over his balls, the cup
of his hand to the right of them, the thumb touching. With his
shoulders rolling, his head bobbing to the Doors' "Crawling
Kingsnake," snapping his fingers, he diddybops across the hootch
dragging his left foot slightly. "It ain't nothin' for a stepper,
Hollywood — Mutherfucker!"*

"Mutherfucker," I say.

Run! (Tell me something: how long, asshole, are you
going to keep your ass hanging out in this speed trail?)

Get your ass off this here speed trail! The first place you
can, jump in.

No, run! Get some distance on that place.

Try and keep your head. Try and keep your head. Stay
cool.

Run!

Charley's going to be all over there. Keep running.
How long? Charley's going to be coming up this here speed
trail and he's going to grease your ass, Tommyboy. What you
going to do?

Just run. Did you shit your pants? Did you piss them?
Who cares? Run. Just run. Are you afraid, Tommyboy?

No, I'm not afraid. This shit is all a big movie. It isn't
happening, but if it is happening, I can hack it. I can hack it.

I found a creek and decided to turn around and go back
down the mountain, back into the valley. The next day I hid,
slept even, crashing bad from those "greenies." At night I ate
a biscuit from a packet of "C's," felt stuffed by it, and cautiously I moved out again.

Dawn. The creek got bigger and fed into a small river.
Two gooks in black pajamas picked me up and started firing

from a hundred meters. I ran along the edge of the river, slipping, falling.

I'm back in the ring at the Northwest Armory, semifinals, Chicago Golden Gloves, tall for a middleweight, with long arms and a fairly decent left jab followed by the crisp straight right. I had nothing much more than that — just those two punches. But it was so easy, setting them up with that jab, I almost feel sorry for them, short little fuckers, fireplugs, mighty tough little bastards but they didn't have a chance. I could keep them off with the jab. Punish them with it, then work the right. Getting mad at myself when I dropped them too soon. I liked making it last, making their pain and their fear endure. I wanted them to know how it felt. *"Someday you'll show them all, Tommy."*

What the fuck am I doing in Vietnam? These gooks are hot on my ass. I drop down and fire a burst off in their direction. They separate. One of them cleaves to the river while the other starts crawling west to pull a flanking move on me. I have to conserve my ammunition. At least I had the sense to grab Mason's spare ammunition. I fire a shot at each of the gooks and get up and run. I wonder if I should dump my ruck. Not a good idea.

The psycho ward for the criminally insane at the Oregon State Hospital: go up there just out of boot camp and see the old man. He's doing ten years. All he wants to know, all he's got to say to me — how much are Marlboros on the street? They're screwing me at the hospital canteen, he says. I show a picture of my mother. "Who's that?" he says. He doesn't care, doesn't give a shit about anything.

Downriver I found more jungle, set down and caught the two little dinks just five minutes behind me. I let them walk past me and gave each of them a round in the back of the head.

One of them had an NVA pack and I took it off him. The NVA field pack had the USMC pack beat by a mile. I felt like a little kid on Christmas over this pack. As I transferred my gear into the new pack, I was so wrapped up in what I was doing that I barely had time to hug the earth when I heard the metal cork pop of an RPG rocket go off. The grenade sailed over my head and exploded when I heard the bark of AK-47 fire and the unmistakable tinny pops of an M-16. Suddenly a hand clamped itself over my mouth and I felt a sharp blade at my throat. "Your ass is *dead*, Marine." Then I saw Baggit's boot step on my rifle and when he let me go, I turned over and looked up at him. "Recon," he said. "Shit," and then just as quickly as he had come he disappeared into the jungle. I got up and scrambled around the area. There were seven dead NVA apart from the two I had shot. All of them had their noses sliced off and in the mouths of each was a black Ace of Spades with a Navy SEAL emblem on the backside. Fucking Baggit had saved my ass and I wanted to kill him for it but he was gone, no doubt thinking that he would be safer alone than with me. As I moved out of the jungle again with my new pack, I sounded like a couple of skeletons fucking on a tin roof and had to stop and repack it. When I moved into the sun, it steamed the wetness out of my uniform and my gear but it couldn't steam away my own humiliation for acting like such a cherry. I almost wish Baggit would have let me walk into that RPG round. I wouldn't have felt a thing.

For two days I followed the river and finally felt safe enough to be hungry. My fucking C-rats were ham and lima beans, but I had some hot sauce and cool halazone-flavored water. This was the best meal I've ever eaten. *Better than crackers and milk in the dark kitchen back at the store?*

Yes, better.

On the fourth day I spotted a radio tower near a bend in the river. Someone had blown a paddy dike to flood the field, turning it into waist-deep mud. With my field glasses, I spotted a U.S. Marine in the watchtower watching me coming in with his own binoculars. He smiled at me and flashed a "V" sign. I held my rifle in one hand and flashed the "V" sign back. I slogged through the field, and it seemed to take forever.

As I got closer in, I saw that it was a small outpost surrounded by razor wire. There was a pair of half buried "conex" cargo containers inside the perimeter covered with sandbags. The Marine on watch signaled for me to move over toward the river and two Popular Force soldiers came out to walk me in, away from the mines. I told them I wanted to soak in the river a moment, to get the fetid-smelling mud off of me.

Baggit, Gerber, Singh, and our ARVN Rangers and Kit Carson were inside the wire. They had just come in, like an hour before me. Baggit's thumb had been partly severed and I had barely set my gear down when he started begging me to cut it off. Everyone on the team had a specialty — light arms, demolitions, communications, cartography, and so on — and each of us tried to learn backup skills. I had learned some "meatball" surgery from Mason.

"Cut the goddamn thing off. I can't take it anymore. I don't need it. Cut it off."

It occurred to me that if I cut Baggit's thumb off he would get to go home. I was running on the last dregs of adrenaline, feeling really ragged, but I still had Mason's medical kit and I pulled it out of my pack to examine the contents. I just about shit when I find a pound of M&M's and two single-serving boxes of Sugar Pops. I started sorting through the medical equipment.

"I can clean that up. I can sew it back on," I said.

"Fuck that. Cut it off. I don't need the goddamn thing. I don't want it," Baggit said.

"Then cut it off yourself," I said. "But you cut that bone and you will feel pain. Bone pain is bad pain."

A Marine captain came over and asked me, "Are you with these people?"

"That's right, Captain."

"Are you a corpsman?"

"Our corpsman is dead and we've been running. Charley is out there big time, sir, and I'm thinking this place is in a world of shit."

I found a packet of morphine Syrettes, like little toothpaste tubes fixed with needles. Each contained a quarter grain of morphine sulfate. I took three of the tubes and set them apart on the canvas cover of the medical kit. I found a bottle of orange malaria tablets and a number of Kotex pads, which make excellent field dressings. I found Betadine and set this on the lid of the kit. I found the suture kit and a bottle of antibiotics. I shook a couple of tablets into my hand and handed them to Baggit. "Take these so you don't get an infection," I said.

Baggit obeyed me like a small boy.

"I'm going to tie off a vein and hit you with morphine. These are small needles. If you don't like needles, turn your head — as soon as you feel the rush I'm going to start sewing —"

"Recon," the captain said, chewing on the word as if it were a turd. "You people think you are a law unto yourselves."

"Captain," I said. "There are NVA all over the place. I would secure the perimeter, sir —"

"I think we've got it covered, Marine. Antipersonnel mines, beehives, illumination. We've got that paddy field ass deep with mud."

"The NVA has got flyweight sappers, sir. They can hop over that mud like Jesus walking on water. I weigh a hundred and eighty pounds. Charley has got rubber sandals and he can go. I know this. He's been chasing me for four days and he knows how to scooter."

Baggit let out a sigh as the morphine began to hit home. I squeezed in the last few drops. First he threw his head back and then he let it fall forward.

"I'm going to clean out the wound, now," I said.

As soon as I started to scrub Baggit's thumb, he drew it back. "Fuck!"

One morphine Syrette mainlined would be enough to kill most people but I had seen Baggit smoking heroin and chugging whiskey at China Beach. I had seen him do six "greenies" at the beginning of this mission and I knew he had an unreal tolerance for drugs. I took another morphine Syrette and popped it in Baggit's thigh, squeezed the tube, and then waited. Ondine was crashed alongside one of the cargo containers. It was getting to be the midafternoon and the heat was kicking in hard; the sun was baking hot and I knew that no matter how long Ondine crashed, he wasn't going to get any real rest.

"What the fuck happened to you, Hollywood? And what happened to Mason?" Gerber said.

"Yeah?" Singh said.

"Mason bought it the minute we came in. I got pinned down by .31-caliber fire. Those fuckers wanted me so bad they burned up a machine gun —"

"Oh, man, that shit is so . . . good . . . man!" Baggit's body slumped forward.

As Baggit continued to nod, I cleaned the wound as best I could. I could see that while much of the meat of his thumb had been torn away, the little blood vessels on the attached portion were still intact. I pulled the flesh down around the back side of his thumb where the bone was exposed and sewed the flesh together. The sight of exposed ivory bone was getting to me. For a moment I felt as though I would faint. I hurried the job and when I had finished stitching, I wrapped a field dressing over the thumb and taped it over with duct tape. Baggit fell into a drugged sleep, and Gerber, Singh, and I carried him into a slit trench, shading him with a poncho liner. It was all we could do to get him that far.

Singh, Jensen, Gerber, and I cleaned our weapons, and after that we all fell asleep as the heat of the day took over. We were all too exhausted to exchange stories.

I awoke at nightfall to the sound of incoming artillery — *Ka-rump! Ka-rump! Ka-rump!* Suddenly there were explosions all over the place. Singh shook me and said, "We have to get out past the wire. They've got beehive rounds in that fucking cargo container."

No, Tommy, when you die, you just die.

I jumped up and followed Singh. We got out past the wire into a deep trench when the illumination rounds started popping off, casting an eerie glow across the paddy field. There were NVA in tan cotton uniforms all over the place setting off mines as they came in, blowing the shit out of themselves, only to reveal more of them coming in behind. Baggit and Gerber jumped into the trench with us on the wrong side of the wire and we were all firing at the human wave assault. I kept waiting for the beehives but when I looked back at the compound, all of the Popular Forces were down and scared shitless. The only movement I saw came from the handful of Marines from the communications team.

I turned around again and started shooting gooks. They were blowing holes through the wires with bangalor torpedoes. A man I took to be one of our own jumped into the trench and jabbed Gerber in the back with a bayonet. Singh saw it happening as I did and reached up on top of the trench where he had set his .45, picked it up, turned, and fired the gun in the man's face. Because the man was wearing a helmet, the concussive effect of the round blew his face away. Gerber was lucky. He was wearing his flak jacket and the soldier had only made an arm thrust with the bayonet. If he had followed through with a full body thrust, he could have buried it into the hilt. As it was, Gerber hardly acknowledged the wound although I could see blood running down his pant leg, saturating it.

There was too much happening to do anything except shoot. Gooks were getting past us and getting through the wire and the Marines inside the perimeter were firing 60s. *"Tom, this is your uncle John, you better sit down; I've got bad news. Your father hanged himself up at that nuthouse."*

In a while the Phantoms came in with white phosphorus and then, best of all, an Air Force gunship, Puff the Magic Dragon, made an appearance and started pouring out so much fire with its miniguns that tracer rounds looked like orange lightning bolts.

When it was too late to do any good, the Popular Forces let go with the beehives, the flechettes sounding like whiplashes. We decided to lay low in the trench long after the captain called a cease-fire. I stuck one of Mason's Kotex pads on

Gerber's wound and pressure-taped it with the last of the duct tape. Gerber said that the wound didn't hurt. The only thing that bugged him was that he could feel blood squishing in his boot. "How bad is it, Hollywood? I don't even want to look."

"Gerber, you're tougher than shoe leather. You are almost as tough as Ondine. You don't have to worry about nothin', man. Bleeding's quit."

When we moved back inside the wire at dawn, I saw Ondine and Jensen in a trench covering the river. I hollered at them and they turned to look at me. Both of them had a mirror and their razors out and the sight of them clean shaven caused me to laugh.

Around 0700 the Marine Corps sent in a medevac chopper and we got Gerber out along with another of the Marines who had taken shrapnel and lost an eye. There was room for Baggit, but he said he was okay and wanted to stay with the team. There were no choppers for *Break on Through* and we were ordered to proceed to a ville of friendlies four klicks downriver where there would be motor transport. Everybody was feeling pretty raggedy, but we moved out after the communications captain presented us two bottles of Jack Daniel's and a thank-you.

We made the ville before noon and started in on the Black Label. I had some beef and potato "C's" and although I hadn't eaten much in days, I couldn't face them. Singh, who spoke Vietnamese, paid an old woman to fix us some chow. She was barbecuing paddy rat and served it to us on skewers along with fluffy overcooked rice. Baggit said the meat was delicious, what was it, and we all gave him a look like don't ask, until everybody started laughing. Singh was the one who told him we were eating paddy rats.

Baggit ran out of the hootch and threw up, which was a

shame considering he had finished off at least a third of a bottle of Jack. I was a little surprised at this display of fussiness since out in the bush he was the complete primal man. All of a sudden I heard him raising hell and then heard the old woman and when I went out into the sun I saw that Baggit had sliced the heads off of two geese. He shot a pig with his .45 and started chopping that up with his machete and when the old woman tried to stop him, she grabbed his sore thumb and wouldn't let go until he smashed her in the face with the barrel of his .45.

Ondine ordered him to knock it off, which he did for a time, pacing back and forth in front of the hootch, slugging down whiskey like it was iced tea; then he went for a one-armed old man, cuffing at him with an open hand. The old man meant nothing to me. If Baggit had shot him, I don't think I would have given it a second thought. I wasn't used to seeing that many villagers and when I did, there was such a wall between us, that it was as though they weren't human beings at all.

Jensen, the heavyweight boxer, threw a body slam at Baggit and the old fellow scrambled away.

"That's it. That's enough, Baggit. He's innocent old man. These people are friendlies. What the hell's the matter with you?"

I wondered if Jensen really cared about the old man or if he was just picking his moment to fight. The words were barely out of his mouth when Baggit bayed, "Yaawww!" and clipped Jensen in the head with a roundhouse karate kick. Jensen dropped to one knee, and before he got up Baggit hit him in the face with a front kick and then tried another of the roundhouse kicks but Jensen managed to catch his foot and pull him to the ground. They rolled around in the dirt cursing each other until Baggit was on Jensen's chest slamming punches into Jensen's face with his bad hand as well as his good. Jensen had his arms up and I could see him rolling to avoid the punches, but Baggit was getting him pretty good.

Ondine adroitly stepped up behind Baggit and grabbed his sore thumb, twisting the whole arm behind Baggit's back as he frog-marched him away from Jensen. "That's it, man. Have you got it?"

"Let go!"

"Reading loud and clear?"

"Affirmative."

"Well, you just better get your shit together or I'm going to take you out!"

As soon as Ondine let go of Baggit's hand, Baggit shot a head butt into Ondine's face and punched him three quick blows with his good hand. Ondine fell on his ass and held his nose with both hands, dazed and glassy-eyed, catching the blood, trying to keep it off his uniform.

Jensen rushed in and grabbed Baggit by his fatigue shirt, flung him face-first to the ground and then whenever Baggit tried to get up, Jensen pounded him down again with rabbit punches to the back of Baggit's neck. Baggit would get himself in the approximation of a push-up and Jensen would knock him down again.

"Yawwhhh!" Baggit screamed, and at last he was able to get up and set himself in his karate stance, but Jensen moved in and started bouncing his fists off Baggit's head. Baggit rushed forward with his forehead and the two men collided heads. It sounded like two bowling balls clanking together, and now Jensen stalled. It seemed that Baggit was going to kick him, but then he walked by and went over to hold on to a bamboo post that supported a little porch in the front of the hootch. Choking, Jensen got up and removed his soaked fatigue shirt and dropped it to the ground as if it was too heavy to fight in. "C'mon, Baggit, is that all you got?"

Baggit was hanging on to the pole. "Fuck it, you win," he said. "I've had enough." Baggit sunk to his knees and began to vomit when Jensen rushed him and started in with the rabbit punches again until I thought he was going to kill Baggit. He shoved Baggit's face into a hot slick puddle of vomit and said, "You'll quit, when I say you'll quit, you cocksucker."

At last Ondine and I intervened. "Jesus Christ, Jack, you're going to kill him," I said. I helped Baggit over to the village well and poured water over his head and shoulders. He tried to refuse my help but I said, "Hey, man, you fuckin' saved my ass. You're on the team, brother. Everything is cool. You fucking SEALS are fucking hard-core."

"Not bad, huh?"

"Fucking hard-core. Don't worry about Ondine or Jensen. I'll straighten things out."

Baggit looked up at me. It wasn't the psycho look. It was a look of human gratitude and of genuine surprise. "You'll do that for me?"

"We can buddy up. I got a lot to learn —"

"I had you figured. I guess I had you figured wrong."

"You saved my ass, man. What can I say?"

Before long a pair of trucks came in with a platoon of Marines heading up to the communications outpost. The driver talked with Ondine, who had staunched the bleeding of his nose with the green towel he wore under his ruck for padding. Ondine told us the trucks would be back soon. It turned out we were farther north than I thought, up near Dong Ha. We sat in the hootch drinking the last of the Jack. Ondine had taken Baggit's rifle and .45 and kept an eye on him as he sat out on the short veranda of the hootch all by himself.

Jensen also went down to the well to wash himself off and was still there when the trucks came back. Ondine ordered Baggit onto the back of the first one and jumped in with him, telling the rest of us to ride on the second truck.

When we arrived at Camp Clarke, Captain Barnes told us to take a shower and grab a nap, we were going out again the next afternoon. All of us were going, that is, except for Baggit and Gerber who were sent to the aid station and from there to the hospital. When we got back from that next mission, after six weeks in the bush, Gerber was fit for duty and waiting for us. Baggit, Gerber said, had lost his thumb and was stateside waiting for a medical discharge. Some weeks later when we had all but forgotten Baggit, he sent us a postcard from Salinas, California, where he was working in his old man's body and fender shop. He said the Navy had restored all his medals and had given him his stripes back. He received an honorable discharge and a disability pension. There was a parade given in his honor because of his Medal of Honor and all. He said he wished us all the best. That he was "Proud to claim the title" (of U.S. Marine) and so on. No one on the team said much about it at the time. I think someone said that he had done pretty good for a guy that was supposed to be on death row, or something like that. I do know that none of us could remember his first name. Judging by the childish scrawl, you could see that Baggit wasn't used to writing letters. Maybe this was the only card he had written in his life, but I could tell that Baggit *had* to write that card. Baggit was writing to say thanks for saving him. He was two steps from the abyss until Jensen started hammering the shit out of him with those rabbit punches. Jensen had beat him savagely, within an inch of death, but within that inch, there was a kind of temporary redemption. And then, too, maybe Ondine laid something

heavy on him during that ride back to Camp Clarke. Whatever, Baggit had run into something that was tougher and
meaner than he was and it caused him to recover his psychic
ballast for a time. So I think he wrote to tell us that he was
going to be okay and to say thanks. Thanks for the scare.
Thanks for the bad beating. I had seen enough of them on my
own in boxing to know that sometimes a bad beating could do
a fellow a world of good, but I also knew that for a guy like
Baggit there was no permanent cure. A few months after *Break
on Through* rotated back to Pendleton, Baggit made the front
page of the *Los Angeles Times*. He had barricaded himself for
fourteen hours in a Salinas, California, beauty parlor with his
estranged old lady before he shot her and shot himself. When
the police got inside and found the bodies, a bag of heroin,
narcotics paraphernalia, and a blood-stained Medal of Honor,
Jim Morrison of the Doors was singing "The End" on Mrs.
Baggit's radio, the article said. It was July 9, 1971, the day
James Douglas Morrison's death had been revealed to the
world and all you could hear on the radio waves were the
Doors. Morrison had already been buried in the "Poet's
Corner" of the Père-Lachaise Cemetery in Paris. I remember
that day far more clearly than the day Kennedy was shot, when
I was a shavetail private just out of boot camp, and really
didn't have a clue about life. The death of Jim Morrison
revealed on July 9, 1971, a hot and clear day at Pendleton, hurt
me a lot more and hurt it still does. In a matter of days *Break
on Through* lost it's raison d'être and a man who wasn't good
for much on the streets of America but knew the purple fields
better than anyone I knew. I guess you could say it was a good
thing that the war was finally over.

The Black
Lights

COMMANDER ANDY HAWKINS, chief psychiatrist of
the neuropsych ward at Camp Pendleton, received the
inevitable nickname Eaglebeak, or Eagle, early in his first tour
in Vietnam when a crazy Marine attacked him out of the clear
blue and bit off his nose. It became a serious medical event
when Commander Hawkins developed a resistant staph infection in his sinuses, which quickly spread to his brain — a danger that is always present with face wounds. To complicate
matters, Hawkins was allergic to the first antibiotics adminis-
tered to him and went into anaphylactic shock. When that was
finally controlled, his kidneys shut down, and he had to be
placed on dialysis, as the infection continued to run rampant
through his system. Hawkins developed a raging fever and had
to be wrapped in ice blankets for two days, and weeks later,
after his kidneys and immune system kicked in again, he came
down with hepatitis B and nearly died from that. He resigned
his commission, quit doctoring altogether for a time, and went
to the Menninger Foundation in Kansas, where he did some
work — work on himself. He wanted to regain some compas-
sion for his fellowman before trying to go back into private

practice, but his dreams of a successful civilian career were destroyed by the fact that he had no nose. He wore a tin nose, complete with a head strap, crafted by a Vietnamese peasant, and it made him an object of ridicule, led to a divorce from his wife, and prompted him to rejoin the Navy, where it didn't really matter that much what you looked like if you had enough rank. It mattered socially — at the Officers' Club and so on — but not on the job.

Commander Hawkins started out with a plastic prosthetic nose, but it was easily detectable, so he decided to make the best of a bad situation by wearing the tin nose and being up front about it. He was always quick to point out that he, more than anyone, realized how absurd his condition was, and in doing so he attenuated in part the sniggering he was subjected to for wearing a tin nose. What bothered him more was what he imagined people said about it in private. He became a virtual paranoid in this regard.

I was sent to Pendleton's neuropsych facility — that bleak, austere nuthouse — some weeks after defending my title as the 1st Marine Division Middleweight Champ in a boxing smoker at Camp Las Pulgas. I lost on a K.O. My injuries resulted in a shocking loss of weight, headaches, double vision, and strange, otherworldly spells. EEG readings taken at the hospital indicated that I had a lesion on my left temporal lobe from a punch to the temple that had put me out cold for over an hour. I was a boxer with over a hundred and fifty fights, and I had taken a lot of shots, but this last punch was the hardest I had ever received and the first punch ever to put me down. I had seen stars before from big punches; I had seen pinwheels; but after that shot to the temple I saw the worst thing you ever see in boxing — I saw the black lights.

★   ★   ★

There I sat in a corner of the dayroom on the kelly-green floor tiles, dressed in a uniform of pajamas and bathrobe, next to a small, tightly coiled catatonic named Joe, who wore a towel on his shoulder. Here in this corner — the most out-of-the-way place in the ward — was one of the few windows. Occasionally a Marine would freak out and bolt for the window, jump up on the sill, shake the security screen, and scream "I want to die!" or "I can't take it anymore, let me out of this motherfucker!" At these times Joe would actually move a little. By that I mean he would tilt to the left to give the screamer a little space. Except for me and one of the corpsmen, Joe would not let anyone touch him or feed him or change him.

As I said, Joe wore a towel on his shoulder. He drooled constantly, and he would grunt in gratitude when I dabbed his mouth dry. Joe gave off a smell. Schizophrenics give off a smell, and you get used to it. Sometimes, however, it would get so bad that I could swear I saw colors coming off Joe — shades of blue, red, and violet — and to get away from it I would get up and walk over to the wall-mounted cigarette lighter, a spiral electrical device much like the cigarette lighters in cars. The staff didn't trust us with open flames or razor blades.

Sitting next to Joe, I would chain-smoke Camels until the Thorazine and phenobarbital that Eagle had prescribed to contain my agitated restlessness got to be too much and I fell into heavy, unpleasant dreams, or I had a fit and woke up on the tile with piss and shit in my pants — alone, neglected, a pariah. The same corpsman who changed Joe would change me. The others would let you lie in your filth until the occasional doctor or nurse came in and demanded that they take action.

I was having ten to twenty spells a day during my first month, and I was so depressed that I refused to talk to anyone, especially when some of the fits marched into full-blown grand-mal seizures, which caused me much shame and confusion. I refused to see the buddies from my outfit who came by to visit me, and I did not answer my mail or take calls from my family. But as I got used to the Thorazine I began to snap out of my fits quicker. I began to shave and brush my teeth, and mingle with the rest of the neuropsych population. With Eagle as my living example, I had decided I would make the best of a bad situation; I would adjust to it and get on with my life.

As a rule, there were about thirty men in our ward — the Security Ward, where they kept the craziest, most volatile marines in all of Pendleton. Eagle seemed to regard me as super-volatile, although I was anything but at the time. He always kept me at arm's length, but he would get right in and mix with really dangerous, really spooky whacked-out freaks. I figured he was afraid of me because of my history as a recon marine with three tours in Nam, or because I had been a boxer. But he was a doctor, and his professional fear made me wonder about myself.

One day a great big black man named Gothia came into the ward. I had been there about two months, and this was the first new admission I had witnessed. He was extra-big, extra-black, extra-muscular, and extra-crazy. Gothia was into a manic episode and talking fast: there was a Buick waiting outside with a general in it, and he and Gothia were going to fly off to the Vatican, where the pope urgently awaited Gothia's expertise concerning the impending apocalypse. He kept repeating, "It's going to come like a thief in the night — a thief in the night!" until he had everyone half believing that the end of the world was at hand. I immediately liked Gothia. He made things interesting in the ward. As my hair got long, Gothia arranged with the other brothers to give me a hair treatment, a kind of pompadour. It looked like shit, but I was flat-tered to be admitted into the company of the brothers, which was difficult, my being white and a sergeant and a lifer and all.

A few weeks after he arrived, Gothia bolted unseen up the fence in the exercise yard, did the Fosbury Flop over the barbed wire that topped it, and returned with a six-pack of cold malt liquor. I drank three as fast as possible on an empty stomach and had my first cheap satori — though whether it was epilepsy or the blast from the alcohol is difficult to say. As I finished a fourth can of the malt liquor, sitting against the fence in the warmth of the golden sun, I realized that everything was for the best. Years later, I read a passage from Nietzsche that articulated what I felt in that fifteen-second realization: "Becoming is justified . . . war is a means to achieve balance. . . . Is the world full of guilt, injustice, contradiction and suffering? Yes, cries Heraclitus, but only for the limited man who does not see the total design; not for the con-tuitive God; for him all contradiction is harmonized."

Weird. Sleeping in the neuropsych ward at night, I sensed the presence of a very large rabbit under my bunk. A seven-foot rabbit with brown fur and skin sores, who took long, raking breaths. I didn't want to do it, but I had to keep getting out of bed to look. Gothia, who never slept, finally came over and asked me what was the matter, and when I told him about the rabbit he chuckled sympathetically. "Hey, man, there's no *rabbit*. Just take it easy and get some rest, baby. Can you dig it? Rabbit. Shit." But by and by my compulsive rabbit checks got on his nerves, until one night he came over to my bed and said, "I told you there was no rabbit under the bed. If you don't stop this shit, I am going to pinch you." He said it louder than he meant to, and the corpsman on watch came over with his flashlight and told Gothia that if he didn't get to bed he was going to write him up. I lay in the darkness and waited and listened to the rabbit breathe like an asthmatic until I had to check again, whereupon Gothia popped up in his bed and pointed his finger at me and shouted, "There ain't no goddamn rabbit, goddamn it! Knock that shit off!"

I shouted back at him. "It's that rabbit on the Br'er Rabbit molasses jar. That rabbit with buckles on his shoes! Bow tie. Yaller teeth! Yaller! Yaller!" For causing such a commotion we were both shot up, and put in isolation rooms. It was my first experience with a straitjacket, and I nearly lost it. I forced myself to lie still, and it seemed that my brain was filled with sawdust and that centipedes, roaches, and other insects were crawling through it. I could taste brown rabbit fur in my teeth. I had a horror that the rabbit would come in the room, lie on my face, and suffocate me.

After my day of isolation, a brig rat, a white marine named Rouse, came up to me and said, "Hey — you can tell me — you're faking this shit so you can get out of the service, aren't you?" Rouse, an S-1 clerk-typist, a "Remington raider" who had picked up a heroin habit in Saigon, had violet slash marks on his arms, and liked to show me a razor-blade half he had in his wallet. He offered to let me use it and often suggested that we use it together. Rouse had a lot of back pay saved up and ordered candy and cigarettes from the commissary, and innumerable plastic airplanes to assemble. He always claimed to have nasal congestion and ordered Vicks Inhalers, which at that time contained Benzedrine. Rouse would break them open and swallow the cottons and then pour airplane glue on a washcloth and roll it into a tube and suck on it. I got high with Rouse once by doing this, but the Benzedrine made me so restless that I begged Thorazine from the guys who used to cheek it and then spit it out after meds were issued.

Actually, Rouse was wrong about me: I didn't have anything to hide, and I wasn't faking anything. At the time, I didn't want out. I intended to make the Marine Corps my home. At group-therapy sessions I reasonably insisted that mine was a straightforward case of epilepsy, and for this I was ridiculed by inmate enemies and the medical staff alike. When I saw I was getting nowhere, I refused to speak at the group-therapy sessions at all, and I spent a month sitting sullenly, listening to everyone argue over an old record-player one of the residents had brought in to spice up the dayroom. The blacks liked Smokey Robinson and the Miracles; the war vets were big on the Doors, the Rolling Stones, and C.C.R. I started getting fat from inactivity — fat, although the food was cold and tasted lousy, and in spite of the fact that I fasted on Fridays, because Thursday's dinner was always rabbit. The thought of eating rabbit after a night of sensing the molasses rabbit under my bed gasping for air, and hearing the air whistle between his yellow teeth as he sucked desperately to live — the sight of fried rabbit put me off food for a solid day.

When I had been on the ward about six months and my fits were under better control, a patient named Chandler was admitted. Chandler was a college graduate. His degree was in French. He had joined the Marine Corps to become a fighter pilot but quickly flunked out of flight school and was left with a six-year enlistment as a grunt, which was unbearable to him. I wasn't sure if he was going out of his way to camp things up so he could get a Section Eight discharge, or if he always acted like a fairy. No one held it against him In fact, a number of the borderline patients quickly became devotees of his and were swishing around with limp wrists, putting on skits and whatnot, and smoking Chandler's cigarette of choice —

Salem. Rouse was the first to join in with Chandler by wearing scarves, kerchiefs, and improvised makeup. Rouse even changed his name to Tallulah.

But Chandler wasn't just some stupid fairy. He was erudite, well read, and well mannered. He had been to Europe. Chandler turned me on to Kafka and Paul Valéry. He knew how to work the library system, and soon I found that as long as I had a good book I did not mind the ward half as much.

Under Chandler's influence, Gothia somehow became convinced that he was Little Richard. After about the five hundredth time I heard Gothia howl, "It's Saturday night and I just got paid," and Chandler respond, "That's better, but try and put a little more pizzazz in your delivery!" I was glad to see Gothia go. They transferred him to a long-term-care psychiatric facility in North Carolina. In truth, Gothia was pretty good as Little Richard. He was better at it than Chandler was at Bette Davis or Marlene Dietrich — although at that time I had never seen Marlene Dietrich and had no basis for comparison.

Overwhelmed by boredom one afternoon in the dayroom, as we watched Chandler execute yet another "grand entrance" (a little pivot with a serious lip pout and a low and sultry "Hello, darlings"), I confided to Rouse that I suspected Eagle of being a "closet" faggot, and shortly afterward I was called into the Eagle's den for a rare appointment. Obviously Rouse had snitched on me. I told Eagle that I thought he was a homosexual because he had surfing posters in his office, and I watched him scribble three pages of notes about this. Eagle's desk was cramped, and his office was hot in spite of a pair of twelve-inch portable fans beating like they could use a couple of shots of lightweight motor oil, and I began to perspire heavily as I watched Eagle write. He was a spectacle — a tall man, cadaverously thin, with his long, angular legs crossed tightly at the knees, his ass perched on the front edge of his chair as he chain-smoked with one hand, flicking ashes into a well-filled ashtray on his desk while he scribbled at the notepad on his lap with his other hand; turning pages, lighting fresh cigarettes off the butts of old ones, scribbling, flipping the pad, seemingly oblivious of me until he looked up and confronted me with that incredible tin nose. "Do you realize that you are sweating?"

"It's hot."

"It's hot," he repeated. He looked down at his notepad and proceeded to write a volume.

By now I was drenched with sweat, having something very much like a panic attack. Without looking up, Eagle said, "You're hyperventilating."

Everything was getting swirly. Eagle dashed out his cigarette and reached into a drawer, withdrawing a stained paper sack from McDonald's. "Here," he said. "Breathe into this."

I took the bag and started breathing into it. "It isn't working," I said between breaths.

"Just give it a minute. Have you ever done this before? Hyperventilated?"

"Oh, God, no." I felt like I was dying.

Eagle pushed himself back in his chair and placed his hands on his knees. "There's more at work here than just a seizure disorder," he said. "I'm seeing some psychopathology."

"It's that fucking nose," I said, gasping. "I'm freaking out."

"You don't like the nose?" Eagle said. "Well, how do you think I feel about the nose? What am I supposed to do, go off on some island like Robinson Crusoe and hide?"

"I didn't mean that," I said. "It's just —"

"It's just too fucking weird, isn't it, Sergeant?"

"Yes, sir," I said. "Not normally, I mean, but I'm on all this medicine. You've got to cut back my dosage. I can't handle it."

"I'll make you a deal. I'm going to cut you back if you do something for me."

The paper bag finally started to work, and everything began to settle down. "What?"

Eagle removed a notepad and pencil from his desk. "Take this. I want you to jot down your feelings every day. This is just between you and me. I mean, it can be anything. If you were a kind of breakfast cereal, for instance, what would you be? Would you be — oatmeal? Would you be — mush? Would you be — FrankenBerries? Would you be — Count Chocula?" Eagle reclined in his chair, extracted a Lucky Strike, and lit it — with the same effeminate gestures, I noted, that Chandler used to light his Salems. Eagle had very broad shoulders for such a thin man. The sleeves of his tropical uniform were rolled up past his elbows. He brushed what few strands of hair he had back across his shiny pate. It was impossible to ignore his nose. He looked like an enormous carrion bird, and although I knew I could break him in pieces, he terrified me. He took a deep drag and exhaled through his tin nose. "Would you be — a Wheatie?"

"Don't try to fuck with my head!" I protested, crushing the McDonald's sack. I got up and stalked out of Eagle's office, but that night, when I went to bed, I found the notepad and pencil on top of my footlocker.

To disprove Eagle's theory that I was borderline psycho, I began to write what I thought were mundane and ordinary things in the diary, things which I thought proved my mental health, e.g., "A good day. Read. Played volleyball and had a good time smoking with the brothers. Picked up a lot of insight in group. Favorite breakfast: Shit on a Shingle. Two hundred push-ups. Happy, happy, happy!" I found such a release in writing that I started a diary of my own — a real one, a secret one, which I recently glanced through, noting that the quality of my penmanship was very shaky.

JANUARY 11, 1975: Sick.

JANUARY 13, 1975: Sick. Managed to read from Schopenhauer.

JANUARY 15, 1975: Borrowed some reading glasses and read Cioran. Sickness unto death. Better in the evening. Constipated. Food here is awful. There are bugs crawling on the wall and through the sawdust that is my brain. My personality is breaking down? I am having a nervous breakdown? Curiously I don't have the "stink" of schizophrenia.

MARCH 14, 1975: Vertigo. Double vision. Sick. Can't eat.

MARCH 18, 1975: There is a smell. A mousy smell.

APRIL 34, 2007: *I am a boxer dog of championship lineage dating back to the late nineteenth century, when the breed was brought to a high point of development in Germany. I have a short, clean brindle coat involving a pattern of black stripes over a base coat of golden fawn. At seventy-five pounds, I am considered large for a female. My muzzle is broad and gracefully carried, giving balance and symmetry to my head. In repose or when I am deep in thought my face is the very picture of dignified nobility.*

APRIL 40: *My under jaw is somewhat longer than the upper jaw and is turned up at the end, as it should be. The jaw projects just enough to afford a maximum of grasping power and holding*

*power (but without the exaggeration and underbite you sometimes
see in poorly bred or inbred boxers). Once my jaws are clamped on
something it cannot escape.*

*My entire muzzle is black. My nose is completely black, the
nostrils wide and flaring. My eyes are of a deep brown and are set
deeply in the skull. I do not have that liquid, soft expression you see
in spaniels, but rather assertive eyes that can create a menacing and
baleful effect when I am irritable. This is particularly the case
when I fix my piercing stare on its target. I can burn a hole through
steel and escape this Mickey Mouse jail anytime I want, and I will
as soon as I get my rest. Arf!*

APRIL 55: *Before my accident I was a circus performer with
the simple-minded animal consciousness of the here-and-now. That
I had been a great hero of the circus — the dog shot from cannons,
the dog that dove from fifty-foot platforms into shallow barrels of
water, the dog that rode galloping stallions bareback — that I was
Boris, the Great One, a celebrated hero of Mother Russia, beloved
by my countrymen meant . . . nothing to me.*

Eagle has me back in his little office, and he confronts me not
only with my fake diary but with my real one as well. I'm pissed
that they've been rummaging through my personal gear.

"Let me get this straight. You say you were this circus
dog in Russia, and you got a brain injury when you were *shot
from a cannon?*"

"I forgot to wear my safety helmet."

"So a famous neurosurgeon put your brains back
together and sent you to a health spa —"

"Only the V.I.P.s went there. Nikita K. was there. I
knew him. Dancers from the Bolshoi. Army generals. K.G.B.
officials. Chess champions."

"And you . . . a dog?"

"I wasn't *just* a dog. I was the Rin Tin Tin of Russia."

"You're pretty bright and well informed. How can you know all this kind of thing?"

"Because it's true," I said.

"How would you like it if I sent you to the brig?"

"Fine. The brig would be fine. I'm a howlin' wolf. Put me in a cage or let me go."

Eagle drummed his fingers on his desk, changing pace. "Tell me something. What does this old saying mean to you? 'People who live in glass houses shouldn't throw stones'?" Finger drumming. "Well?"

"I don't know —"

"'A rolling stone gathers no moss.' What does that mean?"

"Don't know."

Eagle began to write furiously.

"Why would anyone live in a glass house? It would be hot," I said. "And everyone could see you."

"I hear you like to read Kafka. That's heavy stuff for a young guy. You're pretty bright. Have you ever read any books on abnormal psychology?"

"Hey, man, just let me out of this motherfucker. I'm going down in this place. Put me in a normal ward and let me see a real doctor."

"I'll give it some thought. In the meantime, I'd like you to check this out," Eagle said, clapping me on the shoulder. He handed me a copy of *Love Against Hate*, by Karl Menninger.

STARLOG, JANUFEB, 2010: "Gate is straight/Deep and wide/Break on through to the other side. . . ."

*   *   *

There was an old piano in the dayroom. When a Marine freaked out and broke the record-player, Chandler started playing the piano day and night — driving me crazy. "Canadian Sunset" over and over and over again! One night I rubbed cigarette ashes all over myself for camouflage, crawled into the dayroom recon style, and snapped off the little felt hammers inside the piano. Shoulda seen the look on Chandler's face when he sat down to play. This was not insane behavior. I knew I was not really insane. I was just a garden-variety epileptic temporarily off my game. Thrown a little by the war. I laughed and said to Chandler, "Hey man, what's the sound of one hand clapping?"

After I put the piano out of commission, I noticed Chandler was losing weight. They had him on some new medication. He quit camping around and took a troubled leap into the darkness of his own soul. He grew quiet and started sitting in the corner with catatonic Joe. A black Marine, a rotund and powerful murderer from South Carolina named Bobby Dean Steele, was admitted to the ward for observation, and he began to dominate. Despite the charges pending against him, he was buoyant and cheerful. He walked over to Joe's corner a lot and would say, "Joe-be-doe, what's happening? What's the matter, man? You saw some bad shit in the Nam, didn't you? Well, that's okay. We're going to fix you up — not those doctors, but us, the jarheads. We'll help you. I know you can hear me. Go easy, man."

Bobby Dean Steele gave Joe back rubs and wiped his face and in a matter of a few days was leading him around the ward in a rigid, shuffle-step fashion. The patients began to rally around Joe, and soon everyone was giving him hugs and reassuring him. One of the corpsmen warned me that catatonics often snap out of their rigid stupors to perform sudden acts of extreme violence. It was a catatonic who had bitten off Eagle's nose, he said.

For a brief period during Bobby Dean Steele's tenure, my temporal-lobe visions jumped more and more into grand-mal seizures. Just before the fits, instead of having other-worldly spells, I felt only fear and would see the black lights of boxing. I was having very violent fits. In one of these I bit my tongue nearly in half, and for two weeks I sat in Joe's corner with Chandler, overloaded on anticonvulsants. My corpsman came by with a little spray bottle and sprayed my tongue. It had swollen so much that I could not shut my mouth, and it stank. It stank worse than schizophrenia, and even the schizo-phrenics complained. Bobby Dean Steele and I got into a fist-fight over the tongue, and I was amazed at my ability to spring into action, since I felt nearly comatose when he came over to the corner and started jawing at me, kicking at me with his shower shoes. I got up punching and dropped him with a left hook to the jaw. The sound of his huge body hitting the tile was like that of a half-dozen rotten melons dropped on con-crete. Bobby Dean Steele had to be helped to the seclusion room, but I was not required to go there, nor was I shot up. I guess it was because my tongue made me look miserable enough.

When Bobby Dean Steele came out of isolation, he was so heavily loaded on Thorazine that his spunk was gone, and without his antics and good cheer there was suddenly no "character" on the ward. Joe, who had seemed to be coming out of his catatonia, reverted back to it, but rather than seek-ing out his corner, he assumed and maintained impossible positions of waxy flexibility wherever he happened to be. It was like some kind of twisted yoga. I had heard that Joe had been at Khe Sanh during the siege and, like Jake Barnes in *The*

Sun Also Rises, received a groin wound — that he had lost his coconuts. I often wonder why that is considered such a terrible thing. I brought this up and was roundly put down. Better to lose your sight, arms, legs, hearing, said Rouse. Only Chandler, who rarely spoke up anymore, agreed with me. "If there was a hot-fudge sundae on one side of the room and a young Moroccan stud with a cock like a bronze sculpture on the other," he said, "I'd make for the ice cream."

Eagle came to Chandler's rescue, just as he had bailed me out for a while with the diary idea. Eagle appointed Chandler his clerk, and in a few weeks Chandler began to put on weight. As a clerk, he was allowed to leave the ward under the escort of one of the corpsmen. Invariably he went into Oceanside to the bookstores or to restaurants to gorge on big meals. He brought me delicious food in doggie bags, and books: Dostoyevski, Spinoza, Sartre — the writers he insisted I read — and the lighter stuff I preferred. I was reading a lot and having fewer seizures; I had begun to get better. Chandler was better, too, and up to his old mischief. He constantly mimicked his new boss, and his devastating imitations were so accurate that they actually made me realize how much I respected Eagle, who had the advantages of a good education and presumably had a history of confidence and self-esteem, but now, with his tin nose, had been cut adrift from the human race. The humiliation of epilepsy had unmanned me, and I felt empathy for the doctor. At least I looked like a human being. According to Chandler, Eagle had no friends. Chandler also told me that Eagle would get drunk and remove his tin nose and bellow, "I am the Phantom of the Opera. Ah ha ha ha!"

Patients came and went, and time passed — I had been in the nuthouse for fourteen months. I was becoming one of the senior patients on the ward. We got very good meals on the anniversary of the founding of the Marine Corps, on Thanksgiving, at Christmas. In fact, at Christmas, entertainment was brought in. I remember a set of old geezers who constituted a Dixieland band. They did not play that well, but it made for a welcome break in the routine of med calls, of shower shoes flip-flopping across the kelly-green tiles, of young men freaking out at the security screen near Joe's corner, of people getting high on airplane glue and Vicks Inhalers, of people trying to kill themselves by putting their heads in plastic bags, of the long nights in the ward with the bed springs squealing from incessant masturbation, punctuated by nightmares and night terrors and cries of "Incoming!," of the same cold starchy meals over and over again, of a parched mouth from drug dehydration and too many cigarettes, of a life without hope.

When the band took a rest between sets, two old farts, one white and one black, played a banjo duet of "Shanty Town" that brought tears to my eyes. Then a group of square dancers came in. They were miserable-looking middle-aged types in Western getups, the women with fat legs. You could sense their apprehension, and I realized that I had forgotten how frightening someone like Bobby Dean Steele, who had been copping an attitude of late, wearing an Afro and a pair of black gloves, must have seemed to people like them. Once the music began, however, the misery was erased from their faces and replaced by a hypnotic expression as they mechanically went through their paces. From my folding chair, swooning on phenobarbital, overly warm from all the body heat, I was in agony until I saw — with a rare and refined sense of objectivity — that their sufferings and miseries vanished in their dancing, as they fell into the rhythm of the music and the singsong of the caller's instructions. And for a moment I saw myself as well; I saw myself as if from on high, saw the pattern of my whole life with a kind of geometrical precision, like the pattern the dancers were making, and it seemed there was a perfect rightness to it all.

One day after chow, Bobby Dean Steele was summoned to the meds kiosk by one of the doctors, and a corpsman buzzed a pair of enormous brig chasers through the heavy steel door of the ward. They cuffed Bobby Dean Steele, while the resident on duty shrugged his shoulders and told Steele that he was being transferred back to the brig to stand General Court-Martial for three counts of murder in the second degree. It had been decided, Chandler informed us, that Bobby Dean Steele was not especially crazy — at least not according to observation, the M.M.P.I., and the Rorschach. Chandler told us that Steele would end up doing twenty years hard labor in a federal prison.

My own departure was somewhat different. Eagle called me into his office and said, "I'm sending you home. Don't ask me whether you're cured or not. I don't know. I do know you were an outstanding Marine, and I have processed papers for a full disability pension. Good luck to you, Sergeant."

"Thank you." I was dumbfounded.

"When you get home, find yourself a good neurologist. . . . And keep your ass out of the boxing ring."

"Yes, sir."

As I turned to leave, Eagle saluted me. I returned the salute proudly, and I heard his booming, operatic laugh start up after I pulled his door shut behind me.

The next morning I collected over nine thousand dollars in back pay and I went out to the bus stop with my seabag on my shoulder. A master sergeant came by, and I asked him what time the bus came. He told me that I could not leave the base until I got a No. 1 haircut and I told him to forget it, that I was a civilian. A moment later a jeep pulled over and a captain with an M.P. band on his sleeve hopped out. I showed him my discharge papers, the jump wings on my set of blues, the Navy Cross and the two Silvers, and he said, "Big fucking deal. You got a General Discharge, Sergeant. A psychiatric discharge, Sergeant. I want you off this base immediately."

"Well give me a ride and I'll be glad to get off the motherfucker," I said. I was beginning to see cockroaches crawling through the wet sawdust inside my skull, and I kept wiping my nose for fear they would run out and brush across my lips.

"You're a psycho," the master sergeant said. "Go out there and wreak havoc and mayhem on the general population, and good riddance."

"You could cut me some slack," I said. "I was a real Marine, not some rear-echelon blowhard, and by the way, fuck the Corps. Eat the apple, and fuck the Corps. I curse the day I ever joined this green motherfucker."

"I want you off this base and I want you to hump it off this base," the master sergeant said.

"You mean I don't have to get a haircut after all?" I said in my best nellie voice.

"Fucking hit the road, Marine. Haight-Ashbury is that way."

"Well, fuck you," I said.

"And fuck you. Go fuck yourself."

I threw my seabag down and was about to fight when a Marine in a beatup T-bird pulled over to the bus stop and asked me if I needed a lift. Without another word I tossed my seabag in his backseat and hopped into the car. Before I could say thanks he hit me up for five bucks in gas money. "It's twenty-three miles to Oceanside," he said. "And I'm runnin' on empty. I ain't even got a spare tire, no jack, no nothing." He looked at me and laughed, revealing a mouth filled with black cavities. He said, "Hey, man, you wouldn't happen to have a cigarette, would you?" I handed him my pack. "Hey, thanks," he said.

"That's all right," I said.

He lit the cigarette and took a deep drag. "You want to hear some strange shit?"

"Why not?" I said.

"I just got six, six, and a kick." The Marine took another pull off the cigarette and said, "Six months in the brig, six months without pay, and a Bad Conduct Discharge."

"What did you do?" I asked. I was trying to stop the vision of bugs.

"AWOL," he said. "Which is what I'm doing now. I ain't going to do no six months in the fucking brig, man. I did two tours in Nam. I don't deserve this kind of treatment. You want to know something?"

"What's that?"

"I stole this fucking car. Hot-wired the motherfucker."

"Far out," I said. "Which way you going?"

"As far as five bucks in gas will take me."

"I got a little money. Drive me to Haight-Ashbury?"

"Groovy. What are you doing, man, picking your nose?"

"Just checking for cockroaches," I said weakly. I was afraid I was going to have a fit, and I began to see the black lights — they were coming on big time, but I fought them off. "What was your M.O.S.?"

"Oh-three-eleven, communications. I packed a radio over in I Corps. Three Purple Hearts and three Bronze Stars with valor. That's why I ain't doing six months in no brig. I just hope the 'P. waves us through at the gate. I don't want no high-speed chases." The Marine lit another of my cigarettes from the butt of the first one. "Hey, man, were you in the war? You look like you got some hard miles on you. Were you in the war? Did you just get out? You're not going AWOL, too — that ain't no regulation haircut. Man, you got a headful of hair. On the run? How about it? Were you in the war? You got that thousand-yard stare, man. Hey, man, stop picking your nose and tell me about it."

Arf!

"Goddammit, are you zoned or what?"

Bow wow!

"I can't believe this shit. That motherfucker 'P. at the gate is pulling me over. Look at that. Can you believe this shit? They never pull you over at this gate, not at this time of day — and I haven't got any identification. Shit! Buckle up your seat belt, nose-pickin' man, we are gonna motate. This fucking Ford has got a blower on the engine and it can boogie. Haight-Ashbury, here we come or we die tryin'. Save us some of that free love! Just hope you get some of that free lovin' — save me some of that *good* pussy!"

The Marine slammed his foot down full on the accelerator. The T-bird surged like a rocket and blew by the guard post, snapping off the wooden crossbar. For a moment I felt like I was back in the jungle again, a savage in greasepaint, or back in the boxing ring, a primal man — kill or be killed. It was the best feeling. It was ecstasy. The bugs vanished. My skull contained gray matter again. I looked back at the M.P. in the guard post making a frantic call on the telephone. But the crazy Marine at the wheel told me not to worry, he knew the back roads.

Part
II

Wipeout

I believe in the philosophy of rock 'n' roll. Like, "If you want to be happy for the rest of your life, don't make a pretty woman your wife." I mean, who can refute that? Can Immanuel Kant refute that? How can you refute that? I mean, really. Any guy knows this is true, even a shallow, superficial guy like me. Of course, I think almost all women are pretty. You have to make them feel special, make them have the best day of their life, and what woman doesn't look good on the best day of her life?

Don't get me wrong, I go for the really pretty ones, but it all falls in cycles, like the phases of the moon affect my style, or something. I mean, I can go out feeling like I've got a certified guarantee in my pocket that I'll get laid and come home empty, especially in these precautionary times of AIDS. Whenever I'm having a dry spell, I don't really push myself either; you have to take it slow and know your limitations. You have to know what they want and how to treat them. You have to make them come to you and you just can't get emotionally involved. I mean, it's her ball game when you do that, when you start having pet names, knowing one another's favorite color, and she starts springing little anniversaries on you. The next thing you know, you're a daddy, with all that responsibility. You have to play that noninvolvement theme, and work that. Give them a little James Dean or Montgomery Clift or a little Rudolph Valentino action, and when they know they can't own you, they want you all the more and you're the victor. It's very simple. It's just a matter of style. And in this age of Prince and Michael Jackson, affecting the style of the old masters smacks of originality and flair. Rent a bunch of old movies. Check out some Jimmy Cagney, you'll see what I mean.

Anyhow, I was having a dry period. (They aren't bad if they're short, but you get to thinking about your life and all that when they endure and you don't want to dwell on this kind of thing for long. It can make you miserable.) I was overdue, horny, and looking for a sign.

I changed my environment a little and started hitting the state library at lunchtime. It's a good place: lots of females — state workers running the gamut from research assistants to attorneys. You can find young ones, fresh ones there, and as one thing leads to another, on the second afternoon I spot a likely prospect, a brown-eyed girl — medium height, nice figure, no engagement ring, looks about thirty, she'll be just about right, I prefer blondes, but she'll do.

I've got my head down like I'm reading but I'm really watching her through a pair of dark Porsche sunglasses from my post near the card catalogues. I'm wearing a twelve-hundred-dollar Italian suit and standing there with an air of European elegance about me, with a certain devil-may-care flair, an irresistible sort of psychopathic charisma. Waiting for contact. She looks up once or twice and then, bingo! She gives

me the look. In another minute she goes upstairs into the
stacks, philosophy section, and I think, *Philosophy, how interesting,* you know, this is a little bit different, I like this, I'll just
trust myself and go with this. I'm following her upstairs, and
she knows it. Both of us browse for a while, rows apart, and
then she begins to select some books. After she collects an
armful, I catch her coming around a corner and *blam!* plow
into her. And then I do James Dean doing Montgomery Clift
doing Rudolph Valentino doing a Garfield.

I learned how to do Garfields as a little kid watching the
"Garfield Goose Show" on television. What you do is get this
astonished look on your face and simultaneously jump back
suddenly, like you've been surprised or scared by something.
Fraser Thomas, the host of the show, who was some sort of
dignitary who used to talk to Garfield, who was this goose pup-
pet, the king of this faraway goose kingdom, actually, and
whenever Fraser Thomas said something that would astonish
Garfield in any way, the goose, who was a mute, would open
his beak, arch his neck, and hop back, all in one move, this
emphatic double take.

So, like I said, I catch this brown-eyed girl coming
around the corner with a pile of books and I slam into her,
really suddenlike, give her the double Garfield, knocking the
books out of her arms and she says, "Whoa!"

"Oh, boy, am I ever sorry." I say, "Here, let me help
you. Oh, brother! What a dummy I am. What a knuckle-
head!"

Right away I pick up on the fact that she smells clean,
her breath is sweet. *This is good, this is good,* I think, and
she felt firm, this is good, this is good! My precious little
heart is pumping out the drum roll from "Wipeout" by the
Safaris.

"Jeez, I'm really sorry, I thought I was all alone up here; you scared the living crap out of me."

"I was being loud," she says. "I'm a clomper. I'm not a mouse. People hear me when I walk in libraries."

"My mind was a million miles away," I say, a little too much like Columbo. I pick up her books and then box her in against a shelf and look her square in the eyes, big, beautiful, bright brown eyes. "I'm sorry," I say, "what's this? *The Critique of Pure Reason*!" I say, "You can't read this," I say, "you're a girl."

"But of course I can read it," she says, bristling.

"I mean, I'm not saying that you can't read Kant. What I mean is, women don't usually go in for philosophy, as a rule, whereas men don't go in much for . . . sewing."

"Have you read Kant?" she says icily.

"Of course," I say. "I mean, after Kant, what's left to be said? He was the best. The last word."

Her tone begins to soften a little. "Lots of folks are big on Wittgenstein these days," she said.

"That effeminate little pansy," I say. "'Don't think, look'; the folly of language, of concepts. He ripped that off from the Buddhists. And let me tell you something, I think the proof is in the pudding. Guys like Wittgenstein, Nietzsche, Kierkegaard — they were little ninety-eight-pound weaklings. Didn't they have weight lifting in those days or what?"

She laughs at this.

"How can you talk about superman, or soaring with the eagles, when you've got eleven-inch biceps?"

More deep-basso laughter from her.

I say, "Tell me something, who do you think would win, Madison Square Garden, fifteen rounds of boxing, the Dangerous Dane and the Wicked Witt?"

She laughs. "Kierkegaard had a bad back, Wittgenstein would prevail," she says. She had the scariest laugh I had ever heard since *The Exorcist*.

I knew I had an alpha female here, I had an amazon. This chick was tougher than nails. A chick like this can turn the tables on a normal guy. When you go out with an alpha, they think they're screwing you; they think the guy is the piece of ass. This was Emily Brontë, and she was looking for Heathcliff.

Well, good, I thought, a wildcat would be nice for a change, and I can do Heathcliff. Heathcliff comes naturally.

Her name was Simone. Came here from Paris at an early age. She was a lawyer. She liked Plato, she liked the ballet, she played the piano and violin (yawn!). She liked horseback riding. She ran marathons and could swim five miles. She practiced Zen.

I took her to a prizefight and to the track. She took me to see Wagner's *Ring*. I made her read *Lucky Jim* and *A House for Mr. Biswas*, she made me read *Pale Fire*. She had traveled the globe to places like Zanzibar and Rangoon, Burma; she could match me drink for drink, and when we arm wrestled, her right arm could beat my left two times out of three. She had zest, spirit, energy.

And it was like I figured, she was a wildcat in bed, which made all of the horseshit about the opera and the ballet worth sitting still for. She was good.

She put the glide back in my stride, my juices were flowing again. I fell into my rhythm and got all loose and jangly again. I began to pick up side action — a Danish blonde, a redhead from Ireland, a divorcée, a married chick, a couple of them from way back when (never break off harshly with them, it's cruel and unnecessary, and you never know when you might want to replay a golden oldie).

The dry spell was over, I had the ball rolling at last, and when you've got a few of them going like that, you can relax and be yourself. You don't have to put up with any bullshit, because you've got your reserves.

Things were going so well, in fact, I was booked up so heavily, I broke things off with Simone, just quit calling, really — the initial spell had begun to fade, and it's important anyhow to get gone at this point. They really can't take it, being rejected like that, before you get to know the real and wonderful person they are. It's a crucial move and timing is all.

I let a couple of weeks go by and showed up at a regular Friday-afternoon pub get-together Simone had once mentioned. I showed up with Jeannie, the Irish, as if it was entirely coincidental, and there was Simone with a party of her friends from work. We were barely seated way back on the far side of the pub when Jeannie said, "Don't look now, Herbie, but that gal over there just did one of those Garfields of yours and then gave us the most bloody sardonic glare since God told Adam and Eve to pack up and clear out of the Garden."

"Be more precise," I said. "How would you gauge it?"

"It was quite clearly a triple," Jeannie said.

I imagined Simone was thinking something along the lines of *He had her all along, they had a fight, now they're back together again — he was just using me!* When I finally dared to sneak a look over, Simone was a study in nonchalance, but I could see that her breathing was rapid, angry, and barely under control.

I was pasting together just the right sort of improvisational intrigue that would start a real fire. I was cooking up some real passion. (Sometimes it's even better to be seen with a plain one so there's that what-does-he-see-in-her-that-he-doesn't-see-in-me? to it.)

Jeannie and I cleared out pretty fast (you never want to linger), and then I laid low for a couple of weeks so she could soak up what she'd seen until finally I called, all innocentlike, before she'd given up hope completely, and turned the corner on her feelings for me. I called up and asked her to go horse-back riding. There was the slightest pause and then she said with a French accent, "Fuck you, you asshole, go fuck your-self!" *Blam!*

How completely and utterly predictable.

At times like this it's important to become traditional. I sent volleys of roses, special candies, poems (free-and-easy steals from Byron, Shakespeare, and Rimbaud). Every day for a week I sent her a plastic statue of Jesus — a dashboard Jesus. I don't know why, I don't know how such a thing occurred to me, I just did it thinking that if you keep doing the same thing, over and over, no matter how crazy, you can break them down. I mean, picture her alone in her apartment with seven statues of Jesus.

She held out for three weeks, about ten days longer than average, and then finally she picked up the phone.

"Hi, how have you been? . . ."

In no time we were back at it again, candlelight din-ners, sensitive intimate talks until dawn, horseback riding, English style, the sun and the wind in our faces, Heathcliff and Catherine, frolic on the moors, cloud-nine exhilaration and steamy, hot-and-heavy passion. *Body Heat* passion. Passion, like you've never known passion.

It went along nicely all that summer and into the fall and then I got the flu, really got sick with it, and Simone suddenly got domestic with chicken soup, vitamin C, zinc, aspirin, and this Louis Pasteur thing — sterilize the apartment. She wasn't like Louis Pasteur, she *became* Louis Pasteur. She was out to kill every germ in the world. Lysol spray mist. Bleach and ammonia. Boiled cutlery. Microwaved toothbrushes. She even microwaved the pillows. Then she caught the flu and I had to do the nursemaid thing with her.

Lord, have mercy! What a hassle! She looked like hell sick. I mean, they look bad enough in the morning or when you see them sitting on the toilet, but when they get sick it really puts you off. I resolved to get rid of her once and for all, I had fathomed all her mystery, her every dimension, and while she had lasted longer than most, now I was really through. This coupled with her obsessive-compulsive perfectionism — it was irrevocably over. I mean, like, "So long, pretty baby, *comprendez?*"

Before I got around to dumping her, I got sick again. It was worse the second time. It was like bone-break fever. We had to get a doctor to come over and everything, and it was around then that I saw that she really loved me; I mean, I didn't look so hot sick either, but she was there with the soup and back rubs and reading to me and all with a lighthearted touch — with gaiety, wit, and charm. With complete and utter selfless devotion. Meanwhile she's having some kind of lease hassle, and the next thing you know some of her friends haul all of her stuff over, and she's moved in. Quite presumptuous of her, hey, *compadre?* Enough to suffocate you, no?

She's had really nice stuff, including a copy of Paul Gauguin's famous Tahitian painting *Where do we come from? What are we? Where are we going?* She hung it up in the front room, where I lay deranged with an outta-my-mind fever, and

I could not take my eyes off this painting. It seemed to say everything to me, and this "everything" had sinister overtones. Either I was paranoid or she watched me watching it, she was using it as a test. I had fever, I'm talking fever and it's like, "The horror! The horror!" looking at this painting. Things seemed to change in this fever. I was suddenly vulnerable, a tenderhearted sentimentalist. I was on the verge of turning human and having feelings and so on.

I had really gotten to like her, I mean like you like a friend — you just like them for what they are, and yet I couldn't help feeling that she was testing me for weakness, that she was setting me up most diabolically to break my heart. I knew that over the years I had established a lot of bad karma along these lines. She would have been within her rights. But this was all fever, paranoia, and psychological projection. Actually, she was faithful and true and she loved me and I loved her and what got me was that I acted mechanically. I reverted to form. It wasn't really me talking when she said she was pregnant and I told her to pack up her shit and get the fuck out of my life. I couldn't believe the cruel words that spat from my vicious filthy mouth. There was this sense of unreality.

She walked out without a word, without a tear, without a look back. There's a Zen chick for you.

I had a hard time stopping myself from rushing after her and begging her to stay. It was so much worse the weeks after, coming home every night, hoping to see her, wondering where she had gone, what was she going to do about the baby, and so on. Hoping that it had only been a bad dream and that I would wake up with her by my side. There's nothing in the world I wouldn't have done to get her back, but she was gone — like in the FBI federal-witness-program sense of gone. I mean, like, UFO-abducted — Bermuda Triangle–*vanished!* Gone without a trace.

I was plagued with insomnia. I couldn't eat. I lost fifteen pounds in two weeks. The whole world had lost its meaning and color for me. I was filled with a generalized sense of loathing, bitterness, remorse, self-pity, and despair. Life was so lonely without her.

But you have to be true to yourself. What I did sprang from my deepest instincts. The scorpion stings, it can't help itself. There are no choices.

And there really isn't any sense moping. When the word got around about what had happened, I had it better than ever. They like an element of danger. I had more action than ever before. Chicks coming and going. You know, you really can get it down to a perfect art.

Mosquitoes

I guess the reason I can't relate to Clendon: . . . he almost cracked up getting his Ph.D., got weird, and took off to Vermont, bought a Volvo, and married this cool slim blonde with long legs, nine thousand dollars' worth of capped teeth and a heart colder than the dark side of the moon. Victoria. Spoiled single child, rich and indulged. Sarah Lawrence degree in art history. Clothes are DKNY. She drives a BMW and Clendon *worships* her and all the time I was there I saw her make him squirm and humiliate him. I'm thinking he's getting some kind of masochistic thrill out of this. There was something *in that* that has estranged us as brothers and has made us like Cain and Abel. I mean, I can't identify with somebody who won't fight back. I can't work up any sympathy for him.

"The kids," he says. "You have to think of the kids."

Or: "A divorce would leave a psychic scar."

Clendon teaches at Middlebury College in Vermont. Middlebury is really a beautiful place but it's that old bullshit: Greenpeace. You know, I don't want to overgeneralize but it's a style

I find hard to take. They really let you have it up there. Throw it right in your face. Self-righteous do-gooders. I mean, I think we ought to save the dolphins, too. Torpedo those Japanese fishing boats if they don't lay off! But spare me the folksingers!

Anyhow, I went out to see Clendon one summer expecting the weather to be cool, praying that it would be cool that summer, and it was atypically hot and there was some kind of mosquito convocation going on there — every mosquito in the world flew into Vermont that summer.

Historically mosquitoes are among the deadliest enemies of man. Mosquitoes caused the downfall of ancient civilizations around the Mediteranean Sea — sleeping sickness, elephantiasis, dengue, malaria. Plus you know about all of that yellow fever jive when we dug the Panama Canal, right?

Well, great big monster mosquitoes from Siberia, the size of sparrows, made the trip to Vermont that summer, and there were little ones that were, in a way, worse because they had no fear of the blazing sun, thrived under it, and would attack at high noon like Mirage fighter jets. *Aedis aegypti* if you want to get technical. *Aedis aegypti* is completely dependent on human blood and will attack in the full light of day, like Dracula with sunglasses. I mean, they wouldn't light on you and make preliminary moves to give you warning before they injected their hypodermic proboscis into your skin. They were like flying piranhas; they would practically bite you on the wing.

You couldn't buy, beg, or steal insect repellent. There was a run on it. It was more precious than a rhinoceros horn in an Asian bazaar. Clendon was so preoccupied with his marital problems that he scarcely noticed the mosquitoes, but they were all I could think of. There are nearly two thousand species of them and I think most blew in for the big convocation. Mosquito Woodstock.

I hated to watch my brother grovel, the children irritated me, and so I holed up in the guest bedroom with the air conditioner on full blast and a satchel full of medical journals. Victoria had the gall to insist I confine my cigarette smoking to the bedroom. "What kind of doctor has a two-pack-a-day cigarette habit?" she says.

"Smoking is good for you; it makes your heart merry," I say.

"Oh bullshit," she says. "It's such a juvenile habit."

If you were my wife, I thought, *you would be a splat on the wall*.

Clendon had given me a number of literary magazines to read including stories of his own. I'm a reader, I read them but it was always some boring crap about a forty-five-year-old upper-level executive in boat shoes driving around Cape Cod *in a Volvo*. I mean you actually do finish some of them and admit that "technically" they were pretty good but I'd rather go to back-to-back *operas* than read another story like that. It was with relief that I returned to the medical journals.

Boy, that Victoria was a cool one! Chilly. Even with the kids. I made a few points when obese little Jason fell and lacerated his knee. I numbed the knee with lidocaine, debrided the cut, and did a first-class job of suturing the wound. All jokes. No tears. The kids thought Uncle Bob or *Doctor* Bob was great and loved it when I took them out in the Jag V-12 convertible and drove them on the swervy back roads, cutting swaths through the

dark clouds of mosquitoes. Victoria didn't like the Jaguar. It
was too ostentatious, too L.A., for her blue-blood sensibilities
but, hey! I worked like hell to buy that car. And second gear
in a V-12 Jag has got more juice than anything short of an
Apollo 10. *Va-rrroom!*

What really put a frost on the visit was the night I took the kids
out to see *The Exorcist III* and they came home to vomit hot
dogs and ice cream and then Jason woke up the whole house
with a screaming nightmare. The "Bonecrusher" had been
after him. "There, there, baby, Mommy's here and everything
is going to be just fine." Fucking little Jason tells Victoria that
Uncle Bob punched the V-12 up to 130 m.p.h. and the telephone poles were looking like a picket fence. Fucking little
Jason tells Victoria how we fishtailed onto a gravel road, spun
around, knocked over a mailbox, and blew out a rear tire.

I swore the little bastard to secrecy!

In the morning Clendon told me he knew Vickie was having an
affair and while he hated her for it, it excited him to think of
her making love to another man. Clendon told me he was
dicking some of his students and that he couldn't get it up for
Victoria. I said, "Leave that nasty bitch. I can't work up any
sympathy for you, she's runnin' you, man."

"I don't know what to do. You're right. I'm torn. I feel
like Hamlet. Good God, what are you doing?"

"What?"

"Put out that cigarette."

"Are you shittin' me? What the fuck is the matter with
you?"

"Passive smoke, little brother. The kids. And Jesus!

Don't take them out in that goddamn toy anymore either. A hundred and thirty miles an hour?"

"It's not a toy, big brother, it's pure pussy. You're scared shitless, aren't you?" I flipped him the keys to my Jaguar. "Go take it for a ride, motherfucker. Live a little. Go on, drive it; it's good therapy. Primal Scream Therapy."

Clendon went out into the driveway and turned the engine over. He revved the motor and popped the clutch, spinning rubber out into the street. I spotted his reflection in the rearview mirror frozen in the rictus of fear. Not a good sign, I thought. How Clendon could *not* find satisfaction from the rich *thrrraaaghh!* of the duel exhaust system baffled me. It was that sound that made the car worth every bit of the $80-some thousand. I could have thrown the money into a Keogh account but, hey! it was the sound of pure balls.

In a moment the kitchen door opened and Victoria walked in with a tanned young man in his late twenties; both were wearing tennis clothes. I was caught in the act of lighting another cigarette. Victoria introduced me to the young man, Larry, a tennis pro, and exchanged an intimate look with him before she ran upstairs to change. If they thought they were fooling me, and I think they did, they were both dead wrong.

I offered Larry a cigarette and he declined in that particularly annoying Middlebury fashion so I said, "If you weren't such a goddamn faggot, I'd bet you were screwing that bitch."

He began to puff up and I said, "Don't even think about it, motherfucker."

When Victoria came down five minutes later, showered and in fresh sweats, if she missed Larry or was puzzled by his taking leave, she didn't show it, didn't miss a beat, but remained pleasantly aloof and began to whip together a Caesar salad for supper. I was in the mood to tear her head off. Maybe she knew that.

Dinner was consumed with stiff formality, to my thinking, sea trout on a bed of lentils with a coconut crème de caramel for dessert, espresso and brandy. Clendon took the edge off things when he spoke of Victoria's forthcoming show that he had arranged, using his influence with the college art department. Victoria began to talk of her paintings, which were done in the expressionist style. "I like the realists," I said. "What I really like is that trompe l'oeil style. And I always thought Andy Warhol was totally insane and crazy. Have you ever gotten totally insane and crazy, Jason? When your daddy was little, he used to act that way. Are you ever like that, dude?"

"Yeah," Jason said shyly.

"Warhol," Victoria said pompously, "the early Warhol, before he was shot —"

"Where would America be without Andy Warhol?" I said. "He put his stamp on American culture. Think about it, Vickie. He invented superstars and all of that shit. It didn't quit with the Tomato Soup Can. Andy Warhol was a genius. He — what he had, was this great radio antenna. Picked up on all of the cosmic vibrations. He just did it, I don't think he knew the half of it. He was one of those idiot savants, I'm thinking. Your paintings are too goddamn vague, Vick. I can't get a reading on them."

After dinner, Jason and I went into Victoria's studio and painted cans of Campbell's Mushroom Soup. Made a super mess. Pissed her off royally.

In the morning I sat in on a session of Clendon's creative writing class. It didn't take any real brainpower to figure out who his protégé was — a bright bohemian type in black leotards and a turtleneck. She read from a novel in progress in a confident low and sexy voice. She couldn't write and she wasn't really pretty. What she had going for her was the bloom of youth and a headful of platinum blond hair.

She appeared at Victoria's art showing, which was sparsely attended by the faculty, public, and student body. I stuck it through to the bitter end wondering if Larry, from the tennis club, would make an appearance, and the deeper I got into the white wine, the more I hoped he would. He did not. I met a number of Clendon's colleagues that night and began to understand why he had nearly broken down getting his Ph.D. I remembered people like that from medical school. The English faculty had its med school counterparts — the bunch that went into psychiatric residencies. It was those types, the counterpart of those types that considered surgeons to be assholes, but if I have an assholish aspect I can only say — you better go out and get whatever you want on this trip, because this is *the* trip, the only trip.

On the second night of the showing I stayed at home and baby-sat the kids. The next morning Clendon told me there had been a light turnout. Then he asked me quite bluntly if I could wrap up the visit and leave. Victoria considered me an "invader," he said. My presence was provoking migraine headaches. She was up in bed now, wasted with a headache because of me.

"The *invader*. It's your fucking house, man. And you're telling me to go?"

"I don't remember — you never had such a filthy mouth. Is that how they talk in hospitals?"

"Fucking-A. She's got you pussy-whipped. I never figured you for a Ph.D. in English —"

"It's her house. Her parents' money."

"Leave her."

"Right, live in a trailer court. Plastic curtains. Alimony. Child support."

"Well, it will be your trailer. Home sweet home."

"No can do —"

"She looks at you and you wither."

"I can't explain it. I need her."

My blood boiled. I didn't know if I wanted to cock my fist and smash his teeth down his throat or write him a script for some Valium and Elavil.

"Well, fuck it then," I said. "I'm going back to Los Angeles."

I got a little loaded. It was late. The kids were in bed. Clendon was at some sort of university function. I went out into the kitchen to make a sandwich and caught Victoria standing over the sink, her platinum hair pinned up to keep her neck cool. I had startled her and when she turned to me, I realized she wasn't altogether surprised. She was wearing an expensive sheer nightgown and her breasts, just bigger than medium and firm — I mean they were *there* — large erect pinkish-white nipples. They were just absolutely the most beautiful tits in the whole world.

It was a matter of some ambivalence for both of us. Neither of us liked the other. Yet the physical attraction right then and there was incredible. After I kissed her, she led me into the bedroom. She said, "Oh, my God!"

I really gave it to her. I really let her have it.

You take the gorilla . . . I suppose there are probably only about forty of them left on the planet, if that many. Point of fact: the reason the gorilla has such a large brain is not because he has to figure out where to find food or how to make a little nest in the grass. In Gorilla Country food is plentiful; enemies, apart from man, are nonexistent. To find food, make the nest, and then migrate along to the next spot, the gorilla needs a brain the size of a Rice Krispie.

The *reason* the gorilla has such a large brain and the reason it takes so long for the young to mature and develop is because in a gorilla society, in addition to understanding the various nuances of their vocal utterances, they are masters of reading body language. They are skilled psychologists and, in their roughshod way, they are far more diplomatic than a human can ever think of becoming.

In a gorilla troop there is no violence. Everyone gets along. There's a pecking order, true, but everyone has his place and accepts it. Gorillas are happy. They don't need New Balance tennis shoes, or VCRs or Jaguar V-12 convertibles. They don't need DKNY. They don't need crack cocaine. They don't need to write clever stories about some guy driving around Cape Cod with angst. You give a gorilla a banana and a piece of nooky and you've got a happy gorilla; you've got a gorilla that has no desire to commit rape or Murder One, or to paint the Sistine Chapel, or run for president, win a Nobel Prize — any of that. Gorillas don't war upon one another or torture one another. It never happens.

A friend of mine in the ER told me that the animal consciousness is one of the here-and-now and that the human being can approximate it by drinking five martinis while soaking in a hot tub. A Saturday evening condition, if then. The rest of the time . . . well, just read the newspapers and you'll know what I mean. Human behavior, ninety-eight percent of it, is an abomination.

*   *   *

The morning after I screwed Victoria, everyone at the break-fast table *knew*. Humans can read body language, skin color, flushed cheeks, eye pupil size, heads hung in shame, etc., just as well as any gorilla can.

I finished my platter of buttermilk pancakes topped with pure maple syrup and then packed up my valise, gunned the V-12 Jaguar, and roared out of Clendon's life forever. I couldn't wait to get back to the Emergency Room at Valley General in Los Angeles, California, where I practice as a trauma surgeon and save human lives by the score, although I had to drive the Jaguar very carefully. The wheel alignment had been thrown out when I blew the tire and the frame shud-dered behind all of that V-12 power.

I knew that either Clendon would become so pissed that he would leave that nasty-ass bitch or he would weasel under and suffer worse than that alienated hero in the Russian novel *Crime and Punishment*, Clendon's favorite character of all time. I believe the dude's name is Raskolnikov.

How Clendon ever married that pit viper is a mystery to me. In that summer of the mosquitoes, I saw that he had capitu-lated completely . . . for a Volvo, two overweight kids with "blah" for personalities, and a neurotic wife who took separate vacations to Florence, Italy, to look at artwork. Victoria was a good fuck but I kept thinking of those awful paintings she signed with her maiden name and how she made Clendon use his influence with the art department so she could have that pathetic show over there at Middlebury College.

Beyond that, I knew she'd make him think it was his fault that she screwed the young guy at the tennis club, among others, me included.

Well, Clendon is not the world's first cuckold, and he won't be the last. When I saw her turn around from the sink in that sheer nightie with those breasts made in Heaven, those long slim legs, etc., I can understand what must have happened to my big brother and can see how he got suckered in. Romantic love. Romeo and Juliet. No-fucking-body can look six months down the road. It just doesn't last. How come they can't see it? Why can't they anticipate?

Thus the two fat kids, both null and void. It was plain to see they aren't Clendon's. But he can't leave now ("the kids, the psychic scar of divorce proceedings, plastic curtains in the trailer court"). Hey! I tried to do him a favor.

I remember once when we were in high school and I went into a clothing store with him to buy a new suit and fell under the salesman's spell and in no time I had six hundred dollars' worth of garish clothes piled on the sales counter — clothes that were the antithesis of me, horrible clothes. Clendon dragged me outside into the sunlight. "Have you lost your mind?" he said. "You're going to look like a pimp in all of that shit!" Laughing, we ran down the street out of that salesman's life for all time.

I hope by screwing Victoria I snapped him out of his trance. If not, then I've only made things worse.

I had to do something. I had to try.

According to Darwin the species wants to go on and on, forever and forever, but we are diluting and degrading the species by letting the weaklings live. I am guilty of this more than anyone. I took the Hippocratic oath and vowed to patch up junkies, prostitutes, and violent criminals and send them back out on the streets to wreak more havoc and mayhem on themselves and on others. I try not to think of that. I like to hope for the best.

I was just reading about the real Robinson Crusoe. He was this troublemaker that got kicked out of his hometown in Scotland and became a sailor in the Royal Navy and then on a trip off the coast of Chile, he started bitching about the ship and the conditions aboard and told the captain he wanted off and so they rowed him ashore with his sea chest, dropped him off, returned to the ship, and when they pulled up the dinghy and got ready to take off, Robinson Crusoe changed his mind and called to the captain, "I didn't mean it. I'm sorry!"

The captain called back, "That's too goddamn bad! Fuck you!"

And off they went. Robinson Crusoe spent three months on the beach trying to stay awake, thinking that it had all been a bad dream and that they would come back for him. He lived on king crabs. Funny he didn't develop gout or blow out his kidneys on that rich and monotonous diet.

When it dawned on Crusoe that they weren't going to come back, he moved inland and made a hut for himself. He became self-sufficient and industrious out of necessity, and learned to take a special pleasure in doing things patiently and well. There were goats on the island, coconuts, pineapples, fish, edible tubers, breadfruit, etc. Also, Crusoe had a splendid view. In a way it was a kind of tropical paradise. By and by Robinson Crusoe captured a number of goats and cut their Achilles' tendons to keep them near his shack. Rats were a problem and often bit his toes to the bone as he slept, but he found some wild cats, stole some kittens, raised them, and trained them to sleep with him and kill the rats. This formerly bitter, angry man was said to have come close to God and learned to love Him. Living on pure foods, breathing fresh air, taking in sunshine and the tranquil sound of the surf, he became more healthy and his sense of hearing and eyesight became remarkably keen.

He became a prime physical specimen. He could run a goat down, pounce on it and slit its throat with his dirk knife. Once, he jumped on a goat that was feeding on the edge of a thirty-foot precipice obscured by dense brush. They both went over and Crusoe, although he landed on the goat, killing it, was so injured himself that he could not move for three days. When he recovered and went back to his hut, the idea of his old age and inevitable helplessness became an *idée fixe*. Portuguese sailors often stopped at the island for food and water, but to reveal himself to them, he knew, would amount to suicide. If they didn't kill him, they would literally make him a galley slave.

Eventually an English ship laid anchor near his island and he went down to greet them in his beard and goatskins and was rescued. What a tale he had to tell.

The real Robinson Crusoe was quickly disillusioned when he returned to England. After a brief moment of sensational attention, he reverted to his old ways, drinking and making trouble. He lost access to God. Finally, he went off, far off in the country, and lived in a sod hut dreaming of his idyllic days of paradise on his island, where he lived less than six years altogether.

I think human beings are despicable. I am sick of saving their miserable lives. I would like to take a boat and my two German shepherds and go off to a tropical island. If anything happens, I can save my own life, pull my own teeth, perform minor surgery. Before I go, I'd have my appendix removed. I know the medicines I need to take and I can get them. I'm sick of junkies, prostitutes, alcoholic street bums, and killers, but they depress me far less than would, say, a Beverly Hills clientele.

I do love my dogs, however.

I'm scheduled to work the weekend night shift at the Valley General Emergency Room. There's a full moon out. I find that it's kinda hard to find access to God in Valley General's ER, especially on a full-moon weekend.

Dufaye owes me a favor. I'll twist his arm and get him to work my rotation. Tell him I got GI pain, fake a fever, and get someone to slice that appendix.

A guy driving around Cape Cod suffering from existential despair! Clendon and his Volvo. Victoria and her tits. Those fat kids and all of that prosperity. It just depressed the hell out of me!

There are lots of uninhabited islands in Fiji. Me and the dogs, we're going to pull a Robinson Crusoe. Cutter's Insect Repellent. I'm going to take a whole case of that shit.

I can't stand mosquitoes.

Unchain My Heart

IN his glistening wet suit Bocassio emerges from the heaving sea, massive and scary like the creature from the Black Lagoon. Cursing, he drops his weight belt like a ton of bricks on the platform and strips off his face mask while his Cuban tender, Serria, quickly goes to work helping him out of his diving suit. The withered old man works quickly, wordlessly, with an ever-present Pall Mall in his mouth. Bocassio takes the cigarette from Serria's wet mouth and puts it in his own, inhaling so deeply its orange coal flares like a neon sign. He takes another long hard drag on the cigarette, almost crushing it between his powerful fingers; he's been five hours on the bottom; he's got a cigarette jones moderate to medium-heavy and he's complaining that the crane operator, on the platform, swung a length of pipe so quickly that it whiplashed Bocassio with a body blow that knocked the wind out of him and nearly caused him to drown. Not only that, he says, but some "motherfucker" was running a diesel motor near his air-intake pump and he bitches out Serria for being too hung over to care. "If you ever fuck up like that again, you're through," Bocassio says. Mr. Macho. He doesn't know I'm on the rig.

Bocassio smiles broadly when he sees me holding down my skirt against the frigid updrafts of the North Sea. Our eyes meet like lovers in love. Marilyn Monroe on the steam grate in *The Seven Year Itch*, and Jean Paul Belmondo in *Breathless*.

Stripped down to his bathing suit, Bocassio takes me in his arms and kisses me deeply. He smells of sea salt, tobacco, and musk. Barechested, his muscles are taut, hard and slablike beneath his dark sun-baked skin. His hands are blue from the cold of hanging idle at his recompression stops unprotected by gloves. He buries his rough black beard in my bosom and his large hands slide under my skirt. Ashamed of himself, Serria busies himself with Bocassio's gear ignoring us, but the other platform workers stop and gawk. It doesn't bother me. Whenever Bocassio arises from the floor of the ocean, his lovemaking is out of this world. There's a reason for this. He's breathing heavy concentrations of nitrogen and it gives him a hard-on that won't quit. He tells me it's a medically proven fact. He carries me across the platform to his small cabin and gently removes my silk skirt and underwear. We make long slow love. Patient love. Savoring.

Bocassio holds me in his arms. I kiss his enormous hands and run my fingers through his brisk black beard. He cups my breasts with his rough hands — cold, sturdy, scarred, and strong. I have never seen such large hands. Jack the Ripper would envy these hands. I kiss his face and he holds me. When he holds me after we make love, I am past all knowing. His holding me — that's the part I like best. The best part.

On the launch to the mainland Bocassio is having twinges in his knees and shoulders — nitrogen bubbles. He tells me that I shouldn't come to the platform, he says he actually *knew*

I was on the platform and that he rushed through the ascent
table so that he could make love to me, he tells me that at certain depths he knows everything. He knows the stuff Plato and
Socrates knew. The stuff that Jesus of Nazareth knew, that the
Sufis knew, and Zen monks knew. He tells me that he has
experienced eternity and that he hates to come to the surface,
where like having drunk of that mythological river Lethe, the
brain forgets all of the cosmic verities and becomes earthbound
once again. Earthbound and stupid.

He tells me that my breasts are so beautiful that it's not
fair for the other divers to see them. He tells me that my
honey-blond hair was made by God on the eighth day of crea-
tion, my hazel eyes on the ninth, and my legs and ass on the
tenth.

We make love again in my hotel room. I love his raw male
smell. Bocassio pulls me off him with his large square hands.
He wants a hot shower. His joints are hurting worse. I lie in
bed and drowse. His pungent smell lingers in the sheets with
an opium effect and I float as if in clouds of heaven.

Suddenly Bocassio barks my name. He's on the bottom
of the shower doubled over in pain with the bends. It is the
worst case of the bends Bocassio has ever had. Excruciating
pain. A helicopter flies us to the nearest hyperbaric tank in
Aberdeen, Scotland. The doctor permits me inside to help
Bocassio kill time.

I hang my jacket over the thick yellow window and when
the pressure inside the tank is lowered to the fourteenth atmos-
phere, Bocassio's pain is miraculously gone. We make love in
the stale dank oxygen of the tank. When the recompression
cycle is complete, the chamber smells of wildcat animal sex.
Outside one of the medics is listening to the Beatles sing "A
Ticket to Ride" on his radio. If he was about to smirk, one

look from Bocassio dispells that idea. Sonny Liston could give such a look. Or his big hero, Roberto Duran.

Big hands on a burnished wooden steering wheel. Superman hands that could squeeze coal into diamonds. We drive the Ferrari to the English coast and make the channel crossing from Britain to Calais then drive through France, Switzerland, Italy, and finally across to Spain, where Bocassio finally feels warm. In Málaga, a young matador is gored by a bull, tossed and stomped like a rag doll not fifty feet from our seats at the bullfights. Miraculously, he lives. There's a picture of him in his hospital room, smiling for the morning papers. *Un milagro!*

One morning while he sleeps I buy my lover a gold Rolex Submariner. He loves the watch but says its beautiful glitter will attract schools of barracuda. Because of their incredible speed, curiosity, and razor-sharp teeth, Bocassio tells me they are the most dangerous and unpredictable fish in the ocean. He decides he'll wear it anyhow. "'Live fast, die young, and leave a good-looking corpse,'" says Bocassio, who reads to kill time on diving rigs. He probably reads as much as I do who am paid to read for a living. He gives me his battered helium Sea Dweller, which is pressure-proof down to 4000 feet. Bocassio's wrists are so thick the watch fits on my biceps.

A surfer is attacked by a great white shark in the waters just to the north of Málaga. He loses an arm and a shoulder but he, too, lives and smiles for the morning papers. *Un milagro!*

Bocassio tells me that in lean times sharks will sometimes prowl the coastline for dolphins, often forcing them to seek the breaking surf for safety not only from the sharks but from an even more certain death — the killer whales. The dolphins take risky forays out past the shelves and reefs for food and then come back to the surf to hide again. Exhausting work.

Many of them starve when food is scarce, he says, and when it's marginal, they have to hustle around the clock. I tell him of a documentary I have seen on television about the idyllic life of the dolphin, that I had always wanted to be a dolphin and work a forty-five-minute work week, and Bocassio laughs. "If the sharks don't get you, the Jap tuna nets will."

My lover rents some scuba gear and takes me out near the shelf where the surfer was attacked. The ocean becomes increasingly dark and cold the deeper we go. I look up to the surface for the reassuring light of the sun and the silhouette of an object that seems to be the size of a ballistic submarine passes overhead. Back on the beach Bocassio tells me it was nothing too heavy, just a tiger shark. Eight feet, maybe ten. The next day he takes me out to the shelf again and we go down two hundred feet and I get stoned on nitrogen, like taking a hit off a can of whipped cream. I don't see God, but it's not bad.

Near the reef on the way in I grab for a piece of nylon rope and Bocassio shoves me away. Later he tells me it was a sea snake. "But it was just laying there like a rope," I say.

"That's how they do," he says. "With their deadly venom."

In the glove compartment of the Ferrari I find a recent letter from Bocassio's Spanish whore. We fight. I curse and spit and beat my fists against his solid chest. It feels like I'm pounding a tractor tire. Bocassio grabs my wrists and holds me down. He *fucks* me so hard I have orgasms like epilepsy. I love Bocassio even when I hate him.

We drive the Ferrari to Nice. Bocassio shaves his beard. His face is pale and tender like a baby's, yet it looks much older than his twenty-eight years and it unsettles me. He says, "Hard miles on this face."

In Monte Carlo Bocassio starts a fight with two young men he catches sitting in the Ferrari, play-driving. One of them comes on to me. They are young bucks, drunk and cocky but harmless. Bocassio beats them savagely, too much. When I ask him why later, he says, "Because I wanted them to know how it feels."

That night while we are making love, Bocassio complains of pain in his hips. It was the fight, I tell him. He agrees. "Even when you win, you never get off totally scot-free," he says. In the morning he has X rays taken at a clinic. When the doctor learns that he is a diver, he tells Bocassio that he has aseptic bone necrosis. His hip bones are as fragile as honey-combs, the doctor says, from the years of residual nitrogen bubbles trapped in his bone marrow. The doctor tells him he can no longer make the deep saturation dives worth $300 an hour. He will have to become a mud diver or a harbor diver and never again descend deeper than fifty feet. "There isn't any money in harbor diving," Bocassio complains. "And nothing holy happens at fifty feet."

"Is the money worth your life?" the doctor says. "Find some other line of work." Bocassio shrugs. He is an ex-convict with no skills other than bank robbery.

After dinner Bocassio says he knows a way of switching X rays to pass his physicals and keep his certification. I tell him that he will become a cripple. He tells me he doesn't care, that the only place where he is happy is on a dive, the deeper the better. "When I'm on the bottom everything is *so right*. Sitting alone on the bottom of the ocean I've witnessed the holy presence of God."

"You mean God like Jehovah?"

He says, "No, I mean God like physics."

Bocassio tells me he's too deep in back taxes to become a mud diver. The IRS is breathing down his neck. He is so sick of their audits, he has failed to file tax returns for three years and is afraid to come back to New York. The Ferrari payments are in arrears. Neither of us likes to think of these details and instead we make love — bum fucks for both of us.

We drive back to Calais and make the crossing to Britain. All is glum including the weather. I am more than three weeks late for work. Big deal.

Bocassio books a ticket for me on the Concorde and presents me with a two-carat emerald ring. He can afford neither but he insists. I fly back to New York at twice the speed of sound.

My sister Dana tells me that Bocassio's bull terrier, Duran, has killed a neighbor's Yorkie. Snapped its neck and shook it like a rag doll. For this I am being sued. The woman is livid and unreasonable. It costs three thousand to buy her off. I have to borrow the money from my boss, Timothy. Duran is pissed at me for leaving him with Dana and for five consecutive days he pisses on my pillow. He chews furniture. I could die. It takes a year to break in a goose down pillow and mine had just about been perfect. I make do with foam pillows until Duran gets over his mood. Dana tells me I should have Duran neutered. I can't do that, I tell her. Duran belongs to Bocassio.

I lie awake nights and think of Bocassio and how old he looked when he shaved his beard, and yet how tender and pale his face was, like a baby's. I think of the letter I found in his glove compartment from his Spanish whore.

My co-workers are sniping because of "three weeks late." Timothy calls me in officially and tells me I'm being docked for missed time. He says that higher-ups want me fired. I threw the whole place into a tizzy. People had to stay late and cover me. People had to work overtime because of me. When I point out the fact that he has taken major credit for a piece I did in our recent issue, one that drew raves — he folds his hands on his very neat little desk and denies it. "It was my idea, and I had to grind out the rewrite."

"Fuck you, Timothy! You're having delusions of grandeur," I said. As I stomp out of the office, he follows me to the door. "That's very dangerous talk and shows a major lack of gratitude for somebody who went to bat for you! You're running this artistic eccentricity number into the ground."

Half of the office is assembled near the Coke machine next to Timothy's office. I walk past them with my head held high. "I write the fucking shit, Timothy, and you get the promotion. Ain't that the way. Do me a favor and fire me," I say.

"You've got an attitude and you're walking a very thin line, a *very* thin line," he says quietly closing the door. "Bitch!" he whispers.

Timothy isn't going to fire me, he needs me. I pick up the picture of Bocassio from the cluttered desk in my cubicle and plant a big kiss on his mouth leaving a thick ruby red lipstick smear on it and then I take the rest of the afternoon off. I haven't got the poise to play nonchalance after that scene.

When I tell Dana what happened at work, she reminds me of the other jobs I've been fired from, the financial mess I'm in, and the fact that I've got one of the best jobs in publishing. "You *are* walking a thin line," she says, "especially if that ex-convict comes back to New York in a wheelchair, and you don't see what a world of shit you are creating here. You act like some heartsick teenybopper in love. Think about your career. All the talent in the world doesn't mean a thing if you can't play the game. I can't believe the way you act."

Dana has a point. I have not been contrite or penitent enough to suit those rapacious jackals at work. I came home late and the whole crew had to cover for me, make vital decisions and work late many nights to make deadlines . . . all because of me and my insatiable need for Bocassio. I love Bocassio. He is my other half. He is strength, he is courage; he is my conqueror. Fuck these catty bitches with their vicious schemes, their smirking, their feigned exasperation. One night with Bocassio and his nitrogen-stiff cock and they would be on crutches with that loose, shiteating grin that comes after a good earthy fuck. We are animals, after all, and fucking is a part of the deal. Why are they trying to make me feel so guilty?

I pull my hair back in a tight bun Monday morning and wear a chaste suit like Grace Kelly in some kind of nun story. No makeup. Clipped fingernails, no nail polish. Just a pair of modest pearl earrings from pearls Bocassio harvested on a sport dive. In spite of my resolve to be on time, I am forty-five minutes late. On my desk next to the lipstick-stained picture of Bocassio is an artist's rendition of me on my back with my legs apart and the depiction of Bocassio as a centaur fucking me with an enormous penis. The picture is entitled, "The Whore of Babylon." I know the artist by his work and scribble "You made his dick too small" on the picture and send it back through the interoffice mail.

Paranoid. I come in early, stay late, and eat lunch in my cubicle. I put out twice the usual work. I am sweet. I am on the cutting edge of innovation. I am indispensable. And I am really freaked. The handwriting is written in the air — even my friends have turned against me. Nobody wants to go down with the blond *Titanic*, the fuck slut. Everyone is avoiding me or they're sniping. Jennifer James, my so-called friend, is appalled by the photo of Bocassio on my desk, exuding danger and virility. She asks me tactlessly if I'm not worried about getting AIDS. Everyone is frosty, but if they are frosty, I am the Ice Queen.

At least I pretend to be. Dana counsels me to work hard. "This will pass off. You're just the item for now. They will get bored with it and start in on someone else or they'll get busy, you know how that goes, these vendettas are hard to sustain. In the meantime just see that you don't start screaming at people."

I think Dana is wrong. I'm finished. I know it.

Folded in quarters in the top drawer of my file cabinet on a huge piece of sketch paper I find yet another graphic depiction of a twenty-five-inch, uncircumcised pulsating penis covered with huge warts. On the bottom the artist has scribbled, "Is this about right?"

That night when I tell Dana she reflects unsympathetically. "When you become an object of ridicule, hope is gone. Start looking around."

"I'm a walking basket case, Dana — look where?"

If I had a nun's habit I couldn't appear more chaste. When Timothy summons me into his office, my heart begins to pound. I figure this is it — fired! Instead, he hands me a stupid little "shit" assignment. I say, "Thank you, sir. Wouldst thou like a cup of coffee, sir?"

A smile warms his face.

"Sir?"

"Sonny Rollins is playing at the Blue Note tonight. Do you wanna go?"

"If it pleaseth thou, sir."

After Sonny Rollins we hit the clubs and got drunk on tequila. I let Timothy fuck me. I don't remember much about it except that he had a pocketful of ribbed condoms, which weren't so bad at first but later began to feel like a crosscut saw. I can hardly walk afterward and when I'm through barfing tequila and wash my face, I deliberately avoid looking in the mirror because that face in the mirror is the face I hate most of all in the world.

The next morning I'm late for work for the first time in weeks. Either Timothy or the janitor cleaned the lipstick smear off Bocassio's photograph on my desk. I'm thinking it was Timothy because my computer screen was dusty. When the janitor is in the mood to dust, that's usually the one thing he dusts.

I wonder why Bocassio hasn't called me. He is way overdue. I feel guilty and pissed at the same time. If Bocassio has a Spanish whore, he has English ones, too. The Whore of Babylon throws herself into her work.

Timothy knows trendy restaurants, movies, off-Broadway theater. I let him fuck me with his French ticklers — I need the physical release, but I kick him out before dawn. I cannot endure the thought of having breakfast with Timothy, of watching him butter his toast with his tiny wrists and his woman's fingers.

Dana thinks Timothy is a "catch." He has impeccable manners and he's a good dresser, she says. I want to say, "Dana, don't you know what that man has put me through?" But I know she doesn't see things my way.

On Friday afternoons I take home as many manuscripts from the slush pile as I can carry and I read them in bed over the weekend. Most of them are junk. Ninety-nine times out of a hundred I bail out after the first paragraph. I slap a form rejection on the manuscript, put it in the self-addressed enclosed envelope, and lick the mucilage on the envelope flaps until I get a stomachache from the taste of glue. I know that out there in the heartland would-be writers are devastated by these sterile rejection slips and maybe even commit suicide over them but my own little stomachache means more to me than all of the life on the planet. Yet I am too lazy to get a sponge from the kitchen.

It bugs me to think of how hard I have to work to earn so little. I am getting paid to find gold from the slush pile, the second-rate agents, and the little literary magazines, where if it is to be found, it comes not in large nuggets but in the smallest of grains. Timothy, pontificating in his newer and larger office, says the typical reader is always some cunt who just graduated from Smith College and is more interested in looking for a husband than a career in publishing. Most of my female colleagues, though cruel, are moral and conscientious about their work, but I don't argue the point, not after their jungle ambush.

I dream Bocassio has made me pregnant with a baby boy who will grow up, become the heavyweight champion of the world, and avenge me against all of my enemies. I will name him Dempsey.

When I find a story I like and give it to Timothy, he puts me off. I keep bugging him until he finally reads it. He tells me it's a piece of shit. I bring him a better one. He tells me that it's fair but not right for our magazine. I bring yet another and he becomes exasperated and tells me he seriously wonders about my judgment.

"Timothy, I wonder about *your* judgment. You keep

going for these safe, neat little stories. You pick stories like you fuck. Safety first. How can you live with yourself?"

"Little girl, don't cross the line on me —"

As always I can't get home fast enough to turn on the answering machine hoping for a message from my lover. He doesn't call.

As I wake up puking I think of how I tried to stand on my head to let Bocassio's sperm saturate my womb. My breasts are getting bigger than basketballs. They're sore. They hurt. I have to pee constantly. I wonder why people want to fuck at all. ("It seemed like a good idea at the time?") The whole idea of labor and childbirth sounds like a total bummer. I feel like I've got a time bomb in my belly. I feel like a cow. Suddenly the whole idea of pregnancy is humiliating. I do feel like the Whore of Babylon. They should take me out and stone me.

I miss my true love. I wonder why he hasn't called, why he hasn't written. I have written him volumes. I have told him the story . . . the jackals at work have back molars that can crush industrial-grade diamonds; they have not put me away with a quick kill but they have ground me down. Does he despise me for my weakness? Does he find me pathetic? Even when he's angry with me he calls up to hear his dog bark. I sometimes think this is the "only" reason he calls. I am glad I have not written him the news that I'm pregnant.

In the slush pile I find a wonderful manuscript, not a mere grain of gold but rather a boulder. A writer with an authentic new voice — vibrant, powerful, compelling. It is an absolutely stunning piece. I go over Timothy's head and give it to Jerry. I can't take any more of Timothy's mealymouthed shit, haven't got time for it.

I stand over Jerry's shoulder and watch him read the story. He's *gaga* over it, I can tell. When Jerry is finished he leans back in his chair. "Wow!" he says. "This is the *real* thing. Who *is* this writer?"

"All I've got is a name and an address."

"Run down a phone number and call her. Make a bunch of copies of the story and pass them around. You did good. This is major, major!"

"We're buying?"

"I hope so. Make copies. I'll pass them myself."

Jerry takes me to lunch and we get drunk on champagne. When I get back to the office there is a message and a number to call in England. I dial immediately. I want to tell Bocassio how I miss him, how I love him and that I'm in "the family way." I want to tell him to stay out of the deep sea. I need his hips to be strong. I need him to fuck my brains out. I love him. I am a fool for love and I don't care.

Serria answers the phone. He is drunk, overcome. Speaking a mixture of Spanish and English, he tells me that Bocassio drowned when the crane operator dropped a pipe on his air line. There was a sudden storm. It wasn't really any-one's fault. Bocassio tried to make a rapid ascent but he had been far too deep and had gone down without his "bailout" bottle. A week later I got a small box with Bocassio's gold Submariner. Serria told me the Ferrari had been repossessed. There was no funeral. After Bocassio was cremated on the mainland his ashes were scattered at sea.

My sister Dana convinced me to abort the baby. Bocassio wasn't our kind, she said. "Personally, I never could under-stand what you saw in him. He was crude. His face was all pockmarked. He had those hideous tattoos and his friends were psychotic."

"He knew how to love me like nobody before. He was so real," I said wistfully. "And who are you to talk? Look at these fucking lives we live. Have you ever taken a look, Dana? Don't you ever get tired of being sensible?"

"Stupid! Stupid!" Dana said. "Get the abortion."

I am numb. I let my big sister push me. The jackals have done their work, now it's time for the vulture to pick the bones clean. I put my feet in the stainless-steel stirrups and the future heavyweight champion of the world is tossed into a plastic offal bag without throwing a punch. Funny. If Bocassio hadn't shaved his beard, I know I would have had the baby.

You could say that he did me a favor, saved me a lot of pain by shaving his glorious black beard. I turned Duran in to the animal control department. Maybe someone will adopt him, maybe not, I think. He does have a pedigree. It is such a relief to be rid of that goddamn dog, I really don't care either way. I treat myself to a new goose down pillow.

Jerry gives me a promotion, not because of the story I found but because he knew more about what was going on in the office than he let on, that Timothy was taking credit for my work, playing one against another and destroying the fabric of team spirit. Jerry says I'm audacious, a loose cannon, and that it's important to treat people right. He gives me a copy of *How to Win Friends and Influence People*. "You might think this is corny, but it's one of the most important books I've ever read," he says. I read the book and I don't know if he's putting me on or what. My new job has got so many responsibilities, I don't know if he's done me a favor or not. One thing: I bail Duran out from death row. Just in the nick of time. Like, an hour before they were going to do him. In his gratitude, Duran pisses on my new pillow. He's a real pistol. I take him to Central Park and run him. We both need to blow off steam. With

Duran at my side, I know I can jog in complete safety *any*
time.

Dana introduces me to a Marine Corps fighter pilot. He
takes me up in his Mirage fighter jet and it was quite a thrill
when he kicked in the afterburners and we crashed the envelope. I mean, the Red Baron he ain't, but he knows all about
speed and he's kind of cute in his leather bomber jacket and his
Rolex Cosmograph. I've learned deep, now I want to learn
speed.

———

Part
III

"As of July 6, I Am Responsible for No Debts Other Than My Own"

MY mother looked like a movie star, but my father, J. Z. (pronounced *Jayzee!*) Magill, had been the world's fifth-rated heavyweight contender before the war. He was a good friend of Joe Louis, who I got to know as a little kid. J.Z. thought he was going to win the heavyweight title at the age of thirty-two, screw a bunch of bleach-bottle blondes, and drive around in a brand-new Cadillac all the time. "Get me a new one when the ashtrays are full," he'd say. Or, "Buy me a different one if I don't like the sound of the ray-dio."

When he came back from World War II, my father, a much decorated Raider Marine, won a couple of fights including a knockout victory over an old and fading Jamaica Kid, took a look around to see which way the wind was blowing, and split with a fistful of greenbacks in his pocket. He left my mother a silver bracelet on which he had inscribed "you are nothing but a shell of your former self." J.Z. was a tit man and I later heard that his big bitch was the fact that my mother breast-fed me, causing hers to soften up.

My mother was the kind of woman that had to have a man, and she began to date Frank Coles after a series of botched suicide attempts and nervous breakdowns precipitated by the grandiose dreams of J.Z. My father was always around town and would sometimes come to see me for Saturday visitations with a blonde smelling of face powder and other heavenly scents. We were always going to fly a kite or something, which usually meant I got to stand out in a field alone somewhere while he was screwing his girlfriend in the back of the car. He could do it for hours, or so it seemed to me.

I was four years old when Frank Coles came into my life with expensive toys and phony affection. I was just a kid, but even so, I knew he was a louse and that he hated me. I was afraid to be left in the same room with him. The first time he beat me for wetting my bed I told him I was going to send Joe Louis over to get him and he never laid a hand on me again. But his presence unnerved me and I hated him.

Frank was working the graveyard shift at some factory. No doubt it was a horrible place, and there Frank nourished unrealistic dreams of his own. I remember coming home from first grade on sun-short winter afternoons to find him asleep alone in his bedroom lair. He was not a handsome man. He was prematurely bald and the white skin of his head was covered with thick protruding blue skull veins like that Carpathian vampire, Nosferatu. His ears stuck out like translucent fans. To complete the picture, he had overlong canine teeth that he bared in his sleep. Watching him slumber frightened me. He would get up around 6 P.M. to watch Walter Cronkite on the "CBS Evening News." But before he did, I would go stand outside under the streetlight, clutching a butcher knife under my coat, and wait for my mother to come home. I was afraid that Frank Coles might come after me, and if he did I was going to shove the blade into his vampire heart.

My mother also had some sort of factory job: semi–swing shift, variable hours. My mother, who used to look like a movie star until her tits went soft breast-feeding me. Frank Coles didn't win her heart with love so much as he bullied and pressured her into marrying him. I guess he told her he loved her, adored her, and made all sorts of ridiculous vows of devotion. A lot of beautiful women marry strange, love-struck guys who spare no expense or time winning and wooing them. Beautiful women, unless they know who they are and what they want, may fall for guys like Frank Coles. Such men keep at them with relentless pressure, over and over, until they give in. This is what happened to my mother. She was a living doll, but she didn't have much going for her in the way of sales resistance.

As the economy picked up after the war, Frank gave up factory work and earned lower-class semi-respectability by selling used cars. He liked to wear sharkskin suits. He was the kind of guy who always wore a suit, even when he lay on the couch watching Walter Cronkite deliver the news. I don't think he owned any leisure clothes.

I remember I must have been about eight when I rushed into their sex-steamy bedroom one Sunday afternoon. The door was shut and Frank popped out of bed naked with an enormous erection bobbing in the air like a red-hot poker. He grabbed me by the shoulders and shook me until I thought my neck was going to snap and then stuck his finger in my face and said, "When the door is closed don't you ever, ever, come into this bedroom. Never! Ever!"

I had never seen an erection before, and to this day have

never seen another man with a penis in the same league as Frank Coles's. As much as she grew to hate him, my mother always said he was pretty good in the hay.

Some people live for doing "it." Take ten, fifteen percent of the population. They're hyper-sexed. But if you get married to screw and you haven't married a friend, you're in big trouble. Check out the divorce statistics. What are you left with when the glow passes? You're left in a lifelong trap of a bad marriage or child support. My mother and Frank never became friends, but they had two children of their own, a boy and a girl.

We called my mother "the driver," my sister and I, because of slapstick events that occurred whenever she got behind the wheel of a car. I remember the time her Chevrolet Impala was in the shop and she had to drive my four-speed Austin Healy. She had long since forgotten how to drive a stick shift and burned out the clutch on the brand-new Healy.

My grandmother bought that car for me. My grandmother had four girls and a boy who died at six weeks. I was the son she had always wanted and had lost. She loved me more than anything in the world. She told me that I would grow up and make something of myself — show everybody. She warned me about the futility of life and prepared me as much as anyone can. Her name was Margaret Carpenter. She ran an old grocery store. Margaret Carpenter loved me unconditionally and because of this I'm still on the streets, not in some psycho ward or jail, or dead from a heroin overdose or an alcoholic street fight.

My real father, J. Z. Magill, never realized his dream of becoming heavyweight champion. He ended up in the state mental institution in Salem, Oregon, where they filmed *One Flew Over the Cuckoo's Nest*. They had him in the ward for the

criminally insane. He had knocked some jack roller's eye out
with a single punch of his "dynamite right" in a skid-row street
fight and got ten years. I visited him right after my tour as a
Marine in Vietnam and I remember that ward. The smell of
urine, the awful noise and tension, and the violent insane people prowling the ward like great white sharks in frenzied,
bloody waters. In fact, the craziness there was a lot like what I
had seen in Vietnam. It was intense, psychedelic craziness.

One of the inmates slapped me across the face so hard I
went over backwards in my chair. My father, who was so
depressed he could hardly tell what time of day it was, said you
always have to sit with your back to the wall. Didn't I know
anything? he asked. We watched while the staff shot up the
inmate who'd struck me with Thorazine and whipped a
straitjacket on him.

When I showed my father a picture of my mother, he
said, "Who is that?"

"That's Mooney, your wife," I answered.

He looked at me like I was putting him on. He was
paranoid — certifiably so — and wanted to know how much
Marlboro cigarettes cost on the streets. That was more important to him than the beautiful woman in the photograph. He
thought they were screwing him at the hospital canteen.

I wanted to get the f-u-č-k out of that place, so I promised to send him all of my old *Ring* magazines and a used
banjo, and I headed for the exit. As I was standing near the
steel door waiting for an orderly to let me out, my father put
up his dukes, threw a few punches in the air, and cried, "My
name is Jayzee Magill and I can lick any son of a bitch in the
world!" He started moving his feet and swinging wildly in the
air — an old, burned-out fighter. Talk about being a shell of
your former self. I had to look away. It hurt too much to

watch. I was afraid they might shoot him up with Thorazine, too. I had to get away from that place.

I was on my way to the University of Iowa to get a degree in medicine. I did send J.Z. the magazines, but I got so busy with my studies I didn't find a banjo. I'd hardly tried when one day my uncle John called and said, "You better sit down. Your father hanged himself in that nuthouse."

What he had done was hide in the bathroom after lunch and hang himself in a stall with a towel torn in strips and knotted together. They buried him in Potter's Field. I'd always loved my father and I pray for him to this day, but really he was little more than a stranger to me. Number five in the world. Not bad considering he wasn't much more than a blown-up light-heavyweight.

When I was a sophomore in high school I went down to the fight gym to learn how to box like the old man. I came home with a broken nose and said I was quitting.

"No you aren't," said Frank, sticking his finger in my chest. He made me go back to the gym every night and take ass-whippings. I didn't have Joe Louis around to protect me anymore. I learned how to fight.

Outside the confines of our humble home, Frank was known as a decent person, an honest man, an all-round good guy. Everybody liked him. The sales manager at the Chevrolet dealership had this hot idea: They would sell swimming pools. Frank would be their ace salesman. I guess Frank thought he was going to hit it big with this swimming pool scheme, become a millionaire, a Los Angeles, California, big shot.

Actually it was a Willy Loman, *Death of a Salesman* delusion of grandeur. He was counting his chickens before they hatched. But he was so sure the scheme would work that he took a mistress and came right out with it, bragging about it.

He gave my mother a dose of gonorrhea along with crabs. When our doctor, a strict Catholic, treated her, he encouraged her to divorce Frank. There *were* limits.

I saw one of the crabs drowned in the toilet bowl. It was a frightening sight, almost as bad as my childhood vision of Frank as a bat-eared Nosferatu, sleeping off the day in that little bedroom which smelled like a coffin.

A few days after the V.D. episode, Frank got into a fight with my mother and the next thing I knew he'd carried a half-dozen sharkskin suits out of the closet down to his car, a turquoise Impala station wagon with a "Colonial Pools" logo on the driver's door. On the second trip down he had an A&P shopping bag loaded with underwear, T-shirts, his Gillette safety razor, a can of Burma Shave, and his Man-Tan.

I was in my Pony League baseball uniform and my mother was out in the front yard, hysterical, begging him not to leave. Some really heavy scene. The neighbors all came out, saw what was going on, and were appalled. It was embarrassing for me, but worth it. I was glad to see him go and hoped he would never come back.

That's when he put the ad in the paper: "As of July 6, I, Frank Coles, am responsible for no debts other than my own."

Two weeks later when he came home with his tail between his legs, he was uncommonly nice and penitent. Reality had put the quash on his dream — the swimming pool scheme hadn't panned out. But there was something else different about him. His white skin was ghastly pale in spite of his Man-Tan treatments, he had lost weight, and he had this cough. Frank had gotten cancer from incessant cigarette smoking. He was forty-two.

By the time the surgeon got to it, the cancer had spread to both lungs. He took the left lung out and part of the right.

The surgeon told my mother there was no hope. He would be dead in three days.

Hate to admit it, but I was glad. I wanted to do cartwheels. I wanted to burst into song. My mother made me go to the hospital to say goodbye to Frank. The big, bad vampire was now shrunken, tiny, and frightened. He was begging my mother to pray for him. I think he had one of those near-death calls and actually entered into the inferno for a few moments.

"Pray for me, Mooney, I don't want to go to hell! Pray to Jesus for me, please!" he cried.

Pray she did. My mother's prayers were answered and my counterprayers were not. Frank pulled through the immediate crisis. When he got back on his feet again, a cousin with some spare time drove him to the Orange County V.A. Hospital for radiation treatments. The surgeon said the treatments could buy him some time, but no cure was possible. So there was Frank, sick from radiation, lying around the house wearing blue-green pajamas rather than sharkskin suits.

One morning before school, hurrying through breakfast, I accidentally stepped on my sister's foot in front of the kitchen sink. She screamed a he's-picking-on-me-again scream. Frank was down the stairs and into the kitchen in a heartbeat.

"God damn you," he said. "You keep your hands off her, you little shit!"

He trapped me against the Kenmore refrigerator and began to cuff me. When I pushed back he cried, "How *dare* you? You son of a bitch. You bastard!" He was huffing for air, his long, yellow teeth bared, and he slathered like a mad dog, spraying me with saliva.

He was unloading all his anger, fear, and frustration on

me. He forgot that I was a boxer and trained to take blows. Then he went too far and I finally lost my fear of him, unleashing a left hook to his jaw, a straight right to his nose, another left hook to the solar plexus — a crushing shot — and then a left and right uppercut to the jaw. I had lived long enough to grow up, get big, and get even.

I don't know how Babe Ruth felt when he connected with the bat on that famous centerfield home run he is said to have brashly called in Wrigley Field, but I threw crisp, clean, hard punches and could feel them reverberate along my arms, up into my shoulders. I took two steps back and watched Frank Coles collapse in sections to the kitchen floor.

He was a sick man. It really wasn't even fair. Still, it had to be the best feeling I had experienced in the first sixteen years of my melancholy life. I grabbed my schoolbooks and was out the door and walking down the hill to school when I saw my girlfriend, Stephanie, who was coming to the street corner where we met every day.

"Joey, what's wrong?" she asked. "Why are you crying? Who scratched your face? How come you're wearing *pajama tops?*"

Funny. Those radiation treatments at the V.A. Hospital worked, and against all odds Frank was cured of his cancer. If you want it bad enough, you can defy the odds. Frank went right back to smoking. I was living with my grandmother by then so there were no more beefs between the two of us. And his brush with death had made him one of the nicest people you would ever want to know. I began to see why most people liked him. We became pretty good friends, the two of us, and I could see that he loved me just as much as the two children he had with my mother; that wasn't much, but it was all the love he had in him. Frank Coles lived another twenty years, got a toupee and a set of false teeth that looked more normal than his own, and eventually died of a heart attack.

My mother, what with her looks still holding up even at the age of fifty-five, got lucky her third time out, married a schoolteacher. Pretty nice guy. She could have been patient, waited it out and got a doctor or lawyer, she was *that* beautiful. But she had to have a man. She couldn't wait for the dust to settle before she married the schoolteacher, the first guy who came along. But it's worked out great. They're happy together. She doesn't worry that he's out cheating on her, which was her main priority.

Because Frank wouldn't let me quit, I had stuck with boxing. I became good at it even though at the time I thought it was a low sport and was ashamed of it, in spite of my trophies and prizes. I won a hundred and fifty amateur fights and then I fought this guy in the Marines. I had been in with heavyweights and super-heavyweights in my Golden Glove days. I'd taken big shots and so on, but until that Marine I didn't know anyone could punch that hard. J. Z. Magill used to eat guys like him for breakfast, but I wasn't my old man. I suffered three broken ribs, a broken nose, and a broken eye socket. I pissed blood for two weeks, developed a fever, and went into a delirium. I thought I was going to die. You take a beating like that and it puts the fear of God into you. That was it. No more boxing for me. There is always someone bigger and badder than you.

Yet from boxing I learned self-respect, discipline, and the mental strength to achieve goals through hard work and unwavering perseverance. Those skills got me through medical school. Now I work as a trauma surgeon in the emergency room at Valley General in L.A. I patch up junkies and alcoholic street bums and say, "Go out there and give 'em hell, slugger." That's what I tell them.

It's not a bad job. I'm the best trauma "blade" in the city, and I've got all the toys. A solid gold Rolex, a Jag V-12 ragtop, three boxer dogs. The boxers are absolute sweethearts and all the company I need. I don't want a wife. There are plenty of nurses to screw and I don't want to be suffocated. I wish I didn't screw at all, but nothing makes me hotter than a nurse in uniform. I guess it's okay, I just don't want to end up like either of my parents. My grandmother, who lived forty-two years without a man, she didn't screw. She wasn't perfect, she wasn't Mother Teresa, but she loved me. I try to be like her, to sublimate my libidinal energy into my work. Maybe, even, I do some good in this horrible world, this Outer Mongolia of spirituality.

I have forgiven Frank Coles and I have forgiven myself. Until you forgive yourself you cannot love anyone or do a drop of good anywhere or anyhow.

It's just that one thing sticks in my craw. My mother was the one who hauled off to work every day, paid the bills, cleaned the house, raised three kids, paid off Frank's gambling debts, looked the other way when he went out and screwed whores, and nursed him through his cancer while he sat on that couch in his suit watching television, chain-smoking, and eating Cheez-its. So where does he get off with a line like "As of July 6, I am responsible for no debts other than my own"?

Silhouettes

WINDOW fell for Catherine his senior year in high school when both were given special education assignments in East High School's laundry room. The job didn't pay much but it gave them a little spending money, which Catherine spent buying Marlboro cigarettes, Thunderbird wine, candy bars, blotter acid, and marijuana, and which Window spend on Catherine.

Their boss, Meldrick, immediately saw potential in Window but found Catherine useless and had her transferred to lunch room duty. Meldrick was the custodian in charge of the washer, dryer, and the centrifugal extractor in the laundry room, a comfortable hideaway attached to the boiler room where he could sit and read while his bunch of "special ed" assistants washed and folded the P.E. towels. Meldrick expected little from the students but because there were so many, if they performed even minimally, most of his own work was done. When this was the case he permitted the students to clown around and indulge in a kind of Fagin's Band brand of tomfoolery. Their antics were a welcome reprieve after a forty-five-minute dose of Spinoza or David Hume. Sometimes Meldrick would join in the fun and perform a rendition of "Hambone" by rhythmically slapping his chest and thighs with his palms and fingertips, and then when he was finished, he would imitate Ricky Ricardo from "I Love Lucy" and say, "Eet's so ree-diculous!"

A journeyman custodian, Meldrick owned the most advanced college degrees in the school and was working diligently on his doctorate although he was convinced he would never find a better job. This was especially true when he discovered Window, whose capacity for work amazed him. Window was trustworthy and responsible, so much so that Meldrick found that he could hand Window his keys and turn him loose in the shop area where he would do an A-number-one job without screwing up, so that all Meldrick had to do was a casual inspection afterward to make sure the paper towel dispensers were full, the glass was spotless, the floors properly mopped, and that all the lights were out and the doors were locked. On days when Window was focused and his powers of concentration were high, Meldrick didn't even bother to check.

Meldrick's penchant for investigating the riddle of existence caused the other janitors to avoid him, and Meldrick found little in common with anyone on the faculty, with their state university degrees, who would get a glazed-over look in their eyes when he wanted to expound on some philosopher who obsessed him. Meldrick sometimes thought he was the only person at the school, perhaps the only regular job-holder in the whole country, with the leisure to read philosophy, and thanks to Window he had an abundance of time. Moreover, it was only with Window that he felt completely at ease, with whom he could talk and simply be himself — Window, who didn't have a very high-priced vocabulary but who would patiently watch while Meldrick took him into a classroom and illustrated concepts like "nihilism" or "existentialism" on the chalkboard and explained to Window how they were relevant to his own situation, including those times when Window was lovesick over Catherine and would zone out so badly that Meldrick actually had to clean the shops himself or even dump the filthy cloth bag of his "Pig," a noisy but durable commercial vacuum cleaner. Thus Meldrick attempted to instruct Window on such topics as love between the sexes and other practical matters taking an airy, detached, and theoretical view that made the problems of life seem simple and resolvable. Meldrick could get on a kick and rave for an hour until Window would practically topple over like a chicken that had been hypnotized by having its beak placed on a line scratched in the dirt.

Although Meldrick repeatedly warned Window about Catherine, who was notorious at East High for her temper tantrums and sexual escapades, once she let Window have sex with her, Window was deaf to all advice. Like Odysseus, he had heard the "lovely tones" from the Siren's isle and had lost all sense of reason.

Meldrick became exasperated. "I talk to you until I am blue in the face. You just won't listen. What's the matter with you, huh? Hello dere, is anybody home?"

"I'm home, Meldrick."

"Why, mercy, Window. I thought you were lost in space."

"No, Meldrick. Window's on earth today."

"Then perhaps we can work the conundrum through. Perhaps we can slash the Gordian knot. Let's try something new. Listen closely, Window, this is serious. As I count forward from one to seven, you will become more and more relaxed. I want you to picture yourself walking down a set of stairs, and with each step you will find yourself going deeper and deeper into relaxation. One . . . two . . . three . . . (you are becoming more and more relaxed). Please wipe that shit-eating grin off your face, Window — four . . . five . . . six . . . seven. There! You are now in touch with the Higher Power, that part of you which knows all. What does it say?"

Window began to guffaw. "I know, I know, Meldrick. Leave the bitch alone!"

"You've got it, pal. Keep clear from that woman. Man, she's bad. She's gonna drive you crazy."

"I steer clear."

"You promise?"

"Yes."

"Okay, now as I count back from seven to one, you will emerge from the dank basement of your subconscious mind and step into the glorious sunshine of life unbound from the snarls and tangles of that evil black magic web the nasty spider has ensnared you with. Seven . . . six . . . five — stop smiling, Window! Four . . . three . . . two . . . one — bingo. How do you feel, Window?"

"I have pain in my head."

"Ooh, this is so ree-diculous!" Meldrick said. "Take two aspirin and I'll see you tomorrow. You can go."

Meldrick liked to sit in the laundry room with a cup of coffee and a thick book, listening to the comforting sound of the dryer while Window managed all of his jobs. Window had a bubble butt and short feet, and when he ran back and forth into the laundry room to get supplies with short mincing steps, Meldrick was reminded of Kirby Puckett legging out a triple for the Minnesota Twins and would have to chuckle. He knew Window was hustling so that he would have time to find Catherine and steal a kiss or two from his beloved, the love of his life. Meldrick was aware of these shenanigans but ignored them as long as Window performed.

Catherine did not especially like Window. She was still pining over a guy who knocked her up her junior year and then moved off to Spokane, leaving her and her parents to cope with the abortion. She did not like Window because he was such a square and because he had ambitions of graduating from high school and becoming a full-time custodian. But Catherine's parents liked Window and encouraged his visits to their trailer home out on the Hoquiam Indian Reservation even if he was a blue-eyed, fair-skinned ultra-white boy. Window was so white he was almost translucent — you could almost see through him, thus the nickname. His real name was Albert Thomas. Albert Thomas or Window — it didn't matter to Catherine's parents — he was a "prospect" and they felt he would calm Catherine down. She had a wild streak in her and she needed taming. Maybe, even, Window would be their savior and marry Catherine. For this reason they looked the other way when Catherine took Window into her room, where the two lovers soon had the whole trailer rocking like a small boat on the high seas. It was almost impossible to watch television, especially during the sexual climaxes, but the parents quickly accommodated themselves to these sessions and even laughed about them.

Meldrick and the other custodians at East High continued to dissuade Window from seeing Catherine and told him outright that she was no good. Josie, the matron, who had to break up the cat fights the female students got into at lunch or attend to Catherine during her pseudo-epileptic fits, did not warn Window so much as she told Meldrick to use his limited powers over Window to destroy the relationship. It was a shame, she said, because Window was such a good kid and Catherine was nothing but trouble, upside and down, but Meldrick would protest weakly, "It's the metaphysics of the sexes — my hands are tied. Every time the bitch comes around, his eyes turn into two stars."

Packard, a graveyard-shift custodian, confronted Window one morning when, after he went out to turn off the alarms in the greenhouse, he caught Catherine and the school's worst troublemaker screwing shamelessly in the bushes. "You want to know who she was fucking, dipstick? She was fucking Centrick Cline; need I say more? That bitch is insane, Window, and she's taking you for a ride. She's *hustling* you, man!"

When Meldrick came in on swing shift and heard of the incident, he became genuinely angry and harangued Window in the laundry room until Window blushed red. Seeing that he was getting through, Meldrick amplified his argument with the exaggerated body posturing of a courtroom lawyer and threatened to fire Window. It was just play-acting, but Meldrick got so carried away that all Window could do was let his head slump forward and say, "I know. I know. She's no good." Window worked an extra hour on his own time that night and before he left he came up to Meldrick and apologized for letting him down.

"You dope, you say that shit but you don't mean it. You're crazy, man. That bitch is going to bring you down." Meldrick's censure caused Window to writhe in agony. "Dammit, Window, you're breaking my heart with this shit. I go out of my way to help you, I try to be your friend and look what you do to me. Why don't you just drink a bottle of Drano and get it over with? I can't stand watching you go through this bullshit."

"That's right," Josie said. "She's a whore. Keep away from her. Tell him, Meldrick."

"I'm telling him, dammit, but it isn't sinking in. Window, you're completely out of control. We're your friends: listen! What's the matter with you, anyhow? You aren't dumb. Quit giving me dumb. I'm sick of that fucking act. Use your head."

In the ensuing weeks Meldrick browbeat Window into agreeing to stay away from Catherine, and for a time Window avoided her. This was a source of consternation for Catherine since she thought she had Window in her pocket, and when he stopped calling or avoided her at school, a strange kind of emptiness welled up in her and she began to tell her friends that she was in love with Window and was carrying his baby.

Window then came to Meldrick and reported that he "had" to marry Catherine, and rather than scream a diatribe, Meldrick shook his head in resignation and said, "Well, if you really love her, go ahead and do it. My good thing is over. I knew it was too good to be true. I'm going to have to fucking work for a change."

Window asked Meldrick to be his best man after Window's special ed buddy, Paul Palmer, who was slated for this honor, had an epileptic seizure in his bed and suffocated facedown in his pillow. Meldrick refused to be a party to the wedding. In the meantime, Catherine and Window pressed forward and made plans.

In the first part of June, a few weeks before school was out, the librarians went into one of the custodian closets to get a two-wheeled cart and there they found the custodian Mancini, a known alcoholic, passed out on the floor with an alarm clock ticking by his ear and a six-pack of Olympia beer at his side. Mancini, in a full-length beard and filthy flannel shirt, lay on the floor with one shoe missing. He was breathing erratically and the frightened librarians summoned the head custodian, who got the principal. The principal was unable to rouse Mancini, but he had seen enough drunks to know that Mancini would revive and merely wrote a note — "You're fired!" — dated it, signed it, and taped it to the six-pack. Meldrick waited a few days and then made a pitch to the principal that Window, a product of the school's special education program, was a good worker — reliable, cheerful and an excellent candidate for the job. The principal heard him out and then said that Window was too young. Meldrick said, "He's nineteen. What good is the vocational program if it can't get its graduates jobs?"

This was a telling point, and the principal told Meldrick to have Window submit an application and said that he would consider it. While Window cleaned Meldrick's area that night, Meldrick went into the business area and typed out the application forms including a short essay, written in the style of Window's speech, and after Window read and signed the forms, Meldrick neatly folded them and stuck them in the principal's box.

Window was interviewed a week later and hired to replace Mancini. Catherine's parents were ecstatic over the

news and threw an impromptu party for Window out on the
reservation. The school district paid well and had an excellent
health and retirement program. They encouraged Window
even when Catherine lost the baby. That summer when all of
the custodians reverted to day shift, Meldrick, Packard, and
Josie gang-banged Window, launching a new assault against
Catherine, and Catherine, relieved over the miscarriage, lost
interest in Window, called him boring, and flung his ring in his
face.

Catherine refused to see Window and in a matter of ten
days, Window, who apart from his fat ass verged on slender,
lost twelve pounds and began to look like a concentration
camp victim. At work he seemed distracted, and when the custodians took their frequent breaks, Window dozed off at the
table.

Ted Frank Page, the gymnasium custodian, would laugh
as Window's mouth fell open. "He's doing an 'O,'" Page
would say, or if Window exposed his tongue, however slightly,
Page would slap the table and proclaim that Window was
doing a "Q." The custodians would roar with laughter and
Window, who was painfully shy, would jerk awake and blush
like a beet. Sometimes he would bolt away from the table
and disappear for hours. Although the janitors were familiar with all of the hiding spots, no one could find Window
when he was off somewhere nursing his hurt. There was speculation that he went up on the roof to do this and most of
them were too lazy and out of shape to climb the iron-rung
ladder that led to the roof. Generally Window would later
turn up in Meldrick's area to see if he had been missed, and
just as Meldrick could berate Window, at these times he
would calm Window by painting pictures of a new and
better life — Thunderbirds and motorcycles, a healthier body

through a better diet and physical training, sharp clothes, braces to straighten his teeth, Window's very own apartment, and the ultimate prize — a beautiful wife. Soon Window would forget all about Catherine and spin out his fantasies about Whitney Houston or Paula Abdul, singers that Meldrick was barely familiar with. Meldrick cautioned Window to be realistic but he did not entirely discount the possibility. "You're a really neat guy, Window. Who knows. Play your cards right and maybe it will happen, dude. You know the universe is filled with abundance. Sometimes all you got to do is ask."

With his full-time paychecks Window bought the old Citroën behind the autoshop, and the autoshop teacher, who was teaching a summer school course, got it running for him. The janitors kidded Window about the Citroën, which looked like a flying saucer, and Ted Frank Page said, "Well, how else do you expect him to get back and forth from the Planet Fringus except in some sort of a spacecraft?"

The head custodian laughed and said, "I guess you can't drive there in a Ford?" He belly-bumped the table with his big stomach and tossed his head back to laugh. "I can't believe this place."

Late that summer, Window seduced Catherine with presents and protestations of love. Stewing in boredom out on the reservation, Catherine had really begun to hate her parents, especially her father, who drew disability pay because of a bad back and nagged Catherine to wait on him. Catherine often came over to East High with her friend Lutetia, a fat girl who always walked behind her rather than at her side. The janitors were curious about this, but Lutetia was also a product of the special education program and that seemed to explain just about any eccentricity. The purpose of Catherine's visits to the high school was almost always money, and if Window did not have any, Catherine would clutch her fists at her sides, scrunch down in a rage, and scream at Window through clenched teeth. Window would turn red and hang his head submissively and try to appease her. "Please, Catherine, relax or you'll have a seizure."

"If I have a goddamn seizure, it will be your stupid fault, Window. You fucking asshole. You son of a bitch. You motherfucking cocksucker. I hate you!"

These scenes caused Packard and Meldrick to renew their efforts to destroy the relationship, and while Window agreed that Catherine was too wild for him, he also became stubborn. He was stubborn because he had a full-time job and was flush with money (his janitor's pay was a relative fortune for a nineteen-year-old) and Window didn't really care at times what Meldrick thought. Meldrick suspected there was more to it than this and one afternoon up in the library he used his guile to extract a confession from Window that Catherine was pregnant again. Window said that he knew for sure that it was his baby. He told Meldrick that he loved her and once they got their own place and she was away from the firecracker tension of her parents' trailer, where her dad was often drunk, everything would be fine.

In the meantime, the head custodian warned Window that he was sick of Catherine coming over to the school, sick of her rages, and told him to keep his personal life separate from his professional life. After the head man left the custodian's room, Meldrick gave Window an ironic look and said, "He's right, Window. This special ed shit has got to stop. You're a janitor now. Act like a professional."

*   *   *

Shortly after the birth of his son, Joey, Window began to gain weight. Meldrick accused Window of seeking substitute gratification, but Window refused to acknowledge any problems between himself and Catherine. After the swing shift was over, however, rather than rush home to be with his bride, Window liked to play volleyball with the custodians in the gym. Ted Frank Page organized these games and came in early to play before his graveyard shift started. Meldrick and Page hit the weight room after the games and encouraged Window to lift weights and take better care of his body. In the weight room Window finally confessed that Catherine refused absolutely to have sex with him after the birth of their son, that she had run up a shitload of credit card charges and that he was forced to have his brother, Roy, move into their apartment in order to help pay the bills.

Although Roy was Window's brother, and also a product of East High's special education program, he was tall and good looking. He had better teeth than Window. Ted Frank Page teased Window that while Window was busting his ass on the swing shift, Roy was home dicking Catherine. *That* was the reason she wouldn't sleep with Window. One night at the dinner break after Meldrick and Window dined on Meldrick's "macrobiotic special" — a combination of brown rice, black beans and raisins — Meldrick went into one of his classrooms and found Window watching television as he ate from a half gallon carton of Neopolitan ice cream into which he had stirred a pound of M&M's. A six-pack of iced cappuccino was at his side. "Aha, caught you!" Meldrick said as he assumed his district attorney posture. "Have you gone totally insane?"

Window gave Meldrick a startled look and then looked down at his bowl of ice cream and began to guffaw.

"You're completely out of control," Meldrick said, parroting the vice-principal. "Something has got to be done. We're looking at six thousand calories here." Meldrick shook his head and told Window he was going to take a nap in the library workroom. "Make sure I'm awake by ten, okay? I need a nappy-poo. My yin-yang is all out of whack."

"Get your beauty rest, Meldrick, I wake you up at ten."

"Come in whistling, so I know it's you. I almost got caught last night. Ray's been sneaking around. I think he's keeping a journal. He thinks he's in the KGB or something."

A few days later, an exotic package arrived from Marseilles, France, addressed to Window. The package aroused the curiosity of the office staff and for a solid day caused much speculation among them. Even the administrators were intrigued by it, until Window showed up at two P.M., opened the mysterious box, and revealed a rebuilt starter for his Citroën, which had sat in the back parking lot with a flat tire all summer. Meldrick and Ted Frank Page installed the starter that evening, but the Citroën was soon abandoned in the back parking lot again when the radiator overheated and blew. Window did not have the money to have it rebuilt.

Meldrick gave Window a lecture about blowing all of his money on junk food, porno flicks and pornographic magazines. "Are you oversexed or what?" Meldrick said. "I know you're nineteen but you are really driving this into the ground. The librarians found one of your porno magazines in their workroom and it totally grossed them out. Ray told them a student left it and covered your ass, but use your head, dammit. Think."

One evening Window sought out Meldrick and, much

alarmed, told him that Catherine had paged him at work and said she was going to have another baby in two weeks. Window asked Meldrick how it could be possible since he hadn't slept with her in over a year. "She says I did once when we got drunk and that I don't remember, but she lies."

Meldrick said, "Page is right, Roy is dicking her. Geez! Your own brother! This *is* ridiculous!"

Meldrick immediately demanded to know how Catherine could be eight and a half months pregnant without Window's knowing it. Window hung his head down and said, "She's so fat, I couldn't tell."

Later, Window showed Meldrick phone bills to Catherine's first love, the old boyfriend in Spokane. Meldrick asked Window if he might be the culprit, but Window was sure it was Roy. He remembered a night back in the fall when he was in the next door apartment mediating a fight between the couple that lived there. "You see, Johnny hit Karen on the back of the head with a frying pan and they were crashing furniture. I told them fighting wasn't the answer and that they should talk things out. Karen said, 'What I hear you saying, Johnny, is that *Another World* is dumb, that Carl Hutchins is a skinny-ass, short crotch with a greasy ponytail and that I've got a TV crush on him, but I —'"

Meldrick said, "Window, I don't want to hear a fucking soap opera plot!"

"Okay, okay, but listen to this — when they calmed down I went back home and the shade was down and I saw their shadows. Catherine and Roy were on the couch, kissing. He had her bra off. I could see her big hard tits through the shade."

"He saw silhouettes," Meldrick told Ted Frank Page that

night at volleyball. "Silhouettes on the shade —" Everyone fell silent at this declaration, and Meldrick's words continued to resonate through the unusual acoustics of the gym.

Finally Ted Frank Page said, "Window, why didn't you go in and kick ass?"

Window began to strut around the basketball court with his fist on his hips and his bubble butt high. "There's this loose rock in the yard. I'm always tripping on it in the night. I'm so mad at Roy and Catherine, I tried to dig up the rock with my fingers until I'm breaking my fingernails and chipped my tooth."

"He was biting the rock," Meldrick said. "It's solid granite. I've seen that rock."

"It kept wobbling in the ground like it would come out easy but I can't get it out until I get the jack handle out of my trunk and dig it up —"

"How big?" Page said. "What did you do?"

"Plenty big," Window said. "A bowling ball, only heavier. I ran up to the window and threw the fucker in — *Boom!*" Window took his janitor keys from his belt and heaved them against the glass blackboard at the far end of the gym. Then he kicked a number of volleyballs so hard they cracked ceiling tiles. The janitors waited for Window to finish with his tantrum.

"Well, what did they do, Window? What did Catherine and Roy do? What the fuck happened?" Page asked.

"He ran and hid in the bushes," Meldrick said.

"You didn't go inside and kick ass?" Page asked. "Jesus, Window."

"I was afraid I would get arrested. Catherine called the cops. I stayed in the bushes until the police officers left. Then I went back to Johnny and Karen's and had beer —"

"Eventually you went home. What did you *say*?" Page said.

"I didn't say anything. Catherine said some crazy person chunked a boulder in the window. A dope fiend or some nut who escaped from Eastern State Hospital."

"And you didn't kick ass?" Page asked.

"I puked up the beer in the toilet," Window said.

"He was upset," Meldrick said. "And he can't argue with this manipulative and domineering woman. She's trying to sell him a story that he knocked her up when he was drunk one night. And half the time she's going around with Roy's hickeys on her neck. Mercy me! I fear this is not the idyllic dream of connubial bliss Window had envisioned."

Ted Frank Page stood in the center of the gym bouncing a volleyball. "Ha, ha, ha, fucking Meldrick! 'Connubial bliss.' Where did you come up with that shit? 'Connubial bliss.' Ah, ha, ha — fuck!"

Meldrick turned serious. "Think, Window. You know for certain that you did not sleep with your wife for at least nine months?"

Window looked up, his eyes wide. "I don't think so," he said. "I'm pretty sure."

"Then get a blood test when the kid is born. Divorce the bitch —"

Window could not sleep or eat and rushed through his area every night so that he could go upstairs and help Meldrick, so that Meldrick, in his gratitude, would offer him psychological consolation. Meldrick was the only custodian who didn't dismiss him with an "I told you so."

"I know it's Roy's baby, it looks just like him," Window said. "It's got his Bugs Bunny nose —"

"Window, think. When was the last time you slept with Catherine? Are you sure there is no possibility?"

"It can't be mine, Meldrick. I just know it. Can we ask the *I Ching*?"

Meldrick took Window into the library and got the *I Ching* from the shelves. The two custodians went into the librarian's office and while Window tossed the coins, Meldrick wrote down the resulting hexagram — Number 29.

"What does it mean?" Window said.

"Bad. It means bad," Meldrick said.

"Meldrick," Window said with some hope, "can you ask it if I'm going to win the lottery?"

"Window. Geez! Are you still pissing your money away on lottery tickets? What's the fucking use? You won't listen. This is futile, pure and simple futile."

Catherine initiated divorce proceedings against Window and got everything except for the useless Citroën. The court ordered Window to pay six hundred dollars a month in child support and after his lawyer's monthly payment, the credit card charges and room and board at his parents' home, Window was left with a pathetic seventy dollars for pin money. He walked six miles to work and six miles home again. Ted Frank Page liked to take out a pencil and paper at the janitor's table and calculate how much Roy's baby would ultimately cost Window . . . a figure well over sixty thousand dollars. "You could have gone to that ranch in Las Vegas and got some *good pussy* for that kind of money, Window."

Josie sat down with Window one afternoon and tried to calculate a way to pay off his outstanding bills and save enough money to initiate a blood test to determine the father of Catherine's second baby.

"My dad said the test won't work on two brothers."

"They've got a new test. It will work, believe me," Josie said.

Whenever Window mentioned the possibility of going to a lawyer to get a court order for DNA testing, Catherine clenched her fists, scrunched down, and flew into a rage.

"You see," Meldrick said, "if she wasn't worried, she'd just laugh in your face and call you a fool. She's guilty as hell, and she's scared."

Yet no matter how Josie figured it, there was no way Window could come up with the two thousand dollars for legal and medical fees necessary for the blood test. "Can't your parents loan you the money?" Josie asked.

"They said I'm on my own," Window said. "I think they are — you know — embarrassed —"

"Because of what your brother did. It really is low. They ought to be embarrassed."

"That's fucking special ed for you," Ted Frank Page said.

"We told you not to marry the bitch," Meldrick said, puffing on a cigarillo in the janitor's room.

"Think," Page said, "of all the high-class pussy you could have had for all that bread you're laying out. What an idiot!"

"Window," Josie said, "the next time you want a date, go to church and meet a girl there. A girl with virtue."

Window took to blowing his seventy dollars cash the first day he got it each month. Invariably he spent the money on pornography and junk food. While his mother provided Window with board, she did not supply junk food, so Window used his key to the student store and began to raid the candy supplies until the diversified occupations teacher had the lock

changed. Then Window began taking the cook's key to the
freezer and started stealing student pizzas. One day, when he
went for the key in the top drawer of the cook's desk, he found
that it was gone. "They're on to you," Packard said. "Don't
admit anything. If you get called in, deny it."

"If I get *called in*?" Window said with real fear in his
voice.

"Yeah, if you get called in and they grill you — lie,
motherfucker."

"Called in?" Window said. *"Into the office?"*

"I don't know why in the fuck you are worried," Ted
Frank Page said. "You are the motherfucker who's busting ass
and — hey! who is collecting? I'll tell you, it's that fat-ass ex-
wife and your brother, taking your money, welfare and all the
rest of it. If I was you, I'd hop in that Citroën and fly off to
Fringus, go back among your own kind. If they fired you they
would be doing you a favor."

"He's right, Window," Meldrick said. "You are a noble
spirit, an innocent — a pure soul and much too good for this
pitiless brutal planet. You deserve a better fate than this."

The vice-principal began to write Window up for tiny infrac-
tions. Once Window left his vacuum cleaner in the band room
and the band instructor complained to the office. "The next
time it happens," the vice-principal said jauntily, displaying
his palm with a flourish, "probation."

On another occasion Window forgot there was a senior
parents' meeting and took a shortcut to the Coke machine,
bursting into the conference room in a T-shirt with his
Walkman blasting *Fine Young Cannibals*. The vice-principal
wrote him up for not wearing his custodian's shirt and for listening to a headset, a safety hazard. Window finally made pro-

bation when another custodian claimed Window used his mop and bucket and left it dirty in the janitor's closet. It was not a major crime, but there had been an accumulation of misdemeanors.

Window put his nose to the grindstone for six months, but two weeks after the probation was officially lifted, he left the vacuum cleaner in the band room again. "If you do this once more," the vice-principal said, "you will be fired."

Window received an unexpected windfall on his income tax return — eleven hundred dollars. Josie immediately made an appointment with Window's attorney only to learn that the cost of the blood test had gone up substantially. Window was so upset he frittered away the money and then he left his vacuum cleaner in the band room for the third time. When the vice-principal read the union contract and learned that he could not fire Window for this offense, he instructed the head custodian to give Window more area to clean and to ride him, but the head custodian only paid lip service to the order. For one thing, Window never gave him any guff and for another, Ted Frank Page, who was bench-pressing over three hundred and fifty pounds, physically threatened the head custodian. It was not entirely for Window's sake. Ted Frank Page learned that the head custodian had been bad-mouthing Page for laziness and like everything that was said at the janitor's table, it worked its way around the grapevine in less than a day.

When a clutch cable for Window's Citroën arrived from the auto supply house in Marseilles, a note went up on the custodians' bulletin board stating that no custodian was to receive personal mail at the school.

Meldrick and Ted Frank Page installed the clutch cable and the auto instructor boiled out the radiator on the Citroën, but scarcely two weeks after it was running, the clutch cable snapped. It had been installed backwards and the Citroën sat in its accustomed home in the back parking lot for three more months until another cable was dispatched from Marseilles, France.

Window learned to consult the *I Ching* on his own and spent hours in the library asking it questions. Ray, the custodian who worked the special education area, asked Meldrick what Window was doing. Mystified, Ray hid by the library door and watched. "He shakes pennies in his hand and then tosses them down on the desk and writes something down and then he looks something up in a book. What is he doing?"

"It's beyond comprehension," Meldrick said. "Don't even attempt an understanding."

Meldrick and Packard installed the second clutch cable on the Citroën in the correct fashion and a week after it was running, Window came into the school clutching a check for five thousand dollars. A car collector spotted the Citroën and had given Window a check on the spot. The head custodian called the buyer a fool while Ted Frank Page insisted that Window could have gotten three times that amount. Before Window could cash the check, Josie called his lawyer and then personally drove him to the bank and then to the law office where the blood test was paid for — in full, in advance.

Catherine came by the school and had a tantrum. She had court papers in her hand directing her to submit to blood tests. She screamed at Window and told her that the welfare lawyer told her Window wasn't going to get to first base since the blood tests were a "cruel invasion" and that she had recently become a Jehovah's Witness and would not, under any circumstances, spill a drop of her own blood.

"Is that how you act," Ted Frank Page said, "when you

get religion, cursing and having tantrums?" Catherine stalked out of the building with her friend Lutetia trailing after her.

"Yeah," Window said, puffing up, "you should wash your mouth out with soap."

The blood tests proved conclusively that Window's brother, Roy, was the father of Catherine's second child and Window's lawyer got the double child support payment lifted from Window's check. Because of the rise in income, welfare immediately seized a larger payment for Window's uncontested son.

The custodian who had Window written up for using his mop bucket sneered, "All that fucking rigamarole to save a hundred bucks a month. That's what you get for listening to that asshole, Meldrick," he said.

For his part, Meldrick consoled Window by telling him that life wasn't fair.

Josie placed a call to Window's attorney and asked if the brother would have to pay the child support retroactively. The attorney said Roy would have to make the retroactive payments but that Window would not receive any of the money. "So you mean welfare is collecting *twice*?"

"Yes, we could appeal, but I would advise against it. It's going to cost a lot of dough."

Window used the balance of his Citroën money to pay off his debts and buy new clothes. Ted Frank Page, always appalled by Window's taste, found the new clothes especially bad. "Fucking special ed. Don't fucking *buy* clothes, Window, unless you take me along. Where did you get that shit?"

"At D&R's. What's the matter with these clothes? My ma says they look snazzy."

"Your mother came from the old country, Window. You

look like you just hopped off the boat yourself. The Neon Boat."

"Don't talk to me like that," Window said sharply.

"Well, fuck you," Ted Frank Page said.

"Hey," Meldrick said, "it's his money, his clothes."

"So how much did you save after all of this shit? Anything?" Page asked.

"In the long run, he saves fourteen thousand," Josie said. "Next time you want a date, Window, go to church. Meet a nice girl. A girl with virtues."

"I can't go to the damn church without falling asleep," Window said, "and all the church girls are ugly. Plus, *Ted Frank Page*, I didn't do it for the money! I just wanted to know if the baby was mine. If it was mine, I pay gladly. Now in my heart I'm satisfied." Window looked at Page squarely and Ted Frank Page returned the look.

"Well good for you, Window. I am sorry I said that. Please accept my humble apology."

"And no more special ed jokes!" Window said.

"I'm going to shut my mouth," Page said.

The head custodian said, "Window has become a man. He's making inroads. Now let's go scrub that lower hall." It was Christmas break and the custodians were all working the day shift. The school was quiet and they had taken an hour-long break which was now becoming oppressively long.

Window said, "I'm tired of being the mop jockey."

"Window runs the scrubber," Page said. "I'll sling the mops."

The custodial crew set out the yellow caution signs in the lower hallway and without a word, each picked out a task. One laid down the stripper solution. Another took the doodle bug and began edging the sides of the hall. Yet another set up the wet vac while Window plugged in the scrubber, looked to his left and right to see that everyone was in position and then squeezed the power trigger. The black stripping pad was dry, causing the scrubber to lurch violently for a few seconds. Window had to muscle the big machine until it picked up enough water and then began to sing as it glided effortlessly over the scuffed tile. When Ray turned on a country/western station on the radio, Window said, "Turn off that hillbilly shit and play some rock and roll." As the designated operator of the scrubber, Window had that right since at East High, the designated operator of the scrubber was janitor king of the day.

I Want to
Live!

SHE wondered how many times a week he had to do this. Plenty, no doubt. At least every day. Maybe twice . . . three times. Maybe, on a big day, five times. It was the ultimate bad news, and he delivered it dryly, like Sergeant Joe Friday. He was a young man, but his was a tough business and he had gone freeze-dried already. Hey, the bad news wasn't really a surprise! She . . . *knew*. Of course, you always hope for the best. She heard but she didn't hear.

"What?" she offered timidly. She had hoped . . . for better. Geez! Give me a break! What was he saying? Breast and uterus? Double trouble! She *knew* it would be the uterus. There had been the discharge. The bloating, the cramps. The fatigue. But it was common and easily curable provided you got it at stage one. Eighty percent cure. But the breast — that one came out of the blue and that could be really tricky — that was fifty-fifty. Strip out the lymph nodes down your arm and guaranteed chemo. God! Chemo. The worst thing in the world. Goodbye hair — there'd be scarves, wigs, a prosthetic breast, crying your heart out in "support" groups. Et cetera.

"Mrs. Wilson?" The voice seemed to come out of a can. Now the truth was revealed and all was out in the open. Yet how — tell me this — how would it ever be possible to have a life again? The voice from the can had chilled her. To the core.

"Mrs. Wilson, your last CA 125 hit the ceiling," he said. "I suspect that this could be an irregular kind of can . . . cer."

Some off-the-wall kind of can . . . cer? A kind of wildfire cancer! Not the easygoing, 80-percent-cure, tortoise, as-slow-as-molasses-in-January cancer!

January. She looked past the thin oncologist, wire-rimmed glasses, white coat, inscrutable. Outside, snowflakes tumbled from the sky, kissing the pavement — each unique, wonderful, worth an hour of study, a microcosm of the Whole: awe-inspiring, absolutely fascinating, a gift of divinity gratis. Yet how abhorrent they seemed. They were white, but the whole world had lost its color for her now that she'd heard those words. The shine was gone from the world. Had she been Queen of the Universe for a million years and witnessed glory after glory, what would it have mattered now that she had come to this?

She . . . came to . . . went out, came back again . . . went out. There was this . . . wonderful show. Cartoons. It was the best show. This wasn't so bad. True, she had cancer but . . . these wonderful cartoons. Dilaudid. On Dilaudid, well, you live, you die — that's how it is . . . life in the Big City. It happens to everyone. It's part of the plan. Who was she to question the plan?

The only bad part was her throat. Her throat was on fire. "Intubation." The nurse said she'd phone the doctor and maybe he'd authorize more dope.

"Oh, God, please. Anything."

"Okay, let's just fudge a little bit, no one needs to know," the nurse said, twisting the knob on Tube Control Central. Dilaudid. Cartoons. Oh, God, thank God, Dilaudid! Who invented that drug? Write him a letter. Knight him. Award the Nobel Prize to Dilaudid Man. Where was that knob? A handy thing to know. Whew! Whammo! Swirling, throbbing ecstasy! And who was that nurse? Florence Nightingale, Mother Teresa would be proud . . . oh, boy! It wasn't just relief from the surgery; she suddenly realized how much psychic pain she had been carrying and now it was gone with one swoop of a magic wand. The cartoons. Bliss . . .

His voice wasn't in a can, never had been. It was a normal voice, maybe a little high for a man. Not that he was effeminate. The whole problem with him was that he didn't seem real. He wasn't a flesh-and-blood kinda guy. Where was the *empathy*? Why did he get into this field if he couldn't empathize? In this field, empathy should be your stock-in-trade.

"The breast is fine, just a benign lump. We brought a specialist in to get it, and I just reviewed the pathology report. It's nothing to worry about. The other part is not . . . so good. I'm afraid your abdomen . . . it's spread throughout your abdomen . . . it looks like little Grape-Nuts, actually. It's exceedingly rare and it's . . . it's a rapid form of . . . can . . . cer. We couldn't really take any of it out. I spent most of my time in there untangling adhesions. We're going to have to give you cisplatin . . . if it weren't for the adhesions, we could pump it into your abdomen directly — you wouldn't get so sick that way — but those adhesions are a problem and may cause problems further along." Her room was freezing, but the thin oncologist was beginning to perspire. "It's a shame," he said, looking down at her chart. "You're in such perfect health . . . otherwise."

She knew this was going to happen yet she heard herself say, "Doctor, do you mean . . . I've got to take —"

"Chemo? Yeah. But don't worry about that yet. Let's just let you heal up for a while." He slammed her chart shut and . . . whiz, bang, he was outta there.

Goodbye, see ya.

The guessing game was over and now it was time for the ordeal. She didn't want to hear any more details — he's said something about a 20 percent five-year survival rate. Might as well bag it. She wasn't a fighter, and she'd seen what chemo had done to her husband, John. This was it. Finis!

She had to laugh. Got giddy. It was like in that song — *Freedom's just another word for nothing left to lose* . . . When you're totally screwed, nothing can get worse, so what's to worry. Of course she could get lucky . . . it would be a thousand-to-one, but maybe . . .

The ovaries and uterus were gone. The root of it all was out. Thank God for that. Those befouled organs were gone. Where? Disposed of. Burned. In a dumpster? Who cares? The source was destroyed. Maybe it wouldn't be so bad. How could it be that bad? After all, the talk about pain from major abdominal surgery was overdone. She was walking with her little cart and tubes by the third day — a daily constitutional through the ward.

Okay, the Dilaudid was permanently off the menu, but morphine sulfate wasn't half bad. No more cartoons but rather a mellow glow. Left, right, left, right. Hup, two, three, four! Even a journey of a thousand miles begins with the first step.

On the morphine she was walking a quarter of an inch off the ground and everything was . . . softer, mercifully so. Maybe she could hack it for a thousand miles.

But those people in the hospital rooms, gray and dying, that was her. Could such a thing be possible? To die? Really? Yes, at some point she guessed you did die. But her? Now? So soon? With so little time to get used to the idea?

No, this was all a bad dream! She'd wake up. She'd wake up back in her little girl room on the farm near Battle Lake, Minnesota. There was a depression, things were a little rough, but big deal. What could beat a sun-kissed morning on Battle Lake and a robin's song? There was an abundance of jays, larks, bluebirds, cardinals, hummingbirds, red-winged blackbirds in those days before acid rain and heavy-metal poisoning, and they came to her yard to eat from the cherry, apple, plum, and pear trees. What they really went for were the mulberries.

Ah, youth! Good looks, a clean complexion, muscle tone, a full head of lustrous hair — her best feature, although her legs were pretty good, too. Strength. Vitality. A happy kid with a bright future. Cheerleader her senior year. Pharmacy scholarship at the college in Fergus Falls. Geez, if her dad hadn't died, she could have been a pharmacist. Her grades were good, but hard-luck stories were the order of the day. It was a Great Depression. She would have to take her chances. Gosh! It had been a great, wide, wonderful world in those days, and no matter what, an adventure lay ahead, something marvelous — a handsome prince and a life happily ever after. Luck was with her. Where had all the time gone? How had all the dreams . . . fallen away? Now she was in the Valley of the Shadow. The morphine sulfate was like a warm and friendly hearth in Gloom City, her one and only consolation.

He was supposed to be a good doctor, one of the best in

the field, but he had absolutely no bedside manner. She really began to hate him when he took away the morphine and put her on Tylenol 3. Then it began to sink in that things might presently go downhill in a hurry.

They worked out a routine. If her brother was busy, her daughter drove her up to the clinic and then back down to the office, and the thin oncologist is . . . called away, or he's . . . running behind, or he's . . . *something*. Couldn't they run a business, get their shit together? Why couldn't they anticipate? It was one thing to wait in line at a bank when you're well, but when you've got cancer and you're this cancer patient and you wait an hour, two hours, or they tell you to come back next week . . . come back for something that's worse than anything, the very worst thing in the world! Hard to get up for that. You really had to brace yourself. Cisplatin, God! Metal mouth, restlessness, pacing. Flop on the couch, but that's no good; get up and pace, but you can't handle that, so you flop on the couch again. Get up and pace. Is this really happening to me? *I can't believe this is really happening to me!* How can such a thing be possible?

Then there were the episodes of simultaneous diarrhea and vomiting that sprayed the bathroom from floor to ceiling! Dry heaves and then dry heaves with bile and then dry heaves with blood. You could drink a quart of tequila and then a quart of rum and have some sloe gin too and eat pink birthday cakes and five pounds of licorice, Epsom salts, a pint of kerosene, some Southern Comfort — and you're on a Sunday picnic compared to cisplatin. Only an archfiend could devise a dilemma where to maybe *get well* you first had to poison yourself within a whisker of death, and in fact if you didn't die, you wished that you had.

There were visitors in droves. Flowers. Various intrusions at all hours. Go away. Leave me alone . . . please, God, leave me . . . alone.

Oh, hi, thanks for coming. Oh, what a lovely — such beautiful flowers . . .

There were moments when she felt that if she had one more episode of diarrhea, she'd jump out of the window. Five stories. Would that be high enough? Or would you lie there for a time and die slowly? Maybe if you took a header right onto the concrete. Maybe then you wouldn't feel a thing. Cisplatin: she had to pace. But she had to lie down, but she was squirrelly as hell and she couldn't lie down. TV was no good — she had double vision, and it was all just a bunch of stupid shit, anyhow. Soap operas — good grief! What absolute crap. Even her old favorites. You only live once, and to think of all the time she pissed away watching soap operas.

If only she could sleep. God, couldn't they give her Dilaudid? No! Wait! Hold that! Somehow Dilaudid would make it even worse. Ether then. Put her out. Wake me up in five days. Just let me sleep. She *had* to get up to pace. She *had* to lie down. She *had* to vomit. *Oh, hi, thanks for coming. Oh, what a lovely — such beautiful flowers.*

The second treatment made the first treatment seem like a month in the country. The third treatment — oh, damn! The whole scenario had been underplayed. Those movie stars who got it and wrote books about it were stoics, valiant warriors compared to her. She had no idea anything could be so horrible. Starving in Bangladesh? No problem, I'll trade. Here's my MasterCard and the keys to the Buick — I'll pull a rickshaw, anything! Anything but this. HIV-positive? Why just sign right here on the dotted line and you've got a deal! I'll trade with anybody! Anybody.

The thin oncologist with the Bugs Bunny voice said the CA 125 number was still up in the stratosphere. He said it was up to her if she wanted to go on with this. What was holding her up? She didn't know, and her own voice came from a can now. She heard herself say, "Doctor, what would you do . . . if you were me?"

He thought it over for a long time. He pulled off his wire rims and pinched his nose, world-weary. "I'd take the next treatment."

It was the worst by far — square root to infinity. Five days: no sleep, pacing, lying down, pacing. Puke and diarrhea. The phone. She wanted to tear it off the wall. After all these years, couldn't they make a quiet bell? — did they have shit for brains or what? *Oh, hi, well . . . just fine. Just dandy. Coming by on Sunday? With the kids? Well . . . no, I feel great. No. No. No. I'd love to see you . . .*

And then one day the thin-timbre voice delivered good news. "Your CA 125 is almost within normal limits. It's working!"

Hallelujah! Oh my God, let it be so! A miracle. Hurrah!

"It is a miracle," he said. He was almost human, Dr. Kildare, Dr. Ben Casey, Marcus Welby, M.D. — take your pick. "Your CA is down to rock bottom. I think we should do one, possibly two more treatments and then go back inside for a look. If we do too few, we may not kill it all but if we do too much — you see, it's toxic to your healthy cells as well. You can get cardiomyopathy in one session of cisplatin and you can die."

"One more is all I can handle."

"Gotcha, Mrs. Wilson. One more and in for a look."

*   *   *

"I hate to tell you this," he said. Was he making the cartoons go away? "I'll be up front about it, Mrs. Wilson, we've still got a problem. The little Grape-Nuts — fewer than in the beginning, but the remaining cells will be resistant to cisplatin, so our options are running thin. We could try a month of an experimental form of hard chemotherapy right here in the hospital — very, very risky stuff. Or we could resume the cisplatin, not so much aiming for a cure but rather as a holding action. Or we could not do anything at all . . ."

Her voice was flat. She said, "What if I don't do anything?"

"Dead in three months, maybe six."

She said, "Dead how?"

"Lungs, liver, or bowel. Don't worry, Mrs. Wilson, there won't be a lot of pain. I'll see to that."

Bingo! He flipped the chart shut and . . . whiz, bang, he was outta there!

She realized that when she got right down to it, she wanted to live, more than anything, on almost any terms, so she took more cisplatin. But the oncologist was right, it couldn't touch those resistant rogue cells; they were like roaches that could live through atomic warfare, grow and thrive. Well then, screw it! At least there wouldn't be pain. What more can you do? She shouldn't have let him open her up again. That had been the worst sort of folly. She'd let him steamroll her with Doctor Knows Best. Air had hit it. No wonder it was a wildfire. A conflagration.

Her friends came by. It was an effort to make small talk. How could they know? How could they *know* what it was like? They loved her, they said, with liquor on their breath. They had to get juiced before they could stand to come by! They came with casseroles and cleaned for her, but she had to sweat out her nights alone. Dark nights of the soul on Tylenol 3 and Xanax. A lot of good that was. But then when she was in her loose, giddy *freedom's just another word for nothing left to lose* mood, about ten days after a treatment, she realized her friends weren't so dumb. They knew that they couldn't really *know*. Bugs Bunny told her there was no point in going on with the cisplatin. He told her she was a very brave lady. He said he was sorry.

A month after she was off that poison, cisplatin, there was a little side benefit. She could see the colors of the earth again and taste food and smell flowers — it was a bittersweet pleasure, to be sure. But her friends took her to Hawaii, where they had this great friend ("You gotta meet him!") and he . . . he made a play for her and brought her flowers every day, expensive roses, et cetera. She had never considered another man since John had died from can . . . cer ten years before. How wonderful to forget it all for a moment here and there. A moment? Qualify that — make that ten, fifteen seconds. How can you forget it? Ever since she got the news she could . . . not . . . forget . . . it.

Now there were stabbing pains, twinges, flutterings — maybe it was normal everyday stuff amplified by the imagination or maybe it was real. How fast would it move, this wildfire brand? Better not to ask.

Suddenly she was horrible again. Those nights alone — killers. Finally one night she broke down and called her daughter. Hated to do it, throw in the towel, but this was the fifteenth round and she didn't have a prayer.

"Oh, hi. I'm just fine" — *blah blah blah* — "but I was thinking maybe I could come down and stay, just a while. I'd like to see Janey and —"

"We'll drive up in the morning."

At least she was with blood. And her darling grand-daughter. What a delight. Playing with the little girl, she could forget. It was even better than Hawaii. After a year of sheer hell, in which all of the good stuff added up to less than an hour and four minutes total, there was a way to forget. She helped with the dishes. A little light cleaning. Watched the game shows, worked the *Times* crossword, but the pains grew worse. Goddammit, it felt like nasty little yellow-tooth rodents or a horde of translucent termites — thousands of them, chewing her guts out! Tylenol 3 couldn't touch it. The new doctor she had been passed to gave her Dilaudid. She was enormously relieved. But what she got was a vial of little pink tablets and after the first dose she realized it wasn't much good in the pill form; you could squeeze by on it but they'd *promised* — no pain! She was losing steam. Grinding down.

They spent a couple of days on the Oregon coast. The son-in-law — somehow it was easy to be with him. He didn't pretend that things were other than they were. He could be a pain in the bun, like everyone, bitching over trivialities, smoking Kool cigarettes, strong ones — jolters! A pack a day easy, although he was considerate enough to go outside and do it. She wanted to tell him, "Fool! Your health is your greatest fortune!" But she was the one who'd let six months pass after that first discharge.

The Oregon coast was lovely, although the surf was too cold for actual swimming. She sat in the hotel whirlpool and watched her granddaughter swim a whole length of the pool all on her own, a kind of dog-paddle thing but not bad for a kid going on seven. They saw a show of shooting stars one night but it was exhausting to keep up a good front and not to be morbid, losing weight big time. After a shower, standing at the mirror, scars zigzagging all over the joint like the Bride of Frankenstein, it was just awful. She was bald, scrawny, ashen, yet with a bloated belly. She couldn't look. Sometimes she would sink to the floor and just lie there, too sick to even cry, too weak to even get dressed, yet somehow she did get dressed, slapped on that hot, goddamn wig, and showed up for dinner. It was easier to do that if you pretended that it wasn't real, if you pretended it was all on TV.

She felt like a naughty little girl sitting before the table looking at meals her daughter was killing herself to make — old favorites that now tasted like a combination of forty-weight Texaco oil and sawdust. It was a relief to get back to the couch and work crossword puzzles. It was hell imposing on her daughter but she was frightened. Terrified! They were her blood. They *had* to take her. Oh, to come to this!

The son-in-law worked swing shift and he cheered her in the morning when he got up and made coffee. He was full of life. He was real. He was authentic. He even interjected little pockets of hope. Not that he pushed macrobiotics or any of that foolishness, but it was a fact — if you were happy, if you had something to live for, if you loved life, you lived. It had been a mistake for her to hole up there in the mountains after John died. The Will to Live was more important than doctors and medicines. You had to reinvigorate the Will to Live. The granddaughter was good for that. She just couldn't go the meditation-tape route, imagining microscopic, ravenous, good-guy little sharks eating the bad cancer cells, et cetera. At least the son-in-law didn't suggest that or come on strong with a theology trip. She noticed he read the King James Bible, though.

She couldn't eat. There was a milk-shake diet she choked down. Vanilla, chocolate fudge, strawberry — your choice. Would Madame like a bottle of wine with dinner? Ha, ha, ha.

Dilaudid. It wasn't working, there was serious pain, especially in her chest, dagger thrusts — *Et tu, Brute?* She watched the clock like a hawk and had her pills out and ready every four hours — and that last hour was getting to be murder, a morbid sweat began popping out of her in the last fifteen minutes. One morning she caved in and timidly asked the son-in-law, "Can I take three?"

He said, "Hell, take four. It's a safe drug. If you have bad pain, take four." Her eyes were popping out of her head. "Here, drink it with coffee and it will kick in faster."

He was right. He knew more than the doctor. You just can't do everything by the book. Maybe that had been her trouble all along — she was too compliant, one of those "cancer" personalities. She believed in the rules. She was one of those kind who wanted to leave the world a better place than she found it. She had been a good person, had always done the right thing — this just wasn't right. It wasn't fair. She was so . . . angry!

The next day, over the phone, her son-in-law bullied a prescription of methadone from the cancer doctor. She heard one side of a lengthy heated exchange while the son-in-law made a persuasive case for methadone. He came on like Clarence Darrow or F. Lee Bailey. It was a commanding performance. She'd never heard of anyone giving a doctor hell before. God bless him for not backing down! On methadone tablets a warm orange glow sprang forth and bloomed like a glorious, time-lapse rose in her abdomen and then rolled through her body in orgasmic waves. The sense of relief shattered all fear and doubt though the pain was still there to some extent. It was still there but — so what? And the methadone tablets lasted a very long time — no more of that *every four hours* bullshit.

Purple blotches all over her skin, swollen ankles. Pain in her hips and joints. An ambulance trip to the emergency room. "Oh," they said, "it's nothing . . . vascular purpura. Take aspirin. Who's next?"

Who's next? Why hadn't she taken John's old .38 revolver the very day she heard that voice in the can? Stuck it in the back of her mouth and pulled the trigger? She had no fear of hellfire. She was a decent, moral person but she did not believe. Neither was she the Hamlet type — what lies on the other side? It was probably the same thing that occurred before you were born — zilch. And zilch wasn't that bad. What was wrong with zilch?

One morning she waited overlong for the son-in-law to get up, almost smashed a candy dish to get him out of bed. Was he going to sleep forever? Actually, he got up at his usual time.

"I can't. Get. My breath," she told him.

"You probably have water in your lungs," the son-in-law said. He knew she didn't want to go to the clinic. "We've got some diuretic. They were Boxer's when she had congestive heart failure — dog medicine, but it's the same thing they give humans. Boxer weighed fifty-five pounds. Let me see . . . take four, no, take three. To be cautious. Do you feel like you have to cough?"

"Yes." *Kaff, kaff, kaff.*

"This might draw the water out of your lungs. It's pretty

safe. Try to eat a banana or a potato skin to keep your potassium up. If it doesn't work, we can go over to the clinic."

How would he know something like that? But he was right. It worked like magic. She had to pee like crazy but she could breathe. The panic to end all panics was over. If she could only go . . . number two. Well, the methadone slows you down. "Try some Metamucil," the son-in-law said.

It worked. Kind of, but it sure wasn't anything to write home about.

"I can't breathe. The diuretics aren't working."

The son-in-law said they could tap her lung. It would mean another drive to the clinic, but the procedure was almost painless and provided instantaneous relief. It worked but it was three days of exhaustion after that one. The waiting room. Why so long? Why couldn't they anticipate? You didn't have to be a genius to know which way the wildfire was spreading. Would the methadone keep that internal orange glow going or would they run out of ammo? Was methadone the ultimate or were there bigger guns? Street heroin? She'd have to put on her wig and go out and score China White.

The little girl began to tune out. Gramma wasn't so much fun anymore; she just lay there and gave off this smell. There was no more dressing up; it was just the bathrobe. In fact, she felt the best in her old red-and-black tartan pattern, flannel, ratty-ass bathrobe, not the good one. The crosswords — forget it, too depressing. You could live the life of Cleopatra but if it came down to this, what was the point?

The son-in-law understood. Of all the people to come through. It's bad and it gets worse and so on until the worst of all. "I don't know how you can handle this," he'd say. "What does it feel like? Does it feel like a hangover? Worse than a hangover? Not like a hangover. Then what? Like drinking ten pots of boiled coffee? Like that? Really? Jittery! Oh, God, that must be awful. How can you stand it? Is it just like drinking too much coffee or is there some other aspect? Your fingers are numb? Blurred vision? It takes eight years to watch the second hand sweep from twelve to one? Well, if it's like that, how did you handle *five days*? I couldn't — I'd take a bottle of pills, shoot myself. Something. What about the second week? Drained? Washed out? Oh, brother! I had a three-day hangover once — I'd rather die than do that again. I couldn't ride out that hangover again for money. I know I couldn't handle chemo . . ."

One afternoon after he left for work, she found a passage circled in his well-worn copy of Schopenhauer: *In early youth, as we contemplate our coming life, we are like children in a theater before the curtain is raised, sitting there in high spirits and eagerly waiting for the play to begin. It is a blessing that we do not know what is really going to happen.* Yeah! She gave up the crosswords and delved into *The World As Will and Idea*. This Schopenhauer was a genius! Why hadn't anyone told her? She was a reader, she had waded through some philosophy in her time — you just couldn't make any sense out of it. The problem was the terminology! She was a crossword ace, but words like *eschatology* — hey! Yet Schopenhauer got right into the heart of all the important things. The things that really mattered. With Schopenhauer she could take long excursions from the grim specter of impending death. In Schopenhauer, particularly in his aphorisms and reflections, she found an absolute satisfaction, for Schopenhauer spoke the truth and the rest of the world was disseminating lies!

Her son-in-law helped her with unfinished business: will, mortgage, insurance, how shall we do this, that, and the other? Cremation, burial plot, et cetera. He told her the stuff that her daughter couldn't tell her. He waited for the right moment and then got it all in — for instance, he told her that her daughter loved her very much but that it was hard for her to say so. She knew she cringed at this revelation, for it was ditto with her, and she knew that he could see it. Why couldn't she say to her own daughter three simple words, "I love you"? She just couldn't. Somehow it wasn't possible. The son-in-law didn't judge her. He had to be under pressure, too. Was she bringing everyone in the house down? Is that why he was reading Schopenhauer? No, Schopenhauer was his favorite. "Someone had to come out and tell it like it is," he would say of the dour old man with muttonchops whose picture he had pasted on the refrigerator. From what she picked up from the son-in-law, Schopenhauer wrote his major work by his twenty-sixth birthday — a philosophy that was ignored almost entirely in his lifetime and even now, in this day and age, it was thought to be more of a work of art than philosophy in the truest sense. A work of art? Why, it seemed irrefutable! According to the son-in-law, Schopenhauer spent the majority of his life in shabby rooms in the old genteel section of Frankfurt, Germany, that he shared with successions of poodles to keep him company while he read, reflected, and wrote about life at his leisure. He had some kind of small inheritance, just enough to get by, take in the concerts, do a little traveling now and then. He was well versed in several languages. He read virtually everything written from the Greeks on, including the Eastern writers, a classical scholar, and had the mind to chew things over and make something of the puzzle of life. The son-in-law, eager to discourse, said Freud called Schopenhauer one of the six greatest men who ever lived. Nietzsche, Thomas Mann, and Richard Wagner all paid tribute to this genius who had been written off with one word — pessimist. The son-in-law lamented that his works were going out of print, becoming increasingly harder to find. He was planning a trip to Frankfurt, where he hoped to find a little bust of his hero. He had written to officials in Germany making inquiries. They had given him the brush-off. He'd have to fly over himself. And she, too, began to worry that the works of this writer would no longer be available . . . she, who would be worms' meat any day.

Why? Because the *truth* was worthwhile. It was more important than anything, really. She'd had ten years of peaceful retirement, time to think, wonder, contemplate, and had come up with nothing. But new vistas of thought had been opened by the curiously ignored genius with the white mutton-chops, whose books were harder and harder to get and whom the world would consider a mere footnote from the nineteenth century — a crank, a guy with an ax to grind, a hypochondriac, a misogynist, an alarmist who slept with pistols under his pillow, a man with many faults. Well, check anyone out and what do you find?

For God's sake, how were you supposed to make any sense out of this crazy-ass shit called life? If only she could simply push a button and never have been born.

The son-in-law took antidepressants and claimed to be a melancholiac, yet he always seemed upbeat, comical, ready with a laugh. He had a sense of the absurd that she had found annoying back in the old days when she liked to pretend that life was a stroll down Primrose Lane. If she wasn't walking down the "sunny side of the street" at least she was "singin' in the rain." Those were the days.

What a fool!

She encouraged the son-in-law to clown and philoso-
phize, and he flourished when she voiced a small dose of
appreciation or barked out a laugh. There was more and
more pain and discomfort, but she was laughing more, too.
Schopenhauer: *No rose without a thorn. But many a thorn
and no rose*. The son-in-law finessed all of the ugly details that were impossible for her. Of all the people to come
through!

With her lungs temporarily clear and mineral oil enemas
to regulate her, she asked her daughter one last favor. Could
they take her home just once more?

They made an occasion of it and drove her up into the
mountains for her granddaughter's seventh birthday party.
Almost everyone in the picturesque resort town was there, and
if they were appalled by her deterioration they did not show it.
She couldn't go out on the sun porch, had to semi-recline on
the couch, but everyone came in to say hello and all of the bad
stuff fell away for . . . an entire afternoon! She was deeply
touched by the warm affection of her friends. There were . . .
so many of them. My God! They loved her, truly they did. She
could see it. You couldn't bullshit her anymore; she could
see deep into the human heart; she knew what people were.
What wonderful friends. What a perfect afternoon. It was the
last . . . good thing.

When she got back to her daughter's she began to die in ear-
nest. It was in the lungs and the bowel, much as the doctor
said it would be. Hell, it was probably in the liver even. She
was getting yellow, not just the skin but even the whites of her
eyes. There was a week in the hospital, where they tormented
her with tests. That wiped out the last of her physical and emotional stamina.

She fouled her bed after a barium lower G.I. practically turned to cement and they had to give her a powerful enema. Diarrhea in the bed. The worst humiliation. "Happens all the time, don't worry," the orderly said.

She was suffocating. She couldn't get the least bit of air. All the main players were in the room. She knew this was it! Just like that. Bingo! There were whispered conferences outside her room. Suddenly the nurses, those heretofore angels of mercy, began acting mechanically. They could look you over and peg you, down to the last five minutes. She could see them give her that *anytime now* look. A minister dropped in. There! That was the tip-off — the fat lady was singing.

When the son-in-law showed up instead of going to work she looked to him with panic. She'd been fighting it back but now . . . he was there, he would know what to do without being asked, and in a moment he was back with a nurse. They cranked up the morphine sulfate, flipped it on full-bore. Still her back hurt like hell. All that morphine and a backache . . . just give it a minute . . . ahhh! Cartoons.

Someone went out to get hamburgers at McDonald's. Her daughter sat next to her holding her hand. She felt sorry for them. They were the ones who were going to have to stay behind and play out their appointed roles. Like Schopenhauer said, the best they would be able to do for themselves was to secure a little room as far away from the fire as possible, for Hell was surely in the here-and-now, not in the hereafter. Or was it?

She began to nod. She was holding onto a carton of milk. It would spill. Like diarrhea-in-the-bed all over again. Another mess. The daughter tried to take the carton of milk away. She . . . held on defiantly. Forget the Schopenhauer —

what a lot of crap that was! She did not want to cross over. She
wanted to live! She wanted to live!

The daughter wrenched the milk away. The nurse came
back and cranked up the morphine again. They were going for
"comfort." Finally the backache . . . the cartoons . . . all of
that was gone.

(She was back on the farm in Battle Lake, Minnesota.
She was nine years old and she could hear her little red rooster,
Mr. Barnes, crowing at first light. Then came her brother's
heavy work boots clomping downstairs and the vacuum
swoosh as he opened up the storm door, and then his boots
crunch-crunching through the frozen snow. Yes, she was back
on the farm all right. Her brother was making for the outhouse
and presently Barnes would go after him, make a dive-bomb
attack. You couldn't discourage Mr. Barnes. She heard her
brother curse him and the *thwap* of the tin feed pan hitting the
bird. Mr. Barnes's frontal assaults were predictable. From the
sound of it, Fred walloped him good. As far as Mr. Barnes was
concerned, it was his barnyard. In a moment she heard the
outhouse door slam shut and another tin *thwap*. That
Barnes — he was something. She should have taken a lesson.
Puffed out her chest and walked through life — "I want the
biggest and the best and the most of whatever you've got!"
There were people who pulled it off. You really could do it if
you had the attitude.

Her little red rooster was a mean little scoundrel, but he
had a soft spot for her in his heart of steel and he looked out
for her, cooed for her and her alone. Later, when young men
came to see her, they soon arranged to meet her thereafter at
the drugstore soda fountain uptown. One confrontation with
Barnes, even for experienced farm boys, was one too many. He

was some kind of rooster all right, an eccentric. Yeah, she was back on the farm. She . . . could feel her sister shifting awake in the lower bunk. It was time to get up and milk the cows. Her sister always awoke in good humor. Not her. She was cozy under a feather comforter and milking the cows was the last thing she wanted to do. Downstairs she could hear her mother speaking cheerfully to her brother as he came back inside, cursing the damn rooster, threatening to kill it. Her mother laughed it off; she didn't have a mean bone in her body.

She . . . could smell bacon in the pan, the coffeepot was percolating, and her grandmother was up heating milk for her Ovaltine. She hated Ovaltine, particularly when her grand-mother overheated the milk — burned it — but she pre-tended to like it, insisted that she needed it for her bones, and forced it down so she could save up enough labels to get a free decoder ring to get special messages from Captain Cody, that intrepid hero of the airwaves. She really wanted to have that ring, but there was a Great Depression and money was very dear, so she never got the decoder or the secret messages or the degree in pharmacology. Had she been more like that little banty rooster, had she been a real go-getter . . . Well — it was all but over now.)

The main players were assembled in the room. She . . . was nodding in and out but she could hear. There she was, in this apparent stupor, but she was more aware than anyone could know. She heard someone say somebody at McDonald's put "everything" on her hamburger instead of "cheese and ketchup only." They were making an issue out of it. One day, when they were in her shoes, they would learn to ignore this kind of petty stuff, but you couldn't blame them. That was how things were, that's all. Life. That was it. That was what it was. And here she lay . . . dying.

Suddenly she realized that the hard part was all over now. All she had to do was . . . let go. It really wasn't so bad. It wasn't . . . anything special. It just was. She was trying to bring back Barnes one last time — that little memory of him had been fun, why not go out with a little fun? She tried to remember his coloring — orange would be too bright, rust too drab, scarlet too vivid. His head was a combination of green, yellow, and gold, all blended, and his breast and wings a kind of carmine red? No, not carmine. He was just a little red rooster, overly pugnacious, an ingrate. He could have been a beautiful bird if he hadn't gotten into so many fights. He got his comb ripped off by a raccoon he'd caught stealing eggs in the henhouse, a big bull raccoon that Barnes had fought tooth and nail until Fred ran into the henhouse with his .410 and killed the thieving intruder. Those eggs were precious. They were income. Mr. Barnes was a hero that day. She remembered how he used to strut around the barnyard. He always had his eye on all of the hens; they were his main priority, some thirty to forty of them, depending. They were his harem and he was the sheikh. Boy, was he ever. She remembered jotting down marks on a pad of paper one day when she was home sick with chickenpox. Each mark represented an act of rooster fornication. In less than a day, Mr. Barnes had committed the sexual act forty-seven times that she could see — and she didn't have the whole lay of the land from her window by any means. Why, he often went out roving and carousing with hens on other farms. There were bitter complaints from the neighbors. Barnes really could stir things up. She had to go out on her bicycle and round him up. Mr. Barnes was a legend in the country. Mr. Barnes thought the whole world belonged to him and beyond that — the suns, the stars, and the Milky Way — all of it! Did it feel good or was it torment? It must have been a glorious feeling, she decided. Maybe that was what Arthur Schopenhauer was driving at in his theory about the Will to Live. Mr. Barnes was the very personification of it.

Of course it was hard work being a rooster, but Barnes seemed the happiest creature she had ever known. Probably because when you're doing what you really want to do, it isn't work. No matter how dull things got on the farm, she could watch Barnes by the hour. Barnes could even redeem a hot, dog-day afternoon in August. He wasn't afraid of anything or anybody. Did he ever entertain a doubt? Some kind of rooster worry? Never! She tried to conjure up one last picture of him. He was just a little banty, couldn't have weighed three pounds. Maybe Mr. Barnes would be waiting for her on the other side and would greet her there and be her friend again.

She nodded in and out. In and out. The morphine was getting to be too much. Oh, please God. She hoped she wouldn't puke . . . So much left unsaid, undone. Well, that was all part of it. If only she could see Barnes strut his stuff one last time. "Come on, Barnes. Strut your stuff for me." Her brother, Fred, sitting there so sad with his hamburger. After a couple of beers, he could do a pretty good imitation of Mr. Barnes. Could he . . . would he . . . for old time's sake? Her voice was too weak, she couldn't speak. Nowhere near. Not even close. Was she dead already? Fading to black? It was hard to tell. "Don't feel bad, my darling brother. Don't mourn for me. I'm okay" . . . and . . . one last thing — "Sarah, I do love you, darling! Love you! Didn't you know that? Didn't it show? If not, I'm so, so very sorry. . . ." But the words wouldn't come — couldn't come. She . . . was so sick. You can only get so sick and then there was all that dope. Love! She

should have shown it to her daughter instead of . . . assuming.
She should have been more demonstrative, more forthcoming. . . . That's what it was all about. *Love your brother as yourself* and *love the Lord God almighty with all your heart and mind and soul*. You were sent here to love your brother. Do your best. Be kind to animals, obey the Ten Commandments, stuff like that. Was that it? Huh? Or was that all a lot of horseshit?

She . . . nodded in and out. Back and forth. In and out. She went back and forth. In and out. Back and forth . . . in and out. There wasn't any tunnel or white light or any of that. She just . . . died.

Part
IV

A White Horse

A D MAGIC had one of his epileptic premonitions a split
second before the collision, and managed to approximate
a tuck-and-roll position just as the truck smashed into the back
of the mini tour bus. He was seated in the center of the back
row enduring the most horrendous hangover of his life when
the crash projected him halfway down the center aisle like a
human cannonball. There was a moment of stillness after the
accident, and then the bus lurched over to the side of the road.
A group of five men and a woman from Bahrain sitting in the
center of the bus, themselves somewhat discombobulated but
unhurt, got out of their seats to help the peculiar American to
his feet.

Ad Magic had a jawbreaker-size horehound lozenge in his
cheek when the wreck occurred, and now it was caught at the
back of his throat. He attempted to swallow the candy dis-
creetly, lodging it farther into his throat, and when he realized
it was too large to swallow he tried to cough it up. He panicked
as he began to run out of air, however, and dropped to one

knee and choked out a cartoonish series of coughs — *"Kaff, kaff, kaff."*

He could feel a heat wave beneath his breastbone which radiated up to his face and ears, burning like wildfire as he turned to the Bahrainis with furious gesticulations, indicating that he needed someone to perform the Heimlich maneuver on him. The Bahrainis soon got the gist of his problem and began slapping Ad Magic's back, while he clutched his throat like a man being hanged.

At last one of the Bahrainis socked him mightily on the spine with the side of his fist, and, *ka-zeem!*, the lozenge shot out of Ad Magic's mouth, bounced off the windshield of the bus, and fell into the driver's lap. As Ad Magic began to breathe again, a great laugh exploded among the Bahrainis, who were at once relieved and amused by the absurdity of the entire scene. Ad Magic had spent the better part of a day with these people, and while he was grateful to be breathing, he felt that their laughter was tinged with ridicule and hostility, as had been their whole repertoire of Jerry Lewis hilarity. When they cried mocking insults at the enormous statue of a serene, meditating Buddha in the caves of Elephanta, for instance, they stirred up a thousand and one bats, which came screeching past Ad Magic in such profusion that he was buffeted by their wings and their surprisingly hefty bodies. He slipped in bat guano in an attempt to duck under the flock, falling on his knee and hand. The guano was an inch deep and felt like a cold pudding. Fortunately, one of the Bahrainis had a package of Handi Wipes, and he was able to clean the worst of it off, although the stench persisted, and he could still smell it whenever his hand was in proximity to his face.

The bus, with a blown tire, wheeled onto the shoulder of Marine Drive, one of Bombay's busiest streets. Ad Magic

straight-armed the side emergency-exit door and staggered
outside. He could breathe well enough, but his throat felt
bruised. He shucked off his teal-green cashmere V-neck
sweater. It had been madness wearing that. The air outside the
bus was humid and suffocating. Ad Magic recognized Chowpatty Beach and realized he was on a peninsula that extended
into the Arabian Sea like a finger. He knew that Bombay con-
sisted of a series of islands off the coast of India, and that from
this point he was less than a few miles from the Gateway of
India, where the tour had originated.

A small boy, about eight or ten — it was hard to tell,
partly because he had a shaved head — approached Ad Magic,
carrying a rhesus monkey on his shoulder. The monkey,
dressed in a dirty red uniform with epaulets, gold piping, and
a tiny bellman's cap, began an incomprehensible performance
in the art of mime. When it was over, the monkey approached
the American and presented its upturned hat to him as a collection cup. Ad Magic began to cough again as he fished in his
pockets. He placed a half-dozen rupees in the monkey's cap
and tossed his expensive sweater to the boy. "Go ahead," he
said. "Take it. It's all yours."

The Bahraini woman had seen the monkey's performance and emitted a shrill, trilling cry. One of the men, who
could speak a little English, said facetiously, "Bravo. Excellent
monkey."

The tour guide climbed out of the bus and callously ques-
tioned the American about his condition. Ad Magic said he
was all right, and then she chastised him for giving so much
money to the boy. "Not is good," she said with a sneer. Ad
Magic walked away from the guide and the Bahrainis, wanting
nothing more to do with them. He moved from the road onto
the sand of Chowpatty Beach, and when he felt sufficiently

separated from them he turned and watched as the guide skill-
fully led the party of Bahrainis across the whizzing four-lane
traffic of Marine Drive and into a decrepit establishment called
the New Zealand Café.

There were billboards on either side of the grimy, stuc-
coed building. One, in English, advertised Gabriel shock
absorbers. The other, featuring an apparently famous Indian
leading man, who had sort of a Rudolph Valentino look, was
in Hindi. It was an advertisement for men's hairdressing.
Beyond the café, through the filter of buzzing traffic and the
haze of diesel fuel, Ad Magic spotted a cardboard shantytown.
The settlement was centered around a crescent-shaped drain-
age ditch, and people could be seen squatting there, shamelessly relieving themselves, while at the other end of the
obscene ditch, women were washing laundry.

Looking into the restaurant, Ad Magic could see one of
the Bahrainis clutching his throat and pretending to choke
while the rest of the party laughed. Their mouths were opened
wide, revealing an abundance of golden inlays. They waved to
him and cheered heartily. He wondered why they were so
jolly. Why couldn't he be like that?

Out front, the bus driver was quarreling with the driver
of the truck that had rear-ended the tour bus. Ad Magic
turned away again and walked toward the Arabian Sea, out of
the envelope of diesel exhaust into a small, pleasantly pungent
pocket of gardenia, and then back into a zone of a truly ghastly
odor. The tuna cannery in American Samoa had been bad, but
it was nothing compared with these little pockets of smell that
were all over Bombay, and what was worse was that you had to
be nonchalant about it with your fellow-travelers and not com-
plain, for no one else seemed to notice it. Ad Magic was suddenly overcome by a sense of unreality — he wondered if he

had been to American Samoa at all, or if it had been a dream, and, indeed, if the Bombay of the here and now was a dream.

He surveyed the long, deserted stretch of beach, and spotted a small white horse standing forlornly in the surf. As he moved closer to the horse he saw that it was old and swaybacked, covered with oozing sores, and so shrunken that its ribs protruded and its teeth seemed overly large. The horse was having a hard time staying on its feet, and Ad Magic watched it reel. There were plenty of scenes of poverty and desolation in India, but this was the most abject and miserable sight he had ever laid eyes on. Clearly, the horse was going to die — possibly within the hour. Had it been meant to die so completely alone — abandoned? It occurred to Ad Magic that it was the suffering of a horse that had finally driven Friedrich Nietzsche into an irretrievable insanity in the month of January 1889.

Good God! He had done it again. He had abandoned his seizure meds, flipped out, and somehow gotten on a plane, this time bound for India. He frantically searched his pockets for a passport. There was none. He had no wallet, either — only an enormously fat roll of American hundred-dollar bills, some loose smaller bills mixed with Indian currency, and a ball of heavy change that caused his pocket to bulge. He didn't even know his own name; he knew only "Ad Magic," but as he sorted out the loose cash he discovered a room key from the Taj Inter-Continental. "Suite 7" was imprinted on the tag, and Ad Magic knew that the secret to his identity would be found there, although he was in no particular hurry to return to the hotel. Somehow he felt that it would be better not to know, at least not yet.

His throat continued to bother him. As he rifled through his pockets, he found a pack of Marlboro cigarettes and a

beautiful gold lighter. He extracted a cigarette and lit it. The
boy with the monkey appeared at his side and bummed a
smoke. Ad Magic lit it for him, and watched the boy pass the
cigarette to the monkey, who held it in the fashion of an aris-
tocratic S.S. officer in an old black-and-white Second World
War movie. The monkey smoked as though he had a real yen
for nicotine, and after this demonstration he presented his
little bellman's cap for another tip. Ad Magic gave him a five-
dollar bill and then sat down on a small, rusting Ferris wheel,
looking out at the horse again. He took a drag off his cigarette,
and on his wrist he noticed a stainless-steel Med-Alert bracelet
and a solid-gold Rolex. He examined them both with curiosity,
as if he had never seen them before. The little bracelet was
inscribed with the word "Epilepsy."

Epilepsy. Ad Magic did not have epilepsy in the clas-
sic sense, with full-blown, convulsive seizures. He was a
temporal-lobe epileptic. He remembered this now. He had suffered an epileptic fugue. He still wasn't sure what his name
was, where he lived, whether he was married, whether he had
children, or much else, but he did know himself to be an
advertising man. That, and an epileptic. He quite clearly
remembered the voice of his doctor, the large, high-ceilinged
consulting room trimmed in dark oak, a door with a frosted-
glass window, and a hands-clasped-in-prayer statue on the doctor's desk. Ad Magic remembered spending hours from early
adolescence into maturity in that room. He remembered
majestic oak trees, crisp autumn afternoons, the smell of burning leaves, and the palatial brownstone estates of a Midwestern
city, but he could not identify the city, could not picture the
doctor or remember his name. He did know the man had been
more than a doctor to him — he had been a good friend as
well, a man whom Ad Magic loved very much. He suspected

that the doctor was now dead, but he distinctly remembered something the doctor had told him about his condition. "These spells you have, where you go gadding about the world — they could be a form of epileptic fugue, or you could be suffering from the classical form of global amnesia, which is so often depicted on television soap operas. They are very common in television melodrama but almost unheard of in real life. But so, too, are psychomotor fugues, which are a kind of status epilepticus of the left temporal lobe."

Ad Magic didn't know who he was or how he had come to India. He only knew that there were times when he became so depressed and irritable and finally so raving mad that he had to throw his medication away, bolt out, and intoxicate himself or in some way extinguish his consciousness. He felt this way now. He felt a loathing for everything on the face of the earth, including himself — but the suffering of this white horse was something he could not abide. It was a relief, suddenly, to have something other than himself and his hangover on which to fix his attention.

He summoned the boy, who was now proudly wearing the cashmere sweater, and took him and the monkey across the road to the New Zealand Café. The air inside was laden with cooking grease and cigarette smoke, but a pair of ceiling fans beat through the haze like inverted helicopters. A waiter in a dingy white jacket was serving tea and a plate of sticky cookies to the Bahrainis. From the kitchen, a radio blared a tinny version of "Limehouse Blues." Ad Magic pulled a chair up next to the tour guide and said, "Ask the boy who that horse on the beach belongs to."

The guide was a good-looking woman in her late thirties, who fluctuated mercurially between obsequiousness and sullen aggression. She wore an orange sari that seemed immaculately clean. Ad Magic wondered how she managed that, after the boat trip to Elephanta and the long Bombay city tour. He watched her interrogate the boy. Then she turned to Ad Magic and said, "Horse belongs to circus man, and cannot work anymore. Wandering horse now. Free to come and go."

Ad Magic asked the guide whether she could make a phone call and summon a veterinarian.

"Veterinarian?" she said, reacting to the word bitterly, as if he had made an indecent request.

"You're right. That's silly, isn't it. There must not be any veterinarians, or, if any, relatively few on call, even in such a sophisticated city as Bombay — and you've been through a long day, and now the bus has been wrecked. Forgive me. I'm not feeling very well today. Let me ask you. Can you tell me at which hotel I am staying?"

"The Taj," she said.

"Right, the Taj. That's what I thought." Ad Magic placed a half-dozen American ten-dollar bills on the table. "Please accept this little gratuity. You've been marvelous. Now, I wonder if you can call a *real* doctor. Tell him I will make it truly worth his while. The boy and I will wait for him across the road, on the beach. I'll get back to the hotel on my own. It is the Taj, isn't it?" The woman nodded.

Ad Magic and the boy, with the monkey on his shoulder, crossed the road again and sat on a pair of broken merry-go-round horses that were detached from an abandoned carousel. Next to the carousel was the small Ferris wheel, contrived to be powered by a horse or mule rather than a motor. Nearby was a ticket kiosk decorated with elephant-men and monkey-men painted in brilliant, bubblegum colors. The carnival was defunct and depressing. Ad Magic remembered bright lights — a carnival of his childhood, before he had picked up

on the tawdriness of carnivals and saw only the enchanting
splendor of them. He couldn't have been more than four. He
was sitting in a red miniature car when he saw one of a different color — yellow — that he liked better. Impulsively, he
scrambled for the better car. Just as he unbuckled his seat belt
and was halfway out of the red one, the ride began and he fell,
catching his arm under the car, wrenching and skinning his
elbow, and bashing his face against the little vehicle's fake
door. Suddenly he was plucked free by a man in a felt hat and
a raincoat, who smelled pleasantly of after-shave. His father?
A stranger? He wasn't sure; there was no face, as there had
been no face on the doctor.

   He searched his pockets for his cigarettes and discovered a small, flat, green-and-black tin of Powell's Headache
Tablets. He took two of these, dry-swallowed them, and then
lit up another cigarette. He spotted an empty tour bus pulling
up alongside the damaged bus he had arrived in, and from his
seat on the rusting pony Ad Magic watched his party emerge
from the New Zealand Café, board the new bus, and take off.
There was no goodbye wave, even from the friendly Bahrainis.
Again he tried to recover his name and city of origin, but it was
hopeless. At least he had come to Bombay rather than Lusaka,
or Lima, or Rangoon, or Zanzibar. He remembered coming
into Zanzibar on a steamer, seasick — the odor of the spices
was so powerful he could smell it twenty miles offshore. He
remembered feeling instantly well when the boat reached the
harbor, and how the inhabitants of the city were outside — it
was midnight — marveling at the recently installed streetlights. An Australian tourist told him that Zanzibar was the
last place in the world to get streetlights and that when the
bulbs burned out the streetlights would never glow again
unless Swiss workers were imported to come in and change

them. "The bloody buggers can't even change a light bulb," the Australian said. "It isn't in their makeup." Ad Magic's recollection of Zanzibar was like an Alice-in-Wonderland hallucination. It seemed that he had remained stranded there for weeks, almost penniless, living on bread and oranges.

A faded, light-green Mercedes with a broken rear spring came bouncing too fast across the beach and skidded, sliding sideways as it stopped near the carousel. An elderly European man wearing a white coat over a dirty tropical suit stepped out of the car and stretched. He had a head of unkempt, wiry white hair in the style of Albert Einstein. He brushed it back with his hand and opened the back door of the car. A magnificent boxer dog hopped out and followed the old man over to Ad Magic and the boy.

"Are you a doctor?"

"I am a doctor, yes. You were in a car accident, jah?"

"I was, but it's nothing. I called about the horse. I wondered if you could do something about the horse. What is wrong with that animal?"

The doctor looked out at the sea, lifting his hands to shield his eyes from the afternoon sun. "Probably he has been drinking salt water in desperation. He will die, very soon."

Ad Magic said, "I will give you five hundred American dollars if you can save the horse."

The doctor said, "I can send him to seventh heaven with one shot. Haff him dragged away. Fifty dollars for the whole shebang."

"Look, I don't want to wrangle. If you can save the horse, I will pay you a thousand dollars."

The doctor opened the trunk of the Mercedes and removed a piece of rope. He sent the boy down to the edge of the water and had him lead the horse up onto the dry sand while he backed the car another fifty feet down the beach, where the sand became too loose and he had to stop. Then he got out of the car and removed his medical bag from the back, setting it on the hood. He quickly looked the horse over. "Malnutrition, dehydration, fever." He opened the horse's lips. "Ah! He has infected tooth. This is very bad. . . ."

"What about all the sores? Why does he have so many sores?"

"Quick," the doctor said. "In my trunk I have glucose *und* water. We haff to getting in fluids."

Ad Magic carried two pint-size bottles of glucose and sterile-water solution over to the horse and then stood holding them as the doctor ran drip lines into large veins in the horse's neck. Ad Magic watched the bottles slowly begin to drain as the doctor put on a pair of rubber gloves and began to scrub the sores on the horse's body with a stiff brush and a kind of iodine solution, making a rough, sandpaper sound.

"Doesn't that hurt?"

"Animals don't experience pain in the same fashion humans," the doctor said, with some irritation. "Pain for humans is memories, anticipation, imagination —"

"I don't care about that. What you're doing has got to hurt."

The doctor came around from behind the horse. "How much does he weigh? Unless the liver is bad, I will give him morphine. I am not Superman. I haff not got X-ray vision. Maybe the liver is bad. Parasites. Who knows?" The doctor dug in his bag and removed a large hypodermic syringe. He filled it with morphine and injected it into the horse's shoulder. Then he took the same syringe and filled it with antibiotics and injected these into the horse. After this, he picked up the brush and again began working on the large, putrescent sores on the horse's skin. Ad Magic's arms began to hurt from holding the bottles of liquid.

The doctor looked at him. "You are an American? Jah? Who was scratched your face *und* black eye?"

"Huh? Oh, that," Ad Magic said. "I forgot that. Last night, I gave some money to this street person. A woman with eleven kids. I gave her some money as they were laying down a cloth to sleep on the street —"

"Yes?"

"Well, after I gave her the money — these men had seen me pass it to her, and they took it away from her. Slapped her around. I hit one of them, knocked him down, but there were so many of them. I just couldn't fight them all. They tried to steal my watch. I got drunk — or I was drunk. I can't remember exactly." Ad Magic leaned over and looked at his face in the side mirror of the Mercedes. He did have an incredible black eye. No wonder the tour party found him peculiar.

The doctor took the glucose bottles from Ad Magic and propped them on the inside of the rear door, rolling up the window until they were upright and secure. "In my bag is green bottle. Take two *und* lie down in the back seat." As Ad Magic rummaged in the bag, the doctor came up alongside him and grabbed his wrist. He examined the little stainless-steel bracelet.

"Epilepsy," the doctor said. "Mmm." He presented Ad Magic with a little flask of gin. "Swallow this *und* lie down," he said. "Horse will take time."

It was dark when Ad Magic came to. The boxer dog was standing over him, sniffing his face. Ad Magic rolled over and abruptly jerked himself upright. A number of oily torches had been lit, and there were fires in metal barrels as well as drift-

wood fires burning all up and down the shore, which was now
teeming with activity. There were hundreds of people roaming
the beach, and a brisk breeze blowing off the water offered a
variety of smells: the smell of sewage was replaced by the
pleasant aroma of gardenia, followed by the odor of bitter
orange, of vanilla, of cooked curry, of charcoal, of diesel, and
then again of sewage or salt water, or of the ancient leather
seats of the Mercedes. The boxer, openmouthed, panted in Ad
Magic's face, and from her mouth there was no odor at all.

Ad Magic pulled himself out of the car and took in the
scene. The sights and smells and noises were uncommonly
rich. There were roving bands of musicians, dancers, acrobats,
food vendors, boys selling hashish. There were holy people,
fakirs, snake charmers, more boys with trained monkeys. Ad
Magic's own monkey boy watched him leaning against the
Mercedes, his eyes roving back and forth between the Rolex
and the doctor.

"I can't believe how wonderful I feel," Ad Magic said.
"What was that pill you gave me?"

"Just a little something," the doctor said, crouching in
the sand as he looked through his black doctor's bag. Lined up
by the horse's feet there were a dozen empty glucose bottles
and an enormous black tooth — a molar — in addition to several lesser teeth, long yellow ones.

"Abscess tooth. Very bad," the doctor said. "Pus all over
everything when I pull it. Horse falling down, goes into shock.
I'm having to give him epinephrine. All better now. Then sand
in the sores. Clean them all over twice times."

"Is the horse going to be okay?"

"He is looking much better, don't you think? Almost
frisky, don't you think?"

"Yes, much better. Much, much better."

"Maybe he will live. It's touch and go."

The boxer dog presented Ad Magic with a piece of drift-wood and began a game of tug-of-war. Soon the two were running around the beach and down to the sea. As the small breakers washed over Ad Magic's feet, he noticed human excrement in the water and quickly backed away. He looked out at the sea and took in the sight of fishing dhows, backlit by the moon and glowing with tiny amber lights of their own. The boats were making their way — where? The dog tugged at his pant leg, ragging him, and soon she and Ad Magic were rough-housing — chasing each other, rolling in the sand, wrestling. Then Ad Magic was on his feet, jogging down the beach with the dog beside him. Faster and faster they ran until he was running as fast as he could for the sheer joy of it; he had never felt so good — he ran without getting tired, and it seemed that he never would get tired. Wait a minute. He was a smoker. Or was he? He was running effortlessly, like a trained runner, until at last he did begin to tire a little and sweat. So he and the dog plunged into the sea; he disregarded the filth of it and began to swim out into the surf, and the dog swam with him until they were very far out in the warm water. Then they let the waves carry them back in. Ad Magic walked easily in the sand back to the car and the horse, and when he got to the horse he embraced it and rubbed his face against its neck. "Oh, God, thank you," he said.

"You are okay now?" the doctor said.

"Yes," Ad Magic said. "I think so."

"What is 'ad magic'? You were saying, 'ad magic.' What is that?"

"Oh, that. I am an ad writer, and sometimes I feel magic. I tap into a kind of magic. It's hard to explain."

Ad Magic reached into his pocket and peeled off ten hundred-dollar bills. The roll was so tight that only the outer bills were wet. He handed the money to the doctor. He felt for his cigarettes and found them ruined. His tin of Powell's Headache Tablets was also contaminated with seawater. Ad Magic studied the container for a moment. He said, "Listen to this — ad magic. 'It was a hot day in tough California traffic when a Los Angeles red light made time stand still and gave me a headache like there was no tomorrow. I took a couple of Powell's Headache Tablets and just like that — beep, beep, toot toot — I was ready to roll again.' Fifty words. That's my magic. It's not that good right now. I'm just getting a little. Just a little is getting through —"

"I see, advertising writer."

"How's this? 'Second-class passage in a Third World railroad car, hotter than the Black Hole of Calcutta, gave me a first-class headache. I traded my Swiss Army knife for two of Powell's Headache Tablets. Home or halfway around the globe, Powell's is my first choice for headache relief.' It's not that hot, but that's how they come, from out of nowhere."

"H'okay; you are a hausfrau shopping at Christmas und very busy und a bik hurry — Powell's Tablets. Fifty words."

"'The day, Christmas Eve; the time, fifteen minutes to midnight; the place, Fox Valley Shopping Center, Aurora, Illinois; the headache, a procrastination special — on a scale of ten, ten. The solution: Powell's Tablets. The happy ending, gaily wrapped presents under a festive tree, a jolly ho ho, and a merry Christmas to all.'"

"Ad magic. Making money for this?"

"Yes. Making money. I think so. Will the horse live? You see, if the horse lives, then I have my magic. That is God's promise to me. I can do even better for Powell's Tablets. I can do much better, and if the horse lives I will have my magic. How old is the horse?"

"At first I am thinking he is older. Maybe he is twenty years —"

"How long can this horse live? Given the best care?"

"With good care, a long life. Thirty-five years."

Ad Magic peeled five hundred-dollar bills off his roll. "I want you to send this horse on a vacation. I want him to have the best food. If he wants other horses to play with, get them for him. I want this horse to have a grassy field. Do horses like music? I heard that once. Get a radio that plays music. I want the horse to have good accommodations. I want you to be the doctor for this horse and get the best people to take care of this horse. What were those pills you gave me? *I feel fantastic!* Is there some way we can ship this horse back to the States? I'll look into it. Can you drive me to the Taj? This is so crazy — I don't even know my name, but I've got a room key. Tell the boy to watch the horse until I get back. Do you have a business card? Here's what we'll do. I've got it. I've got it now. You stay with the horse. I'll take your car. I've been here before. I know Bombay. I'll take the car back. I don't want you to leave the horse. I don't want anything to happen to this horse. When I get home, you send me a picture of the horse. Stand next to the horse with a copy of the *International Herald Tribune*. When I see that the horse is okay, that his health is flourishing, and I see that the date on the paper is current, I will send you six hundred dollars every month. Will that be enough? Like if this horse needs an air-conditioned stall, I want him to have it. Whatever — TV, rock videos, a pool, anything his little horsy heart desires."

"It can be done."

"Excellent. Look, where did you get this great dog? Will you sell me this dog?"

"For no money," the doctor said.

"C'mon, doctor, I love this dog."

"Anyhow, you cannot take her to America."

"Okay," Ad Magic said. "It was just a thought. You're looking at me funny. I know what you're thinking. You don't trust me with the car. Send the boy to flag a cab. I've got to get back to the States. You know those harnesses those Seeing Eye dogs wear? I could wear sunglasses and take the dog back. A white cane. Just let me borrow the dog for a while."

"Mr. Man. She is my best friend. I'm not selling. Not borrowing."

"Okay, okay then. But take care of the horse. I'll send the money. It's a generous amount." Ad Magic reached into his pocket and withdrew his wad of cash, peeling off a few more bills. "See that this kid gets taken care of, okay? Send him to school. C'mon, doctor, don't look at me like that — it's only advertising money. I don't have to *work* for it. *Now I saw when the Lamb opened one of the seven seals, and I heard one of the four living creatures say, as with a voice of thunder, Come! And I saw and behold, a white horse, and its rider had a bow; and a crown was given to him, and he went out conquering and to conquer.*"

When a black-and-yellow Ambassador taxi honked from Marine Drive, Ad Magic gave the horse a final embrace. "Heigh-o, Silver, and *adios amigos*," he said as he hopped into the cab, brandishing a handful of cash, telling the driver to step on it.

*   *   *

Ad Magic gave the driver a hundred dollars for an eighty-cent cab ride and rushed through the lobby of the Taj Inter-Continental, up to his grand suite in the old part of the hotel. He showered, and after toweling himself off he saw his wallet and passport on the bureau. He cautiously opened the wallet, assiduously avoiding his driver's license. The wallet was heavy with credit cards and cash. In it he saw a picture of an attractive blond woman and two children. At that moment he knew his name, knew his wife of fifteen years, knew his children, and knew himself. He threw the wallet down, and began scribbling on a yellow legal pad. There was so much to get down and his mind was racing out of control. The magic was getting through. He was developing advertising concepts, enough for a year. He phoned the desk and had a porter send up a bottle of scotch and a plate of rice curry.

The scotch calmed him some and by dawn he had most of it written down. He dialed the switchboard and placed a call to his wife in Los Angeles.

Rocket Man

THE Quonset hut was immaculate except in these times when W. L. Moore was drinking. Thus when Prestone entered the yard, found it strewn with empty beer cans, and discovered the front door ajar, he was reluctant to step inside and so he hung back a moment, milling in the yard, waiting for inspiration.

Moore's Chevrolet was parked far to the rear of the lot with the driver's door wide open. The nose of the automobile pressed hard against the taut barbed-wire fence that separated the lot from a cow pasture. To Prestone it seemed as if the car was poised to *blast through* into the field. He walked over to the car and closed the door to save the battery and then slowly walked back to the Quonset hut.

Billy Prestone was a large young man. He was a light-heavyweight but the only time he weighed as little as one hundred seventy-five pounds was for the very weigh-in of a fight, when his huge frame of bone and muscle had been tortured down to the official limit. The only way to do that anymore was by dehydrating off the last ten pounds with diuretics. This was dangerous — but as Moore was wont to say, "Like, so what else is new?"

Although Prestone had just fought and won, he was eating already, taking in water and putting on weight, maybe twenty pounds overnight. In combat boots and a double layer of sweats he seemed gigantic. A sinister set of reddish-black stitches bristled under the curve of each eyebrow — either one of the cuts could have cost him the fight but Moore had been in his corner and kept the cuts under control.

Moore had remained cool while the chief second had panicked in a way that had nearly freaked Prestone. Moore had come through for him, but now Prestone felt he would rather go back and face the anguish of the fight all over again than confront his friend.

He pulled off his watch cap, revealing a "high-and-tight" haircut, and carefully blotted the perspiration from each of his blackened eyes. The rest of his face was splotched with red glove burns and stung with sweat. He swung the door open with the toe of his boot. The room was saturated with the sweet sickly smell of stale beer.

W. L. Moore stood astride his old boxer dog, Muggsy. He had the dog's head tilted back and he was carefully pouring Donnagel down the dog's throat, alternately massaging it so she would swallow and then pouring in more of the pastel green fluid. When she had swallowed a considerable amount, Moore seemed satisfied and wiped the dog's square gray muzzle clean with a disposable napkin.

Elton John was singing "Rocket Man" on the radio and when W. L. Moore looked up at Prestone, Moore plaintively spoke the words Elton John was singing — *"I'm not the man they think I am at all — I'm a rocket man . . ."*

For a moment the dog started to gag. W. L. Moore massaged the back of the old dog's neck, rolling the folds of skin back and forth with one hand while he stroked the underside of her belly with the other. "You have to give her digitalis twice a day," he said, "and it upsets her stomach and she goes into this thing where she shits and pukes for three days and then I can't give her any medicine and then her heart weakens and she'll faint or fall down. It gets so bad you hope you'll just walk past one time and find that she's . . . dead."

Moore searched Prestone's face intently, desperately. "You know what I mean? But then it will pass off, she can take the medicine and have a couple of good days." He looked Prestone over suspiciously as he drew himself erect. He grasped at a spasm in his back and then began to gulp air. He seemed to have shriveled and grown old overnight. Prestone looked away.

"She's a good dog," Prestone said. He walked over to the wine-colored leather heavybag suspended from an iron beam at the top of the ceiling. Prestone squeezed back his thumbs, drawing his hand wraps tight, and with sudden fury the young man ripped off a dozen body shots at the inanimate bag, causing it to jerk violently on its chain. After the barrage he swayed from the waist, in a bob-and-weave style, dodging the bag, picking up its rhythm as he raised himself and unleashed a savage flurry of left hooks and straight right hands to the head of the bag. Abruptly he hooked the bag with his elbow to stop it from moving and turned back to W. L. Moore.

"You look like hell, champ," Billy said. "Your face is blue. I don't think you're getting any oxygen. How come you're juicing again, man?"

"I don't know. I wish I knew. How come you're out running already?"

"I just felt like it. I must have done ten miles. I'm all hyper."

The old dog struggled to get on Moore's narrow single bed. W. L. Moore quickly moved over to help her by lifting up her arthritic hips. The dog made a couple of circles on the tight mattress and then plopped down heavily. Moore covered her with an olive-green army blanket, leaving only her head visible. He tenderly framed her face with his large twisted fingers and bent forward to kiss her. The dog looked back to him with sad grateful eyes and swallowed several times.

W. L. Moore reached under the bed and withdrew three sixteen-ounce cans of Hamm's by their plastic retainer ring along with a half pint of Smirnov vodka. These he set on the oilcloth-covered kitchen table. He broke the seal on the vodka bottle and guiltily looked to his friend. "Blue sparks are popping off my fingertips. Every time I look at the wall I see bugs in my peripheral vision. I feel like I'm in the Twilight Zone or something. It's like . . . *psychotic terror.*"

He threw his head back and tossed down more than half the bottle of vodka and then quickly swallowed an entire can of beer. He looked back at Prestone with red watering eyes and took several long breaths, gulping in the air. "I'm on my eleventh day," he said. "I can't get high anymore. I can't even get straight. I want to go to detox, but her stomach won't come around."

Moore walked back to the bed and lowered himself on it, wrapping his own body alongside that of his dog. "That time I fought Red Franklin," Moore said. "It was a very tough fight. I woke up hyper, like you. I remember I went to the store to get all of the papers to read about the fight. I mean, I knew that I had won but he really roughed me up. He was tough. He was a butt-kickin' stud. I was sore all over, but by the time I got back from the store, my back really started to hurt. I realized I had a fever and when I went to piss, I was pissing blood. I was too sick to drive myself to the hospital and I had no phone. I just lay for three days, delirious. I thought I was going to die but gradually I did come out of it. He was a terrific body puncher. That fight, that beating was the beginning of the end for me. I was twenty-four years old and that's how I celebrated winning my title. Coming up through the ranks is hard. The other night was hard. Too hard, if you ask me."

"I didn't smell booze on you, you were completely absolutely stone cool. Tommy wienied out when he saw the cuts. Man, I don't want to hear that shit, 'You're cut to the bone! You lost a quart of blood! We've got to stop it!'"

"Is that what he said? Tommy said that?"

"You don't remember? Yeah, that's what he said. You closed the cuts and Tommy tells me to go out and throw my shooter, knock him out, but he won't go down, he comes back with his head, he's dropping left hooks in over my right hand. I can't see, my second wind is history, I don't know what's holding me up; back in the corner you closed the cuts again —"

"I remember the cuts, I used two bottles of adrenaline and when that didn't work I burned them shut with ferric chloride —"

"You said, 'There's a third wind.' You said, 'Kid, there's a third wind. It's between here and death. Don't be afraid. Go on ahead and grab ahold. The third wind. It's all yours.'"

"I did? That's pure Gurdjieff!"

"You said, 'Go on out there. It's all on instinct now.' It was so strange. Suddenly I had my legs back and I was punch-

ing, really hurting him, but he was taking it. I mean, I knew I
had him but I couldn't believe how he could take it. I feinted a
right, gave him the Fitzsimmons' shift, and nailed him with a
left hook to the solar plexus. Can you believe that? I'm telling
you, I *nailed* him. I drilled that fucker. He made the count,
and I was glad for this because I wasn't through. I trapped him
on the ropes, slid him down to his corner and blew him away.
I threw the shooter. It was the first clear shot I had at his chin
all night. It had some firepower in it. Blam! He went down like
he was shot between the eyes with a .45. Two minutes into the
tenth round."

"The Fitzsimmons' shift," Moore said. He laughed
shortly. "I don't really remember. I was doing some Demerol.
It's all a jumble."

"I'm as brave as a bull," Prestone said, "I fear neither
man nor beast."

Prestone backpedaled away from the table, set his feet,
feinted the right and then quickly executed the Fitzsimmons'
shift, assuming the southpaw stance, and fired a ferocious left
hook to the solar plexus of the heavybag, followed by a crisp
overhand right. He bounced for a second on his toes and then
mechanically tripped off a sequence of uppercuts.

Prestone arrested the swinging of the heavybag and
turned to Moore with his hands on his hips. He said, "This
morning I get a long-distance call. Guess who?"

"Tell me."

"A call from Scotland. Glasgow. McGillian says he saw
me on TV. . . . He says, 'Yer a bluidy tough bloke, I cannae
wait to get it oan.' They want me for July."

"How much?" Moore abruptly demanded.

"Two hundred fifteen thousand and change."

"They want you before the eyes heal right. Did that ring doctor debride those cuts? That tissue is sodden with adrenaline."

"Hey, man," Prestone said, "he cleaned them up righteously and stitched them with silk. I'm not worried about my eyes. I'm worried about McGillian. I'm going to kill the motherfucker."

"I don't like McGillian at all. His style is all wrong for you." W. L. Moore reached under the bed and withdrew another can of Hamm's. He popped it open and stepped over to the table, finished the rest of the vodka, and then chased it with beer. "Am I still blue?"

"No, you've got color."

"The cells — at this point the only language they understand is alcohol. I feel a little bit better. I was getting fucking paranoid."

Moore crossed the room to a row of metal cabinets next to his small kitchen sink. He rummaged through the drawers until he located a fifth of apricot brandy. He took a long pull from the bottle and then grabbed a full six-pack of Rainier Ale from his refrigerator. He flipped a can of ale across the room to Prestone and then opened one for himself. He took a small sip before he walked back to the bed and laboriously arranged himself next to his dog. "I've got to get horizontal," he said. "I feel rough."

Prestone tossed the sweating can of ale from hand to hand. "McGillian has a good jab," he said.

"Aha! I knew it, *the voice of doubt*. You better believe he's got a good jab and no matter how much you think you're going to be ready for it, it will surprise you. His jab will make you see pinwheels, a whole star show. It will curl your toenails.

You will think that you are being hit in the face with a batter-ing ram. This is how it's going to feel — and let me tell you something, buddy, you've got to be ready for that kind of thing or you'll panic. You've never seen a jab like this and it will throw you out of your conception of a safety zone — all these years of feeling comfortable in the ring will go out the door. You will feel like you're on some strange planet and you'll panic and won't know what to do. It's pretty hard to improvise when you're getting the shit kicked out of you. Last night was a Sunday picnic compared to McGillian. You beat a cheese champion. Fight a couple at home and collect some easy money. McGillian is going to be war —"

"I'm good with a righthand countershot —"

"Not that good. You're going to have to eat that jab for five, six rounds, maybe all night, *and* . . . ," Moore said in-credulously, his high girlish voice rising into falsetto, "you're going to be fighting him *in Scotland*? In his ring with all his homeboys cheering him on?"

"I can't make the fucking weight anymore! One more time and I never want to see one seventy-five again. Don't fuckin' worry, I'll get McGillian. I got the juice for him. I'm going to get *audacious* and kick some ass. I'm going to let him have it. That motherfucker is going to be one sorry son of a bitch when I get done with him. He's going to wish he never heard of me. I got his number. He's mine! They're going to say he was a shot fighter after Billy Prestone. I'm going to tell him, 'You better quit, motherfucker, *you ain't got it* no more.' I'm going to lay some shit on him that they have never even heard of yet and then I'm moving up to the heavies, where I belong, and every swinging dick in the division better fucking look out!"

"Well, *say it like you mean it!* Can you hang in with the big man?"

"I can hang with *any*body."

"You can hang with the big guy?"

"I can hang with *any*body!"

Moore came off the bed with his hands up, his head bobbing as he waded in on Prestone. "Can you hang with me?" he cried in mock fury. He was beginning to sound drunk.

Prestone threw a vicious but well-controlled five-punch combination that was so fine he was able to bring it just a few millimeters short of Moore's jaw. "*Any*body!"

Prestone playfully began to wrestle when suddenly Moore began to shiver uncontrollably. He quickly slipped away from Prestone and staggered over to the sink. "Oh my God," he said. Turning away from the sink he rushed to the toilet, which was in open view at the back of the Quonset hut. Moore pitched his head forward into the bowl and began to retch, although he did not vomit. In a moment he got up and walked back to the table with exaggerated precision. His eyes were bloodshot and watering heavily. He picked up a can of ale and did what to Prestone seemed unthinkable — he drank all of it and then clutched himself as he began to tremble again. Prestone helped him settle back down on the bed. Reflexively, Moore reached for the warmth of his dog under the army blanket.

"Are you all right, champ?" Prestone said.

"Brandy on an empty stomach. I just can't seem to get straight. I'm shitfaced and hung over at the same time."

Prestone sat down next to the table and took a swallow of ale. "The first time I saw you, I was walking home from school and you were in here punching the bag. You were playing the

Doors, so I figured you had to be cool and then I saw your bag action and I was hooked immediately. I had me a hero. What moves you had. It was beautiful. It was the most beautiful thing I had ever seen. I fell into the rhythm and everything else in the world seemed to drop away. I knew I was going to be okay then because suddenly I had a dream. I'm in seventh grade and I had a plan for my life. Man, I love boxing. I love everything about it. I love the punches and all the fancy moves. I like sweat and the smell of leather. I love the diet, the training, the structure of each day. I love the individuality, I love the other fighters. I feel privileged to be in their company. Hey, man, I'm like Peter Pan, I don't ever want to go back to reality. I still can't believe it; champion of the world."

Moore's eyes were rolling back into his head; he had passed from a state of lucidity into unconsciousness in a matter of seconds. Prestone felt a bit like a fool when he realized that his soliloquy would go unacknowledged, yet he sighed with relief. This would make a difficult situation easier. He got up from the chair and found a dry sweatshirt in Moore's foot locker. Prestone took off his own (it was wet and heavy) and looked into the large floor-length mirror Moore kept for shadowboxing.

His neck was huge, his chest was thick and flat, the muscles distinct and visible beneath the smooth, almost transparent skin. His arms were pumped from throwing punches and roped with thick, well-dilated blue veins; his waist, a narrow 32 inches, was perfectly ripped. Prestone squatted down into a fighting stance, once more performed the Fitzsimmons' shift, and then assumed the disdainful Daguerreotype-like pose Robert Fitzsimmons struck after knocking down James J. Corbett in their 1897 match. He had studied the picture for years, burned it in his mind, and somehow had made it come true. He was champion of the world. Hands down on his hips, chest thrust out, head held high, Prestone looked about the room in the arrogant king-of-the-hill attitude of "all right, who's next?" So vivid was his play-acting, he cried aloud, "*Anybody!*," surprising himself with his own spontaneity.

His gaze returned to the mirror. Champion of the world. It *was* hard to believe. It was too much, really, and it was different from what he imagined it would be. He somehow felt vaguely cheated. Prestone studied himself another moment before he put on the dry sweatshirt and went back to the foot locker. He began to fill a small duffel bag with fresh underwear, a clean pair of Levi's, a shirt, a pair of moccasins, Moore's shower kit, and finally, the well-worn copy of *The Portable Nietzsche*.

Prestone zipped the bag shut and then coaxed the dog down from the bed and out into the front lot. While he waited for the dog to relieve herself, Prestone gathered up the beer cans that were scattered everywhere and tossed them into the garbage can. Next he combed through Moore's Chevrolet looking for fresh liquor. It would be too easy, if there was an available supply when Moore came home.

Back inside he dumped a pint of brandy into the sink. He located two more hidden cans of Hamm's. He took these and the three remaining cans of ale along with the duffel bag, and placed them in the rear seat of the Chevrolet. When the dog was back on the bed next to her master, Prestone covered her with the army blanket, then he hoisted Moore and carried him out to the car. Once they were moving, Moore stirred to consciousness.

"Hey," he said. "What's going on?"

"We're going to detox, champ. There's five beers back there. You better drink fast. We'll be there in ten minutes."

"Oh God, poor Muggsy . . . she's gonna die!" Moore moaned.

Prestone saw his friend's contorted face in the rearview mirror. This is just what he had hoped to avoid, a maudlin scene.

Moore began to sob. "I can't bury another dog. Not now. God!"

Prestone slapped the rearview mirror askew and flipped on the radio. Once again Elton John was singing "Rocket Man."

The sun fought through dark, heavy clouds and charged the landscape with a bleak and unearthly white light like the light of nuclear winter. Both men, each for his own reasons, clung to a phrase in the song — *it's lonely in outer space* — and froze up for the rest of the ride.

The glove burns had vanished from Prestone's face; the stitches, too, were gone although the cuts under his eyebrows were still flaming red scars only just beginning to heal. The blackened eyes were fading into shades of red and yellow like autumn leaves. Prestone wore a Ralph Lauren khaki shirt with a button-down collar under a navy-blue sleeveless V-neck sweater, cotton chinos, and deck shoes. He led W. L. Moore's boxer dog around the side of the building until he spotted his friend inside the window. At this point he unhooked the dog's leash and began to shadowbox with the animal. The dog was frisky and well, but Prestone quickly ended the game because of her heart. Inside, Moore gave him the high sign and after this, Prestone took the dog back to the car and then came back across the parking lot and entered the hospital.

Moore was seated at a small table in the detox ward dayroom with a large can of apple juice before him, a red-and-white package of Marlboros, an ashtray, and a packet of matches. His hands shook too badly for him to light a cigarette and Prestone did this for him, lighting another for himself.

"Thanks for taking care of Muggsy," Moore said. "I can't tell you — that's a load off my mind. How did you get her to eat?"

"Consuelo does it. She has been mixing up small pieces of chicken with that Heart/Diet stuff you got from the vet. It smells rank but the dog goes for it. How are you doing?"

"I'm on Librium. I've slept through the worst of it."

"What's with all the apple juice?"

"There's fructose in it," Moore said with a great deal of effort. "Cells can burn it . . . alcohol destroys the mitochondria . . . the cells can't handle — they get used to the simple sugars, like fructose — it's . . . accessible to your cells." The speech took Moore's breath away and he began to pant. Moore pressed his palms against his eye sockets and rubbed them vigorously. When he was done, he stared out into space, popeyed, breathing hard. "Air hunger," he said. "Diabetes out of control."

An attractive blond nurse in a crisp white uniform approached Moore with a blood pressure cuff and a stethoscope. "I need to take another reading, Mr. Moore, and see if you're still running high."

W. L. Moore quietly offered her his arm. The good feelings the sight of his dog had evoked had passed off. Now, nothing felt good. He was back to that. He hoped Prestone would leave so that he could go back to his room and lie down. But then he saw Prestone taking in the presence of the nurse and a smile began to play across his lips. "*Under the charm of the Dionysian, not only is the union between man and man reaffirmed, but the nature which has become alienated, hostile, or subjugated celebrates once more her reconciliation with her lost son —"*

"He reads Nietzsche in the German and listens to blues records," Prestone said. "I can't understand philosophers."

"I know," the nurse said, laughing.

"Somebody had to come out and tell it like it is," Moore said. "As for the blues, once you hear Fats Waller play 'The St. Louis Blues,' you will be transformed, your life will never be the same — *Not thinking of good, not thinking of evil, right at this very moment, that is your original face.* It's more far out than even Nietzsche. It will take you past all duality."

"What I like," the nurse said, "is the part in 'Be My Baby' when the Ronettes come in behind the lead singer." Unselfconsciously, the nurse began to sing both parts of the song. She had a melodious, pleasantly low voice. Prestone liked her spontaneity, her good humor, her clean smell. She looked him over with big beautiful green eyes as she picked up the blood pressure cuff and began to fold it. She broke off the song and said, "You're the boxer — the one on the news! I've never met a boxing champ."

"Well, now you know two," Prestone said. "That there guy is — you're taking his pulse, the former undisputed light-heavyweight champion of the world. That man went gave away fourteen pounds and went fifteen rounds with Sonny Liston. That man is holy! That man is consecrated."

The nurse suddenly reverted back into a professional persona, and Prestone became certain that he had frightened her with his intensity. He watched her record Moore's blood pressure and pulse and then she handed Moore a paper cup containing two black and green Librium capsules. Moore popped the capsules and somewhat shakily tilted the can of apple juice to his lips. The nurse was all business as she looked to Prestone. Her voice took on a solemn tone. "You better convince the champ to lay off the booze before he takes a permanent ten count. This is the third time this year."

Moore said, "I know, I'm a believer. I'm quitting. I'll take Antabuse if I have to."

Prestone watched the nurse walk back to the duty station. He looked back to Moore.

"I did it. I signed . . . it's official. I took a fucking on the deal but I want this fight. They sent the papers already. Faxed them. Maybe you can come over and help me train."

"I can't take the dog to Scotland. They've got a quarantine law."

"You've got to be there, man! I can't rely on Tommy anymore. I'll carry him, he was with us at the start, but he's fucking useless anymore. You have to come over, there's no other way. Consuelo will watch the dog. She's got a way with the dog. Don't worry about the dog."

W. L. Moore mashed out his cigarette and shoved his chair back, far away from the table. Prestone wanted to talk strategy. Moore was in no mood for a strategy session and he was offended that Prestone, after all these years, did not read him any better. "How do you beat a jabber?" Moore asked wearily.

"With your own jab. I've been working my jab with three-pound weights — doubles, triples, and then *cross over* with the straight right, and then, *boom boom!* downstairs with the left hook, back up top with the right hand, left hook to the temple, right to the jaw. I'm going to hit him in the liver; I'll get him under the short rib, dammit, I want him to know how it feels! I'm going to say, 'There, you son of a bitch. How do you like that?'"

Prestone was up on his toes pumping out his left hand,

then quickly began to work the right as he gracefully shuffled about the room in a beautiful ballet. "Douzche! Douzche! Douzche! Dit dit dit, pop, pop, pop, la la la, dit dit dit, pop, pop. Man, he went down like he was *shot between the eyes with a forty-five!*"

"What exuberance," Moore said. "Shit. Tell me, can you *hang* with McGillian?"

"I can *hang* with *any*body, but I'm going to roll over McGillian. It's no bullshit, man. I'm going to mow him down, chop him up. I'm going to slice him. I'm going to drop him like a pair of dirty underwear. I'm going to carve him out a new asshole. I am going to fuck him up —"

"Good," Moore said, thinking that now, at last, Prestone would wind up his rap and leave. "You don't need me. You know what you're doing —"

Prestone's face abruptly became a mask of doubt. "I need you for the head part, champ. Tell me about the Apollo, Dionysus an' all that shit."

Moore dragged himself up from the table. "I'm weak," he said. "Let's go into my room. I have got to lay."

Prestone followed W. L. Moore down the short hall past the nurses' station where he saw the attractive nurse, her blond hair up in plaits, carefully charting medical reports. She looked up at him and winked, flashing a smile of gleaming white, even teeth.

In the room Moore hurled himself on his bed and slung his arm over his eyes. "Can you pull the blinds? Is it hot out? Is Muggsy hot out there?"

"It's just right, champ."

Moore closed his eyes for a moment and feverishly began to massage his forehead and scalp. Moore began a hypnotic drone. "You know, all of those Scots are gonna be going nuts;

you're the first real fight McGillian has had in two years, you're in fighting trim, McGillian could very well be shot, like Willard before Dempsey. Or maybe he's got sore hands, a bad back, a blown knee . . . there's always something wrong . . . anyhow, you won't get rattled; you're ready for all of this, it doesn't bother you 'cause you've left *little Billy* in the dressing room. But, alas, who's that coming into the ring in your body? Why, who could that be? *In every human breast there is a fund of hatred, anger, envy, rancour and malice, accumulated like the venom in a serpent's tooth, and waiting only for an opportunity of venting itself, and then, to storm and rage like a demon unchained.* This is the nice little overseas present you have brought for Mr. McGillian. This is what comes into the ring against McGillian, the Will to Power personified in the body of Billy Prestone!"

"I want to hurt him," Prestone said. "I want him to know how it feels —"

"Good! That's good. You're into it. In fact, you will find all of this amusing and it will empower you and you will enter the ring with a much more deeply refined manifestation of the Will to Power. McGillian is a businessman. He's a celebrity, a public man. He's not a prizefighter anymore. When his two or three tricks don't work, he's going to fold. A young, knock-'em-down stud like you fights for the sake of fighting. How can you top that? I mean, we did a little Gurdjieff last time, that was just a warmup. I knew you were for real after that. You started to *glow,* you practically lit up the room; when a fighter does that he's invulnerable. Anyhow, it will all happen automatically and you will do all the right things. His jab will be there, but you will be able to walk through it if you have to, and when he tastes your own very fine jab he will think, 'I'm tight tonight; I can't get off.' You will take him out of his comfort zone. It's his ring, his crowd, but when you start backing him up — and this cocksucker can't fight backing up — fear will set in. Doubt. You will grow stronger and you will make him pay. If you catch him cold, he goes out early; if not, he will find that he's exhausted by the middle rounds. The pressure will be too much for him. He is not going to catch a third wind like you did the other night. That is something rare and only a few fighters have ever found it. McGillian is going to see that you have something that goes far beyond what fighters call *heart*."

"It's going to work, isn't it?"

"Like magic. It's going to one of those nights. It's going to be sweet, kid. It's going to be magic. It's going to be your night — a night like no other. You're into the rhythm. Jump on him right from the start and never look back. And when you take him out, don't bounce around like you're *surprised* you won. No emotional displays. I don't want to see no shit-eating grin. Play it cool, deadpan. Stone face. Dead black eyes. It will scare the next person you fight. It will drench him in fear. He will think, 'This fucker isn't human.' It will put the chill on him before he ever climbs into the ring. Like Norton before Foreman. Like Michael Spinx before Tyson. Fuckin' little bunny rabbits on some strange and frightening planet."

Prestone was on his feet. He put his hands up and pumped out a jab. "And then I move up and go for the big guy."

"Yes, you're making the transition from local hero into the big time and it's a sucker's game and the big ones eat the little ones up there, but you'll make out, and after you win, hang on to that title with your life." Moore reflected a moment and spoke bitterly. "There's nothing more *useless* to the world than a washed-up prizefighter."

Moore twisted around on the bed and came up on his hands and knees. "Are you sure it's not hot out?" He tore away his sheets. "No wonder. This mattress — it's a plastic-coated mattress!"

Moore yanked the bedcover from the adjoining bed, folded it into a thick, body-wide strip, and spread it over his mattress. He lay down and pressed his pillow over his eyes. "I need another couple of days," he said. "Look, I don't mean to be rude, but I just can't talk any longer. That pill is kicking in. Soak your face in brine twice a day and read the man. It's all in there."

Prestone picked up *The Portable Nietzsche*. "Thanks, champ. You clipped me in. I just won the fight. You just won the fight for me. The rest is simple mechanics. McGillian is in a world of hurt and he don't even know. *I am the lizard king; I can do anything*."

"That's right. It's spilling out all over the place. You scared the nurse with it. Did you see her? She wants to fuck you, man, because you *are* a man. You are so real you had her wetting her pants; she ain't seen a real one on the hoof probably for some time. You *are* a man! Think about that." Moore halved the pillow and folded it over his eyes again. Prestone looked down at his friend, a view that had him peering into the nostril's of Moore's misshapen nose. He watched Moore take several long ragged breaths.

A sucker's game. The big ones eat the little ones.

Prestone squeezed Moore's shoulder and spoke, deliberately chopping off his words so his voice wouldn't break. "I love you, champ. I love you more than anything. There's nothing in the world I wouldn't do for you. These are my true feelings. I love you. Don't fucking go south on me."

When he saw that Moore wasn't going to respond, when

in fact he felt him stiffen and clench the pillow to his face all the harder, Billy Prestone respectfully tucked the volume of Nietzsche under his arm and walked out into the hall.

The blond nurse called out "good luck" as he passed the duty station, and then, as Prestone crossed the lawn to the parking lot, he could hear Moore's voice, at once rich, vibrant, and powerful, crying through the thick glass of the window in his room. Prestone turned to see his friend standing with his arms raised triumphantly in the air, shaking his fists. There were tears pouring down Moore's face and he was crying like all the trumpets of Jericho. He was crying, "*Any*body! *Any*body!"